Mu; Legend of a Lost City
M.D. Neu

Contents

~ Chapter One ~

Five years ago.

The dripping crimson on his hands contrasted against the polished blue stone floors in front of him. Iron permeated around him, the scent made him want to vomit. But he couldn't leave or move, he was frozen by pain and action. Soft warm light from the energy crystals reflected off the walls and floor, filling the space with a bright, cheerful glow, reminding Kaimi of all the wonderful memories this chamber held for him. The birth of each of his younger siblings. The day he introduced Makani to his family, followed by the celebration of their marriage two years later. Watching as Nohealani and Malo were joined in the presence of their gods. Seeing each of their children brought forth and presented to the family and the gods upon their births.

So much joy. Now this.

A burble of air. A cough. A gasp of pain forced him to see what lay before him.

"Help!" His voice yelled out.

Everything sparkled in those memories, but now the red slowly muted not only the bright glow of the veins running through the floors but also his pristine white shirt. From this day forward, the crimson liquid and the pungent fragrance of death would taint each of his happy memories.

More memories pushed forward, forcing out what stretched before him. Kaimi witnessed the day Kai Malina received the gift of sight from the gods of Mu, and was welcomed by Mana Lani into the arms of the world of Spiritual healers and *Māhū*. Something Kaimi didn't fully believe in, well, not as much as he did when he was younger, but everyone had been pleased. Even he found himself excited. Past images of joy played out in his mind. The music, the fire dancing, the tumblers and dancers, the fragrances of meats for the prepared feast. So much elation that day.

How had Mana Lani or Kai Malina not seen this coming? They are gifted with foresight. They are the Māhū. Perhaps they only see what suits them.

"No." Kaimi whispered. "Please, someone." His voice called out again. "Help!" He bellowed.

More family memories rushed as his mind continued to process the scene. The recollections of Nohealani, Ulani, Koa, Kai Malina, and him running around when court wasn't in session. Were they all there? He was barely more than thirteen, too old to play with the babies, but somehow, they had managed to engage him. How many times did he and Nohealani have to usher their younger siblings off to bed, or back to bed, after sneaking out of their sleeping chambers only to find them playing here?

A growing collection of scarlet pooled closer to him. Pouring from her body, the thick fluid marred the sparkle of her dress, crystals hand-stitched into the gown to reflect not only the light of the kingdom, but the light of her soul.

This can't be happening. How did this happen? Who would do...

Troubling recent memories leaked into his mind as more crimson oozed through his fingers, even though his hands remained firmly in place. Rust continued to overpower every other scent around him.

The disagreements about how and if to engage the above worlders. The concerns and potential for discovery by those who live in the sun. Koa arguing with both the queen and king about how encounters with those above would be the end of them and their world here in Mu. The queen believing now the time had come to reveal themselves, hoping their presence to be a positive influence on the world above.

"We can help them. Teach them." She pointed to the ceiling. "We have so much to offer each other. Our worlds have been separated for too long."

However, when challenged and asked, neither Kai Malina nor Mana Lani were able to interpret what the Gods had to say on the matter. He wasn't sure what their gods would say, assuming they commented at all. But if the queen believed in joining the world above, who was he to argue the point? The rest of his siblings offered what he hoped to be agreement.

Well, not all. They didn't argue in public, but in private we spoke freely with each other, even loudly when the need arose.

"I need assistance." Kaimi called out, pleading with each word.

In the distance, the splashing of the tide pools outside the windows past the royal gardens filled his ears. Or were the sounds only his recollection bringing the noises to him? So many memories. Now this.—*so much pain.*—He peered over to the jeweled ornate windows, each crystal pane hand carved to reflect as much light as possible, while bringing the scenes of the world they once occupied to life with movement. Small shells from the creatures who filled the tide pools adding to the created images. A small breeze pushed the smells of water through the slightly opened windows, riding the air as more light shone through. The warmth on his skin and the taste of the salt water from the tide pools on his lips tingled all the way to his soul. He wished to be down there now, walking with Makani hand-in-hand, not here.

The blaring of sirens rang out, calling him from his thoughts, the piercing sound canceling out his calls for help. The puddles of red expanded around his knees and feet, beginning to soak his sarong.

A gift from Makani now ruined.

Kaimi forced himself to focus, his hands covered the wound before him. He glared up. As if seeing Koa for the first time. Koa stood over the body of the king on the floor. Koa glanced down, offering no help. Red droplets on his white shirt and tan sarong created a similar pattern as the light crystals shone on the kingdom when the light cycle recharged. At night, the crystals' patterns were beautiful. Here, on Koa, the image made his stomach turn. Koa stayed quiet as he continued to hold the crystal pike in his hand.

Just as I found you. What happened? Why?

"Why?" Kaimi adjusted the pressure on the wound, trying to stem the flow of blood. The chest of the queen raised and lowered slowly, but the inhalations were becoming much more irregular. He forced his stare up at Koa, his eyes moving from the weapon in his hands to the bodies on the palace floor.

"I... It..." Koa backed away, dropping the weapon to the ground, the clatter almost as loud as the siren still screeching to every corner of the palace, if not beyond. His head shook as he stared at his hands.

The main doors of the chamber burst open. "Koa!" A female voice called.

Upon hearing the doors, Koa made for the rear of the chamber.

"No!" Kaimi called out, wanting to rush after him, but if he did, there would be no one to care for the queen or the king.

"Wait!" Nohealani called out as she ran to Kaimi and the queen and king. "Koa!"

Koa stopped and glanced over his shoulder at her. "I'm sorry." He burst through the doors at the rearmost section of the chamber. The doors for his exit crashing open as he pushed passed, vanishing.

"Why?" Nohealani watched Koa rush out the doors.

"The weapon, on the floor, make sure the pike is secured. The firearm will prove what he did or didn't do." Kaimi yelled. "We need to get help... the healers." He cradled the body of the woman on the floor, tears he hadn't noticed now streaming from his eyes. Her pants for air weakening. "Help our father."

Their father lay unattended. Even on the floor laid out with a crystal gash in his chest, he was still an imposing force. His entire torso was covered with tattoos depicting his life and his many accomplishments. Those achievements were something perhaps Kaimi would someday have for his own. The king's wedding necklace made of polished whalebone had fallen on the floor next to him, his hair hid his strong face from Kaimi's site. He would bleed out soon if no one attended to him. Koa had only stood there, a look of dark satisfaction on his face.

Maybe not dark satisfaction, but fear. Or pain. Or regret.

Kaimi shook his head, pushing the sight of his brother and the pike from his mind. The smell of rust and saltwater coldly filled every part of the room.

Why harm our parents?

Within a blink of Kaimi's eyes, Nohealani moved and was at their father's side. She tore fabric from her dress and used the cloth to cover his wound, applying much needed pressure. "Where are the guards and the healers? Where are the advisors? Weren't they in council to-day?" Each question dropping as if on fire from Nohealani's mouth.

"I don't know, but the sirens will alert them, as they did you." Kaimi replied.

This should not be happening. I just spoke with both of them this morning. How can this be?

Nohealani nodded, saying no more.

What had Kaimi seen when he arrived? The bodies. The blood. Koa. The weapon in Koa's hands. Why? He didn't see Koa make the striking blows. However, he had seen enough to put the events together. Only alerted to what had happened upon hearing the yells and the struggle from the halls of the palace as he made his way to meet up with Makani in the science center. Why would Koa do this?—*he wouldn't...would he?*—Did this have to do with Mother's plans? No. They needed to find Koa. They needed to find him before he got away. He would need to answer for his crimes, or at least explain what happened. Could his brother provide a reason for all this? Koa was always a dark soul, touched by the dark waters, Mana Lani said as much on his birth.

He shook his head, "We need to find him, before..."

A pair of strongcallused hands wrenched his shoulders as several people finally started to fill the chamber around him. The hands pulled him away. He peeked up as Makani hauled him from the floor. Makani lifted him gently out of the way. "Come, let the healers work."

Kaimi nodded. "Guards, secure Koa's crystal pike. We need the weapon for evidence."

Nohealani joined them. "Find Koa. He went out those doors." She pointed to the service section of the chamber hall as another group of healers tended to their father. She peered down at the men and women working on their parents. "Why has Koa done this?"

Did he? I didn't see him commit this crime, but he was the only one in here. He had the pike. He didn't help, only watched.

"I don't know." Kaimi's head pounded with blood. He heard his heartbeat like a drum. Deafening. Iron and saltwater continued to fill his nose. He needed air. He needed to get the sight of his mother and father lying in a pool of blood out of his mind. "He will be made to pay for this heinous act."

"Kaimi. Nohealani." A hard voice called out. "Our pulse. A signal has been sent."

"What?" Nohealani moved like an eel and almost as deadly. "Malo, what do you mean, a *pulse* signal? In what direction?"

"On whose authority?" Kaimi rubbed his blood-covered hands on his dark blue sarong and white shirt without thinking.

This couldn't be happening. Why now? And a pulse, for what reason? Those above have done nothing to warrant a pulse strike.

"We don't know." Malo shifted on his feet, standing before them in his grey sarong with his traditional crystal pike still in his hand. His family tattoos covered the left side of his torso and arm. His wedding necklace displayed proudly on his neck. He was a big man, and a trusted guard of his parents. He made an excellent chief of the guards. "Everything is in chaos; several of my guards were not at their posts. Noe was able to cut off the signal before the pulse was sent out worldwide, but the signal will hit the western coast of what the above worlders call the North American Continent."

"What if they take the firing of our device for an attack?" Nohealani gasped.

"We did attack the outsiders, but not one authorized by any of us." Kaimi glanced at Malo, Nohealani and Makani. Unsure of a great many things at the moment.

Nohealani pulled herself together; her back to the healers and their parents in an effort to focus on what they needed to address now. Her dark hair falling over her shoulders once again.

What would Mother and Father do? What will I do? I need to handle this...for the moment.

Kaimi glanced over at the healer's equipment laid out as the elder barked orders to the others as they continued to work on both the queen and king. A pulse. The attack on Mother and Father. The missing guards. What's happening? Why now? "We need to tend to the queen and king as long as there is hope for their recovery, we must see to the both of them. We will deal with the signal later."

"But the above worlders?" Malo glanced between Kaimi and Nohealani.

"Should we warn them?" Makani's voice was hushed.

Nothing can be done now. What will come will come.

Kaimi frowned. "There is nothing we can do about the strike now, as long as no additional pulses are sent out."

Nohealani nodded.

"We need to secure Ulani and Kai Malina." Kaimi commanded. "And call the council together?"

"Several members of the council didn't come to the meeting today," Malo offered as he glanced down at the queen. "The queen canceled the session. I was sent out to make inquires to their absence, which is why I was not here. I should not have gone. I should have stayed by their side. I should have sent an aide to go." He growled out that last bit.

"This is not your fault." Nohealani offered as she continued to glance around the space as if measuring up what to do next. Despite the torn clothes and the blood, she appeared ready to do what was needed, something Kaimi was glad for.

The healers continued to work on their parents, as gurneys were hurried in to move their parents to the medical facility.

Gods, please let them be healed.

"Send only guards you trust to watch over Mother and Father. No one is to see them without my approval." Kaimi's voice grew stronger.

He had work to do. Not only did he need to be strong for his siblings, but he had to be strong for all their people.

At least for now, until Mother and Father are better. Nohealani and I can take care of what needs to be taken care of...for now.

Malo nodded.

"Find Mana Lani and Kai Malina; perhaps they have a message from the Gods or can lead us in a spiritual healing." Nohealani watched their parents being wheeled out. "Please find Allyn and Palani. I want to ensure they are safe."

"I've already sent for our children." Malo nodded as he reached a hand for her, gripping her forearm. "They will be with my parents."

Nohealani offered Malo a weak smile.

"Until our queen and king are healed, Prince Kaimi, you are the acting ruler," Makani faced Kaimi and kneeled. "I will have my best guards assigned to your protection." He flagged over two guards, who flanked Kaimi.

"Let us hope this will be temporary." Kaimi nodded to the guards, both dressed similarly to Malo and both carrying large crystal pikes. "Perhaps, pull the energy guns and rifles to arm the guards for now, until we know what is happening, but let's keep as much quiet as we can for now. We do not need a panic."

"A wise call." Makani nodded and motioned to the others.

"I suggest I, or we, monitor the pulse situation from Noe's lab," Nohealani offered, her focus now on Kaimi and not the scene around them. "I trust Noe was able to stop the pulse from doing any significant damage?"

"We don't know yet." Makani rubbed his forehead. "But even with minimal damage the above worlders are going..." He shook his head. They all knew the potential for devastation.

"Okay, we need to learn what has happened, as Nohealani stated." Malo adjusted how he stood. "Once our queen and king are secure, I'll join you with Noe and the other scientists. See what can be done from here? The rest is in the hands of the Gods."

Makani brushed his dark brown hair out of his face. "Our priority for the moment is to support Kaimi. Everything else will sort itself out."

Kaimi stood watching events happen around him as time slowed down to a trickle and came rushing back like the waterfalls near the crystal caves.

Someone wants to betray us and our people. And start a war with the outside world. What are the Gods possibly playing at?

"We hope everything will work out." Kaimi replied with a pensive glance toward Malo. "We hope."

~ Chapter Two ~

Present

Michael's eyes fluttered open. The soft scent of lavender tickled his nose, and he took a deep breath, enjoying the smells before exhaling. "Who's there?" He mumbled to the empty room as the first rays of the morning were starting to break through the curtains covering his windows. He rolled over onto his back, a sigh breaking from his lips as the softness of the bed and pillow engulfed him. The smile, his chest, and those beautiful thighs. "So real." He glanced at the ceiling fan as the machine spun, a soft moan joining each rotation. The cool air on his exposed shoulders and chest both chilled and tantalized him, especially after such a dream.

He glanced down, seeing the duvet tented up right below his mid-section. "I'll have to take care of that in the shower." He peered up at the ceiling fan as the blades spun around.

He remembered each detail, the taste of his lips as they kissed, the playful bites at his ears and neck. Even how their tongues danced around each other for what seemed like hours. The dream played out like a scene from one of his movies, but this was real, not forced for the camera. A gentle moment of passion shared between two people who desperately wanted each other as their souls merged into one.

Not fake.

His chest dropped as what he assumed was a smile faded from his chilled lips. "Clearly a pleasant dream, but a dream nonetheless." Things like that may happen to everyone else, but not to him. Michael was a pariah, *persona non grata*, when relationships were in play. Sure, people found him attractive, even at forty, but once they found out what he had done in his past. Where he had come from. Where his money came from.

He shook his head.

They couldn't handle his past or present, and they would leave. At least those were the honest ones. The ones who pretended not to know about him, professed to understand, and faked wanting to be with him, those hurt. These guys only really wanting to see what being with him, a former adult entertainer, was like. Once they got what they were after, or found out he was a regular person, with feelings and emotions, not a prop for their fantasies, they would leave.

The alarm from his phone buzzed, forcing him out of his thoughts.

He rubbed his hands over the stubble on his face and chin.

Definitely need a shave today.

Michael reached over and tapped the alarm before picking up the phone, swiping at one of the news alerts reading:

Five years since the Pacific Pulse. Scientists still baffled by the occurrence. Swipe to learn more.

"Baffled...well I guess *baffled* is one word for what happened." He dropped his feet over the edge of the bed, the cool wood chilling the bottom of his bare feet. He remembered the night the strange signal happened, the pulse interrupted everything, phone, radio, computers, cell service, satellites, all technology. Everyone assumed the Pulse was some new weapon from China, Russia or one of the other countries who didn't like the US. The west coast was a mess for hours, everyone freaking out. Not only here in the US, but Canada and Mexico. Michael shook his head.

"So much devastation and still not everyone has recovered."

The Scientists came out and declared they had suffered from a geological abnormality from the Pacific Ocean. "Right." He huffed.

"Boneheads. What did they know?" He chuckled, "What did I know at the time...hell what do I know now?"

He put the phone down on his nightstand, not needing to turn the light on. More and more of the morning light crept over the room. Prickles on his flesh quickly appeared as a shiver raced down his spine. All the money he offered for research; Stanford, Santa Clara University, San Francisco University, University of British Columbia. He even offered money to the University of Alberta in Edmonton to open a research center. He did the same in Mexico. But nothing, well, that wasn't quite true. Sure, people would take the money, but no one wanted to be associated with him or have his name on any of their buildings.

He frowned down to the floor. "Except for my dream man."

A fresh flash of those soft lips and beautiful dark hair tugged at his visual memory. Another shiver danced down his spine, this time not related to the cold.

"To find a love like that." he lamented "in the real world would be nice."

The more he focused on his dream man, the more details returned to him. "Everything about the dream felt so genuine."

There was another ding from his phone. He glanced at his device.

"A text message from Karen." He didn't bother looking at the message long enough to read. "I'll deal with you after I shower and get myself ready for the day." Standing, he allowed the small amount of the duvet covering him to drop to the bed, exposing his nakedness to the morning air. "And now I have to pee."

He made his way to the bathroom to get ready. His day played out ahead of him. He would go to the office early, meet with his development heads; they were working on another site upgrade for each of his three platforms. After that, he had a meeting with his product development group to go over the series of new adult toys. People might snub their nose at the adult entertainment industry, but explain how, if everyone is against porn, the industry pulls in about $20 billion a year. How do you explain his company being on target to have its most profitable year? He laughed.

"Hypocrisy." He mumbled as the water from the shower bounced off his face, waking up every cell as the heat warmed him. He tapped a button on the shower and hints of eucalyptus started to fill the steam and the stress washed away with each drop of water.

He would need to check with Sharon about his meeting with Karen. They were going to meet about her expedition...

He massaged shave oil into his cheeks, chin, and neck. Karen had managed to convince him to fund all her research into the Pulse. To pay for her little trip into the depths of the ocean. He pondered faking his support of her, giving her enough money to keep her busy, but not enough to do any real work. Maybe enough money to play out her theories here on land. But no, Dr. Linn, Karen, believed in her work and wanted answers. Her passion ended up a contagion and he ended up wanting to support her. Help her.

Dr. Karen Linn is that good.

Michael chuckled at the thought.

Sadly, no one believed in her, or her lost continent idea, so he couldn't blame her for her deception with him at first. When she approached him about studying the Pacific Pulse Event. Trying to learn what actually happened. Considering the effect the Pulse had on the west coast of the whole North American Continent and how horrified everyone had been, his conscience wouldn't allow him to say no. The West coast, specifically California, was his home, seeing the impact and the aftermath, had been unbearable. No, he had to do something.

So many unanswered questions. Why hadn't the Pulse happen all over the world, why only along the North American West Coast? Why not all around the Pacific Rim? The governments, scientists, environmentalists, no one had a clue.

Appearing out of nowhere, Dr. Karen Linn showed up. Charming him, playing to his desire to help, and now here they were. Her wanting to find a lost continent of people and him funding her. Was their partnership more about her charm or sheer force of will? He wasn't sure.

I'm crazy.

He finished his shower, running the hot water much too long, but enjoying every second. He toweled off and caught a glimpse of himself in the mirror.

"You're a damn fool." He grinned and checked himself over. "At least you're a damn fool who still looks good naked." Laughter burst out of him, the joyous noise louder than what he considered necessary, but who cared. The house was empty.

Only him.

"Tom would have helped her. So why not invest the money, not like anyone else wanted his money. Plus, she might actually be right, stranger things have happened and who knows, maybe I'll meet a sexy-ass-merman."

His newfound good mood managed to emanate from him and fill the bathroom as he left to get dressed.

*****

"You have your meeting with Dr. Linn at 2 p.m." Sharon reminded, her shoulder length blondish grey hair danced around her neck. "You'll need to leave at 1:30 p.m. if you want to make the appointment on time."

Michael checked his phone. "I'll leave right after lunch."

"Sounds good. Did you want me to order in, or are you going to have your usual yogurt and salad?" Sharon typed on the keyboard, making the change to his calendar.

Michael stood watching her work. She was a whiz at everything. She understood computers, she understood all the latest and greatest tech, she kept him sane, and she didn't judge him. Which was tops on his list.

"What do you think about all this?" He pointed around the office and her desk.

"Which this?" Sharon peeked over her shoulder as she turned to give him her full attention. She glanced from her custom work station with computer, monitors, color printer, and phone, to the filing cabinets across from her, to the guest chairs, and the large China Doll plant that she had had for as long as they worked together. Her office as put together as her.

"Dr. Linn. A lost city. A lost continent in the Pacific Ocean. The Pulse. All of my crazy outside the office projects. Any of it?"

She crossed her arms over her chest. "Michael, the money is yours. This is your company. Who am I to say?"

Michael met her gaze with raised eyebrows.

"You want my opinion, fine." She inhaled. "I don't know." She uncrossed her arms and picked up her mug, taking a sip of her green tea, if his nose worked. "If there's some Atlantis type thing in the Pacific Ocean, why now? Why not long ago? Why at all?"

"But the..."

"All the stuff with our electronics, I know. I remember, nothing worked. I thought we were staring at the end of civilization. Crazy now, I know. But now, no one knows why or how the Pulse happened and there are a million theories." Sharon's tone raised along with her hands and arms as she continued. "The good thing to come out of all that mess was ensuring we were EM pulse ready." She glanced at her computer. "Look, you run three of the most popular adult entertainment sites on the internet and you run a successful adult entertainment movie and merchandise business. People judge you all the time, before they even get to know you." She glared at the phone. "I hear their remarks and rude comments all the time on that damn thing." She pointed. After a moment she faced him and beamed, "you gave her tens of millions of dollars to research what happened, and she did, well sort of, so who knows." Sharon took another sip of tea, not saying anymore.

"What if she's right?"

"Well, you, Michael Donovan, will be part of one of the largest discoveries of all time and no one will ever be able to take that away from you, no matter what." She nodded. "And that will be pretty fantastic." She checked the clock. "Now go to your meetings and I'll see you tomorrow."

"Yes, ma'am."

"I'll be here if you need anything, so call or text."

"Okay." He returned to his office to grab his keys and phone.

"Oh, don't forget you have the awards dinner this weekend. I RSVP'd for you and a date."

"What. You planning on joining me?" He shouted from his office as he scanned his phone, then his desk and conference table, with the blue and purple hand-blown glass bowl (a gift from Sharon) sitting in the center, to ensure he had all the directions, and all the details he needed for his meeting with Karen.

"No. But I'm sure I can get one of the models to go with you." She laughed.

Michael reflected on his days as a model. Taking in the sight of the various awards and accolades he had received both as the head of the company and from his time as a model. His first real encounter with Tom and how their meeting changed everything.

*****

The old guy sat at his desk as Michael stood at the door. Music, classical, if Michael guessed right, played in the background of the office. The room wasn't anything fancy, but the space and the furniture were nice enough and clean. On one of the bookcases were a bunch of awards. Over the sofa hung some print painting of New York during the winter with all the snow. On the desk where Tom sat was a computer and phone, along with a bunch of files and DVD cases. There was another table filled with more papers. Most were designs for some of the movies they made here. Tom was the big boss, he ran the place, and every detail crossed his desk. Michael had only talked to Tom once, maybe twice, so why was he here now?

Tom glanced up and smiled. "Come in, close the door." He pointed to the sofa. "Have a seat."

Oh. This is why. I figured things were too good to be true. Well, at least I know what I'm in for.

Michael did as instructed; closed the door and made his way over to the sofa, where he stopped and started taking off his clothes. The shirt was easy, a tee-shirt, his belt and jeans took a bit more effort. "Do you want me completely naked or can I leave my socks on...my feet get cold." He asked.

"What?" Tom glanced over and watched what the young man was doing.

Michael faced the couch. He was about to drop his pants. "If I would have known, I would have prepared a bit, but if you want to fuck me, I should be fine. Or did you want me to fuck you?"

There was silence as a chair groaned and moved as if its occupant stood.

Here he comes. I heard he had a big dick, too.

"I can jerk-off if you wanna watch." Michael offered and turned around, exposing himself to Tom, his hand already playing with his dick and balls. "I've had a busy week. I might take a minute or two for things to get hard, but once I'm hard, there won't be an issue, unless you want me to get you off, which is cool." He shrugged and continued to watch Tom, who only stood there watching him. "What?"

Tom chuckled. "I didn't call you here for sex." He moved from the desk. "Please put your clothes on and put your dick away, save it for the films."

"Is something wrong?" Michael glanced down at his body. He assumed he had a good shape, and he had a great dick and balls. "Trust me, if you want me to fuck you, I'll make sure...popping into you won't hurt. I've had a lot of practice and know what I'm doing..." He laughed. "I mean, you've seen my movies... haven't you?"

"Michael, put your clothes on and have a seat. I invited you here because I like what I've seen...not in your movies or online, but of you."

"I don't understand." Michael pulled on his pants and tucked away his dick. With another narrowed eye glance at Tom, he picked up his tee and slipped the garment on.

"First, how old are you?"

"How old do you want me to be?" Michael countered, batting his eyelashes and offering Tom his most winning smile.

"Cute." Tom huffed, a frown crossing his lips. "My file says you're 19. Is the file correct?"

Michael shrugged.

"You're not in trouble. I want to know if you're older. Nothing more."

"Fine, I'm 22." Michael's shoulders straightened. He was still young, but dropping a few years never hurt. People, especially older guys, wanted young guys. The younger you could pass for, the better.

Tom nodded, "I thought so." He pulled out his pen and made a note on a piece of paper. "We'll have to get your age sorted. Right, anyway, there's an award ceremony this weekend, and I'd like you to join me." Tom pulled out his guest chair and sat down.

"Like a date." Michael's eyes narrowed.

He's not a bad looking guy, but not my type. But I need this job and I don't want to be doing this my whole life. Fuck.

Again, Tom laughed and shook his head. "No. I'm too old for you, and I doubt an old black guy is your type. Don't get me wrong, in my heyday we'd have had a lot of fun. Still, I would be flattered if I were, but I doubt it." He pointed to the sofa for Michael to sit. "You don't do drugs, you don't party and from everyone I've talked to, you're a good guy, a bit eager and a little gun shy, but..." He shrugged.

"Look, Sir, um... Tom... what do you want?"

"Did you finish high school?"

Michael shook his head.

"Well, for starters, I want you to get your GED. And when you're not acting or modeling, you'll work here in the office with me."

"I don't understand."

"I think you can be more than a model." Tom beamed as he puffed out his chest. "I think you can be more than someone to look at and get off with."

"But..."

"Look, get yourself a nice suit for this weekend. We'll go to this award presentation, unfortunately none of your movies made the deadline for this year, but next year they will and I believe you'll win." Tom's voice filled with pride as he spoke. "If everything goes well at the ceremony, you'll work here when you're not performing, as you get your GED. Once you're done with your lower education, we'll talk about college."

Michael laughed. "College, right? I'm too stupid. Everyone says all the blood meant for my brain ended up in my dick, that's why my dong's so big. I don't need college to screw people. Especially when I have this between my legs." He grabbed his crotch, giving himself a squeeze to show off his size.

"You're not stupid and your dick doesn't define you." Tom pointed to his head. "What's up here does." He lowered his fingers. "How long you think you're gonna work as a model and performer?"

Michael shrugged.

"People look down on us, people ridicule us, but they all pay for us to perform and show off our bodies." Tom started. "The world is full of hypocrites and we need to take advantage of every last one of them. Look at me. Do you know how many movies I did? How many guys and girls I screwed? I bet you can't name one film I performed in. This life, the sucking and screwing, doesn't last forever, you have to make a plan." He stood up, "Consider that your first lesson." He pointed to the door. "Do you have money for a nice suit? Something wearable to a nice restaurant or a play?"

"Um..." Michael froze, not sure how to answer.

I barely have money for rent and food and the cheap POS I drive.

"I can figure some clothes out. I might be able to find something in the studio's wardrobe."

"Hold on." Tom walked over to his desk. Picked up the phone and dialed. After a moment, he spoke.

"Is Freddy there?" Tom asked as he rested the phone between his ear and his shoulder. He picked up a pen from his desk. "Let him know Tom's on the line. Tomas Reed." After a moment. "Thanks." He glanced over at Michael. "Not too many people know my real last name, and I would like to keep it that way. I'm trusting you."

Michael nodded. A lot of people in the business used stage names. His was Mike O'Toole. On account of his big dong.

"Freddy." Tom laughed. "I'm good. You?" He nodded his head.

"Listen, Freddy, I have a friend who I'm going to send to you. He needs a suit for this weekend. I know short notice, but..." Tom fell silent. "You're the best. His name, Michael Donovan." He glanced over at Michael and nodded. "I'll send him now." He nodded again. "Charge my account, don't bother the boy for money... Freddy, you're awful. You know I only have eyes for you." Tom chuckled again. "You're the best." He hung up the phone.

"I'm sending you to this shop in Los Altos," Tom wrote down the information on his notepad and ripped the piece off, handing the details to Michael. "The Los Altos Beaux Vêtements, the store is on Main Street. Freddy, Mister Bisset will take care of you."

"And what do I have to do for him?" Michael crossed his arms over his chest. Not taking the piece of paper offered to him.

"Nothing." Tom's eyes narrowed. "Be polite and professional. Freddy won't ask questions and he'll treat you right. You treat him with respect and he'll do the same."

Michael inhaled, his eyes darting around Tom's office.

A new suit and all I have to do is be polite and professional. No prob.

Tom waved the piece of paper at Michael.

Finally, Michael took the paper with the details.

"I'm putting a lot of faith in you right now. Please don't prove my intuition wrong." Tom put the pen down on his desk.

"Why you helping me?"

"No one helped me, and my life sucked for a few years." Tom frowned as his gaze dropped. "There aren't a lot of folks who get out of the adult entertainment world unscathed, and I think you've been through enough in your life."

"And what if I fuck this all up or you get pissed at me, then what? Am I still gonna be a model?"

"You'll have your GED and some work experience helping you out."

Michael took the piece of paper and stuffed the folded up note in his pocket.

"Okay, I'll get the suit and I'll be nice to this guy you're sending me to. I'll even go to this party thing, but if anything happens, I don't like, I'm out."

"Fair." Tom peered at his desk and around his office. "Now I have paperwork and phone calls to make." He sat down, causing the chair to creak. "Michael?"

Michael turned to face Tom again.

"Remember, you are more than a model. You're a person and you deserve to be treated accordingly. What you do to earn a living doesn't matter. Fucking in front of a camera..." he straightened his shoulders as he adjusted in his chair. He raised a finger and pointed right at Michael. "You are no different than anyone else who reports to an office every day, or the people picking up the trash or cleaning the toilets. Remember that."

Michael made his way to the door.

Guys out of his mind. But, hey, if I get a suit and get to go to a party, nice. Especially if I don't have to suck his dick or fuck him. As for the rest, we'll see.

*****

"Models." Michael bit his lip, a model; arm candy. He remembered what Tom told him all those years ago and how Tom helped him.—*Y ou are more than a model and deserve to be treated accordingly.* — He imagined his dream man from this morning again. Did any of them know how much he wanted something real, something honest? Tom knew. Tom always understood. Sometimes he wondered if Sharon, if any of those around him understood. Everyone had their talents and their features appealing to different people, but none of them caught his attention, well that wasn't a hundred percent true. He turned off his computer. "There's one ." He muttered to himself.

"Did you need me?" Sharon called out.

"No, just leaving." He reflected on the dark-haired guy with the broad shoulders, pouty lips, and dark eyes that, if you allowed them, would engulf you. Not to mention how charismatic and funny he was. He was still a babe, maybe twenty-six or seven. Still. "See if you can get Alister. He's got a brain, knows how to be charming, and doesn't party too much." Michael closed his office door with a satisfied nod.

Reminds me of myself, when Tom took me under his wing.

Alister had potential. He was already asking all the right questions about the business; production, directing, distribution. All the same questions he had asked Tom all those years ago. If Alister doesn't screw up, I'll bring him on and teach him.

I don't want to waste any potential. Even if our professional relationship doesn't turn into anything more.

Michael sighed.

A line Tom never crossed, maybe if I pushed. Nah, we were better as friends. As family.

"Push Alister if you can, Sharon. I think going with him would make the event tolerable. If he needs a suit, send him to Fredrick's and have him charge my account."

"Will do ." Sharon tapped away on her computer, barely responding.

"Oh, and Sharon."

"Yes." He heard her stop.

"Remember, our performers aren't only models, they are people and deserve all the respect and dignity the rest of society refuses to give them." Michael wasn't sure if the words coming out of him were his or Tom's. Either way, the remarks needed to be spoken.

"Yes, of course. I'm sorry... I wasn't thinking." Sharon's voice rang with regret.

Michael laughed as he reached his door. "Happens to me as well. Thank you for all you do and all the support you provide. I couldn't do this without you." He beamed. "Oh, set up a meeting with legal. I have contracts I need them to go over and I want to check into those new government regulations."

"You got it."

"I'll call if I need anything."

"Bye." Sharon called out.

~ Chapter Three ~

One year ago.

They needed to keep going, but where? If they had reached the science center, where Noe and he had been working on the single fin swimmer suits, they had improved the technology so much, increasing the rebreather, they might have used the suits and gone to the surface.

Well, some of them. Not everyone, but maybe they could have brought some help.

They had worked so hard on the design, pulling from the *nai'a* and the *koholā*. Nature had the best designs, so learning from these other mammals only made sense, especially with how they reached such depths. Still, they had so few working suits, perhaps Malo and the children might have gotten to safety. He might have been able to convince Makani to go.

Well, probably not. He's stubborn, still maybe.

Kaimi glanced up at the glowing crystals. He rubbed the polished bone medallion hanging from his neck. The Crystal Caves were not going to be safe for much longer. There had already been scouts spotted near the tidal pools. He ran a hand along the smooth surface of the walls. How long since they stayed in any one place this stable. Not since the rebellion started almost three years ago. Kaimi pushed the tears away from his eyes. Seeing their parents dead on the palace floor. How had the gods allowed this to happen?

But that was only the start. Fear and unrest built like a hot spring until the pressure blew. Now here we are. This is all my fault. If I was stronger, like Mother and Father.

He shuddered at the memory of the palace burning, the crystal windows shattering. Sirens blaring. Their final day. The day his home was overrun and he and the rest of those he loved had to flee.

"Kaimi ." Makani pulled at his arm. "We need to move. Koa and the palace guards have been reported near the Torokina River. They'll close the distance in a short time and they'll find us here." He shook his head. "We should have moved on when the first scouts were found."

"We need time," Kaimi forced himself to focus on what happened around him. They had been on the run too long. All this transpired because of him and Nohealani. No. He couldn't think that way. His negative thoughts weren't going to help anyone. He had to think of what to do next, where to go, where to hide, or get help. Was help even possible?

"Kaimi." Makani grabbed the pack with food and water. He pulled and grabbed whatever else lay about, stuffing all the bits into the already full pack.

"Nohealani and Malo need to get their children out of here." Kaimi tried to force all other thoughts from his mind.

"Time may not be our friend." Makani pulled together their clothes. A case dropped, and he bent down to pick the holder up. "These are the last of the energy crystals."

"Keep them." Kaimi pulled the blanket from the wall, revealing a passage. "I have plenty still."

Makani glanced over his shoulder at him, an eyebrow raised, but he said no more and stood, slipping the case into the pack he filled.

Rocks crumbled around them, and the glowing crystals flickered. Yells came from all directions as their small group of rebels continued rushing to make their escape. Kaimi recognized the battle wasn't far off. He glanced around the small alcove he and Makani had called home for the past few weeks. They couldn't keep doing this; there was nowhere else to go. Koa anticipated all the places he would go. And why shouldn't he? They grew up here, in these caves. Kaimi was at a loss. If only they'd gotten to the suits Noa and he had been working on, maybe they might have made their way to the world above, but that wasn't possible. "Where can we go?" he mumbled.

"What?"

Kaimi continued to glance around the alcove. "Faga Bay." He turned to Makani. "Faga Bay, we'll go to Faga Bay."

"Are you insane? We can't go there, the area is too close to the mouth of the gods. If Koa doesn't kill us, the gods will, or they would send their manō hae after us."

"Well, that's the only hope we have." Kaimi's voice grew stronger. "Maybe we can get out and if we stay out of the water, the manō won't bother us."

"And go where? We can't go to the outside world." Makani stuffed the last of their belongings in his bag, closing the straps tight. "The above worlders would kill us after what happened. We can't trust them."

"No. They've done nothing since—"

"They are still recovering from—"

"Kaimi." A shout from beyond the curve in the passage called out as the cavern shifted and several small shards of crystals clanked to the ground.

"Nohealani. God's, now what?" Kaimi and Makani met her at the break in the rocks. "We need to go. The others are fighting Koa and his guards off. Malo has the children, but..."

"Makani." Kaimi took his husband's hands. "Go with Malo, keep him and Nohealani's children safe."

"What?" Makani shook his head. "I'm not leaving you." His shoulders were as solid and as firm as the day they married.

"Nohealani and I will ensure you escape with the others. You are not leaving me. We will catch up shortly."

"But, Koa."

"Do you think I..." Kaimi looked at Nohealani.

She nodded.

"My sister and I will not fail. We've outmaneuvered him to date. We have the grace of the gods on our side, plus there are places here in the catacombs even Koa doesn't know. Now go." He leaned in and kissed Makani, pulling him tight and taking in the warm orchid scent of his chestnut hair before letting him go. He traced the tattooed lines on his shoulder, the edges of his lips pulled up into what he prayed was a smile. He broke the embrace and pulled at the wedding necklace around his neck. Holding the bone in his hand, "Take this for me. I will collect this from you in a day or two." He pushed the necklace into Makani's hand.

"Makani, I can think of no better to help Malo and the children, they need you too," Nohealani assured him, resting her hand on top of Kaimi's and Makani's.

Makani frowned, and his shoulders softened. "Two days." Makani stuffed the gift in his pocket. "We will keep the young ones safe. See you soon, sister." He hugged Nohealani.

"Thank you, brother." Nohealani returned his embrace.

Makani disappeared down one of the lighted caverns pack pulled over his shoulder. Kaimi was grateful he didn't turn for one more look at him. He didn't think his heart could bear the burden. Or, Makani's gaze.

"Kaimi, where are they going?" Nohealani asked as a loud rumble and energy shots echoed through the caves.

"Better not to say, the fewer who know the safer, but I promise you, Malo and your children will be taken care of." He grabbed Nohealani's hand. Let's go join the fight and give as much escape time to the others as possible."

"For Mother and Father." Nohealani pulled out her energy, pistol checking the power level remaining.

"No, for the rightful queen and king of Mu." Kaimi grabbed his energy rifle.

He wasn't fighting for a few, he fought for all their people. Kao had caused so much hurt and pain, starting with the death of their parents and the Pulse attack on the above worlders. What had he hoped to accomplish by any of this? Did his heart hold so much hate? Would he kill them all? Kill the rest of their family? No, death wouldn't bring stability, only anger and fear. No ruler ever lasted in a kingdom built on tyranny.

We will overcome this. We will restore our world, Mother and Father will be proud.

Kaimi spared a glance to his sister. She looked as determined as he did. They would need all the resolve they could muster. This battle may be lost, but the war would continue as long as he lived. There would always be hope. And even if he fell this day, Malo and Makani would keep his nephew and niece safe, to continue the battle another day. He inhaled, making peace with what was to come. He had no intention of meeting the gods on this day, or any day in the near future. Hopefully, the gods were not eager to meet him either.

~ Chapter Four ~

Present.

Karen hung up the phone. Patting her lips together, — *how did they always get so dry?*—Today's news better than anticipated. The experimental sub. Her sub, well, her sub granted to her by a friend in the French government and military, then outfitted and updated with Michael's money, would be ready in a couple more weeks. She glanced down at the photo of her with her dad and sister. He never doubted anything she did. He was her biggest supporter. She only wished he was still alive to see this.

They were one step closer. She had spent years looking for Atlantis, with nothing to show for her struggle, and those wasted years were fine, because now she realized she was wrong. She had been looking for the wrong city. She should have been looking for Mu. Who knew Dr. Chan Thomas had been correct? And chiefly thanks to the Pacific Pulse incident, she now realized Mu absolutely existed, now she only needed to find the location.

They laughed at her. They called her crazy. They laughed her out of every respectable scientific institute, but who was laughing now? She was. Pulling out her lip balm, she ran the concoction over her lips.

They are nitwits. No one has a clue as to what happened five years ago, but I'll go to Mu and find out. The location will have the answers since the Pulse came from there.

The smile on her face caused her cheeks to ache. A few more weeks and they would be ready to go. The expedition wouldn't be easy and who knew what they would find? Chances were good Mu would be in ruins. A shadow of its former glory. A long dead society from an ancient time. But something, maybe an underwater quake, caused the Pulse, but still, there would be years of research and study. And once Mu revealed herself, they'd study and learn, with her leading the charge. No longer a laughingstock.

Assuming we find Mu.

No, she couldn't think negatively. They were going to find the lost city. The Pulse was real, the chaos the event caused was real, and so Mu would be real too.

Shortly she had her planned meeting with Michael to give him an update. Their relationship wasn't ideal. The poor man had no understanding of science, and his background wasn't the best for her, or their reputation. But he was a decent man who believed in her, and had deep pockets. Plus, he needed this as much as she did. The positive press and the positive attention would do wonders for his public appearance.

Why did he care? He had money and success. Who cares what others think?

She frowned. The last part she understood. As much as everyone blathered on about how other's approval didn't matter, people's admiration always counted. We all want to be accepted and loved for who we are. She shook her head. "He's a respectable man." Their years working together had been difficult and Michael had threatened to pull funding more than once, but Karen still managed to work her charms, even with him. And if charm didn't work, her stubborn force of will did. She supposed he had a soft spot for her; after all, she was old enough to be his mom.

She shuddered at the notion.

Maybe not just his mom.

She caught her reflection in the monitor on her desk. "Not bad for a 65-year-old gal." She watched the grin grow on her face. She fussed with her auburn colored hair, well auburn now, thanks to her hair stylist. She sighed. Michael wasn't interested in her for any reason people may find funny. He wanted to be taken seriously. He wanted to do good in the world. He would. They would. Finding Mu would give them both what they both deserved and longed for.

She glanced at the photo of her father and sister. Her heart filled with pride. "We're almost there Dad. We almost found our lost city."

*****

Karen closed down her laptop and stood up, adjusting the black blazer she pulled on, the blazer older and maybe not in the best condition, but the jacket appeared professional and that was all her outfit needed to be. Fishing out the lip balm from her pocket, she ran soothing wax over her lips. She would be dressed up for the press conference and the gala event before the launch, but for now this was fine. After all, today was only a meeting with Michael. Passing the bathroom, she stopped and peeked in, glancing at her reflection. She rolled her eyes and went in, putting the laptop on the small counter and quickly nabbing the hairbrush, giving her hair a fast comb through, checked her teeth, making sure nothing from lunch marred her smile, and finally she picked up her only bottle of perfume, giving herself a quick spray.

Okay, good enough. Why am I making all this fuss? Ridiculous.

The scent of lilacs drifted up to her nose, and she waved her hands to ensure the scent dissipated.

"Good enough." She gave herself a firm nod and left the bathroom, closing the door behind her. Laptop in her free hand.

She made her way to the front door of the small four-room office she rented off Montague Expressway. The space wasn't bad. The area had been built up over the years, especially with the BART extension and all the new housing. She remembered when this whole area was R&D. Now this office was one of only a few left in the area. Still, the location and the office had everything she needed. There was space for a small team of researchers should she want them. Also, her location put her near The Great Mall, where she'd go walking if she wanted to get some fresh air and stay out of the rain.

The front reception area was empty except for a few boxes she hadn't bothered unpacking yet, a couple of chairs, a reception desk with a phone on top and a mini fridge where she kept her sodas and snacks. After putting the laptop on the desk, she popped open the fridge and pulled out a soda, opening the can, and taking a sip. She pulled over a chair and sat. Michael would be here soon enough.

Two more sips from her soda and a tap on the glass door caught her attention.

Michael stood at the door, a warm smile on his handsome face. His hair trimmed short, a collared striped long sleeve shirt with an extra button unbuttoned at the top and dark jeans, with black dress shoes. He wasn't flashy, but every part of him was put together nicely.

Karen waved at him, put her soda down, got up and walked to the door, unlocking the bolt and granting him access.

This place was a complete letdown compared to his office.

"Hello, Karen."

"Welcome to my little office." Karen moved out of the way, allowing him entry. "You're right on time, as usual." A hint of eucalyptus caught her nose, causing an involuntary twitch.

He always smells so lovely.

"I didn't want to keep you waiting. I know how busy you are." Michael beamed as he glanced around the reception area.

"Ah, you're sweet." Karen winked at him and walked over and pulled over another chair for him to sit in.

"Can I please hire you an assistant or receptionist... please?" He continued to peek around the office, a small frown tugging at his lips.

"What do I need an assistant for?" Karen returned to her seat.

All they do is get in the way and want to organize everything.

"I don't know." He pointed to the boxes. "To help you unpack or pack."

She laughed.

"Considering how much has been invested—"

"Not like I'm going to be here much longer, moving to Moffett Field soon enough. Plus, I don't want to waste your money." Karen pushed her soda out of the way and leaned forward. "I'm many things, but I'm not wasteful... well, when money's involved."

"I wasn't implying..." He found his seat, not finishing his thought.

"I know you weren't. I don't want anyone bugging me unless I need the help. The grad students and interns were enough help when I needed them, now all we have to do is wait. Well, wait until we settle on the new team."

"So nothing new?"

"Oh sure, I have tons of new data, but nothing like what you mean." Karen opened up her laptop, waiting for the screen to come to life. "No new signals from Mu, no signals at all... nothing. The few ships out there looking for where the Pulse came from gave up years ago, so now I'm alone, again."

She watched for his reaction and bit her lower lip. "I do have some data to show you that we can go through. There is something out there. And now, with all the garbage barfed up on the west coast, I'm able to send some deep probes with minimal interference, but..."

Michael crossed his arms. "But still nothing new."

She shook her head. "However, today I got a call, the sub is almost ready. Where everyone has gone wrong is only sending out boats. We're going to have the Explorer Pontus, four levels of every kind of monitoring sensor we can think of. If Mu is out there, we'll find her in the sub." Every part of her tingled with excitement, the research here on land had dried up, she needed to be out there in the water doing the real work. They would never find anything sitting here in the office reviewing satellite images, radar data, and monitoring underwater sonar.

Karen pointed to the computer screen, adding another finger print to the collection. "They can't see the bottom, well they can, but not like we're going to. We have to be there, see what the ocean is hiding, feel the currents. Really explore."

"And when is the sub going to be ready?" Michael opened his tablet and began taking notes.

"The Pontus is coming out for final testing in a few days. That's when the real work starts. Training. Check and double checks. The sub will probably be ready for launch in a month or six weeks." She laughed. "I've been working on putting my team together, ready for you to approve, of course, and getting them up to speed."

He nodded, continuing to tap away on his device.

"You're still planning on joining the team, right?" Karen glanced up at him. She had pulled up the files on the sub, the crew, and the research team for them to go over.

"I wouldn't miss this trip for the world." He peeked up from his tablet.

"Our expedition is going to be amazing." She pulled up the files and expanded the image of the sub so Michael might review everything more clearly.

He moved forward and checked the files. "This is the sub?"

"And the crew who will pilot her."

"Now I know where all my money went." He used the touch-pad to zoom in and examine the details. Four levels, fully outfitted, everything they would need under the sea. But the sub didn't look anything like he had expected. The Explorer Pontus almost resembled something out of a fantasy novel. Something Hollywood, or maybe his studio, would dream up for some cheesy movie. He couldn't help but laugh.

Karen laughed along with him. "Now you know why I didn't want you to waste money on a receptionist or assistant for this place.

"Well, the Pontus is quite a fine piece of machinery. You sure she'll give us everything we need when we're down there? Neither of us can afford to be caught short."

"The Explorer Pontus will take care of us. I have no doubt. And we should be quite comfortable, too."

"Let's look at the team you've assembled." Michael swiped at a few loose strands of hair on his forehead.

"You're gonna love them." Karen ran her hand over the laptop, pulling up more files and images for them to review.

~ Chapter Five ~

Six months ago.

Tossing and turning, images of the past filled Kaimi's mind. He had heard the whispers. He heard what people grumbled about. But their disillusionment wasn't going to dissuade him or his parents. Their world was changing, and the queen understood, so did the king. But not everyone on the council was as open-minded. Even as his Body Attendant massaged soap and water into his skin, he sensed his touch was different, more forced, even as the scents of coconut and lemongrass filled the air.

Timu had been his Body Attendant since they were youths. The man now not only a servant, but another brother to Kaimi, no, more than a brother; a dear friend and confidant. Someone Kaimi easily spoke with, with no fear. Still, Kaimi and Timu may have shared too much, and now Timu pulled away. Did this new distance have to do with his feelings for Ulani? No, his distance had to do with all the rumors about the above worlders and what his parents might do.

Didn't Timu understand their world changed, so they needed to change, too? Kaimi was no longer the child running around the palace playing with his sisters and brothers, often times found out by Timu who would ensure they, well him mostly, found no trouble. Or as little as possible. Now, as an adult, Kaimi needed to take on more responsibility and he needed to support his parents. His king and queen. They all did.

Standing with family is the way of things. We support those who lead and turn to them for advice and guidance. That is how our world has always been, and will need to continue.

The oiled and scented water cascaded over his shoulders and down his back and chest.

"Would you like your feet scrubbed?" Timu's voice melded with the water as his words splashed around Kaimi's head.

"Yes. Please. You always do an amazing job." Kaimi forced what he hoped to be his typical smile. He enjoyed these moments with Timu. Here in the bathing waters they felt like equals, perhaps because they were both undressed and fully exposed to one another. Their crystals and pikes on full display. Their nakedness allowed for a shared vulnerability.

Timu gestured to the edge of the bathing pool and Kaimi slid into the nook, where he would sit. Timu offered a towel to cover Kaimi's pike, protecting his modesty, which was silly, as Timu had seen him fully and recognized Kaimi's body as equal to his own. Timu had viewed Kaimi grow from a young child to a man, similarly Kaimi watched Timu grow. Timu only had four years on him, granting him a slight start on adulthood, but Kaimi had grown taller and broader, surpassing Timu, even when they were younger. Kaimi took the offered towel and placed the heavy material over his lap, taking up the position. Again, he offered Timu what he hoped to be a warm smile.

Timu bowed his head in recognition and picked up Kaimi's left foot, taking stone to water to foot and began scrubbing.

Kaimi's foot twitched. The scrubbing always caused this reaction, especially when Timu began.

"Sorry." Timu paused and gently shifted Kaimi's foot. He reached for one of the containers of oil and rubbed some on Kaimi's foot.

"No need. You know my feet can be sensitive."

"Yes, your highness."

Kaimi's face and heart dropped when the words spilled out of Timu's mouth. "Timu, why?" He took a breath. More of the warm coconut and lemongrass filled his nose and lungs. "You've been with me since we were boys. Please, won't you call me Kaimi, like you used to?"

Timu stopped and placed the scrubbing stone on the solid edge. He lowered Kaimi's foot into the scented warm water. He glanced up at Kaimi and the expression on Timu's face melted Kaimi's heart and made his stomach drop. "I can't support what the queen and king, and by extension you, are planning. Their new ideas worry me. What they want to do may hurt us all." His words barely a murmur.

"What we're doing is going to help."

"You don't know, Kaimi. Our people do not want..." He stopped and glanced to the water.

"Speak freely." Kaimi encouraged and reached out, taking Timu's hand.

"I'm afraid my speaking would be impertinent." Timu removed his hand and picked up the stone and Kaimi's right foot and went to work on his feet.

Kaimi leaned forward and stopped him. He pulled the stone from Timu and waited for his eyes to meet his. He had the full day to wait if needed. "I want to understand your fears and concerns, perhaps I can bring peace to your mind."

Kaimi heard the air enter and leave Timu's body, finally a slight nod and he met Kaimi's gaze. "He's not good enough for you."

Laughter filled the bathing chamber, something the location had greatly missing.

"Timu, if I didn't know better I would say you were jealous."

He remained quiet.

Is Timu jealous, he never showed interest in me. Never the slightest touch or movement out of line. He was the perfect Body Attendant. Plus, I thought his heart beat for Ulani.

There was a time when Kaimi was young, he would fantasize of Timu, despite him not being what most would consider handsome. Still, he was warm, funny, and always spoke plainly. Plus, his smile lit up the room. There were many times when Timu had bathed Kaimi that his young changing body reacted to his touch, but his excitement was to be expected, especially as he grew into manhood. He hardly ever remembered a time when his pike wasn't ready for action, or when his crystals didn't ache for release. Some days, he had to massage himself four to five times, just so he could focus on other tasks. However, Timu was not only his body attendant, but a friend, a dear friend, with nothing more between them.

"I'm not jealous, Kaimi, I'm worried. I'm afraid." Timu's gaze cast toward the water surrounding the two men.

"Makani offers our people nothing to be fearful of." Kaimi fought with his tone to keep as neutral as possible. "Makani is like everyone else and I love him, since the day our eyes met."

"He's not good enough for you. I'm sorry to say so, but he's not. And your ideas are starting to mimic his," Timu countered.

I asked for him to speak plainly and he has. Perhaps I shouldn't have asked.

Kaimi lowered his body into the warmth of the scented waters. "I see, but Timu, are you sure these thoughts aren't my ideas he's mimicking? Perhaps I've rubbed off on him. Maybe I changed his mind on a great many things."

Timu peeked over at Kaimi and returned his gaze to the water. He zoomed in on the stone, which was still in Kaimi's hand. "You will be king someday and you will need an heir; will Makani allow that? Will he accept you taking a woman to your bed so you may have an heir?"

Kaimi sighed. "Makani understands what I must do and we've spoken of this, but times are not like they were. I do not need to take a woman to my bed, we have ways to doing this now. Involving no intimate contact."

"Another change. All these new ways." Timu countered.

"Why is change so bad?" Kaimi stood, now fully warmed and not caring if Timu regarded him fully. "No one was upset when we created the spark, allowing us to see into the night. No one worried when we managed to duplicate our blood, so more people who suffered injuries would be saved. No one was upset when our Scientists discovered the pulse weapon, which in my opinion is far more dangerous." He shook his head as he walked around the pool and Timu. "We no longer dwell in huts. We have treatments for a large number of diseases that would have killed us only fifty years ago; the gods have blessed us with knowledge and learning, allowing us to improve our world. I cannot believe people are worried or fear my ability to create an heir."

"Many of the people fear these additional advancements." Timu turned to meet Kaimi. "They believe they are leading us to them..." He pointed up.

Timu wasn't pointing to the ceiling, but to the world outside, the world belonging to the above worlders.

"They are like us. We've seen them. We've learned about them for as long as we've been here in Mu. We've learned some of their language even. They are, in a way, our kin." Kaimi made his way to leave the bathing pool. He wasn't going to listen to this foolishness. "What is there to be scared of?"

"They may look like us," Timu shook his head, "but they aren't us. They are foreign and are more focused on destroying the world instead of making our only home better. Even their languages hold destruction in them."

Kaimi stopped. He understood now. The fear the people were speaking of, the fear Timu spoke of, this crisis, isn't about him but about the world outside their own.

Yes, the above worlders were different and some even scary, but soon their technologies would match ours. Then what? We should meet them on an equal footing.

"Timu, we've only learned small amounts about these people, but perhaps now is the time to learn. We can't judge them all by the little we know." Kaimi handed him the stone. "Maybe now's the time for us to trust in the gods and each other."

"Yes, Kaimi."

Timu went to make his way out of the bathing pool as well. Kaimi afforded himself a glance to the ceiling, seeing the crystals glimmer with light. He wondered, not for the first time, what would walking and living in the above world be like. Are they as awful as some believe, or are they like him and his people? Curious and willing to learn, perhaps we would find out soon...

*****

Kaimi woke with a start. His heart racing as beads of sweat dripped from his brow. The images of Timu fresh in his mind. Their conversation. He should have listened, he should have not brushed Timu's concerns aside too easily, but he was supporting the vision of his parents, and they were never wrong.

Clearly, we had misjudged. So many mistakes. Why didn't we listen?

Had his Body Attendant survived? Or, had Timu fallen in line with Koa? Kaimi shifted. All he wanted to do now was sleep. Rest. Dream. However, neither would come, not now, maybe never again. He rolled to his side. The unforgiving steel under him offered no comfort as the threadbare blanket barely covered his body. How had this happened? Why hadn't any of them seen this? His mother would have, but she wasn't here anymore. None of them were. Gone, and everything happening since was his fault. No! These events predated him. He couldn't be blamed for everything. They had all caused their current situation. He took a deep gulp as the abominable, musty air terrorized his senses.

I miss the salt air.

"How are you?" A soft whisper of a familiar voice bounced off the stonewalls pulling him from his misery...from their misery.

"How do you think?" Kaimi moaned. "We caused this. This is our fault. I hope the others are doing better." He turned to face Nohealani. The soft glow of the embedded light was enough to illuminate her once beautiful features.

Her long dark hair tangled, hanging in clumps. She had done her best to keep her hair up, but their conditions didn't allow for much. These accommodations were better than they deserved. The twinkle in her deep brown eyes was all but gone. A beauty from heaven was what their father would say, no longer. The years of hiding and running took her youthful appearance from her. Took their naivete from both of them.

"Koa knows as much as we do, probably more. I doubt..."

"We can't think like that. They may have gotten away, they may have reached safety."

"Safety." Nohealani huffed. "Is there such a thing now?" She pulled herself up and got close to the bars separating them. "The world above.

The world outside our own." She laughed. "There is no safety, not anymore. Not after what we caused."

"We don't know that." Kaimi pulled himself up and focused on his sister, trying to present a face of strength and determination, but mainly one of hope.

For a moment, a smile crossed her filthy lips and brightened her face. Happy images of their past filled his mind; playing by the ponds, stealing treats from the kitchens. This was the Nohealani he remembered and wanted to see. But as quickly as the smile appeared, it vanished. "Mother and Father were killed four and a half years ago," she whispered. "If they..." She pointed to the ceiling, before continuing, "were to come, they would have already. They have the technology and we observed what happened along their coastline. Why not come by now?"

Kaimi grew silent. He didn't have an answer for her. They waited, they hid, they fought, they tried to survive as long as possible and now here they were, in cells. Punished for the crimes they supposedly committed, better than the others they were caught with, they were dead, but Koa... he took pity on them. All this, and for what?

Four and a half years. So much time running and hiding and for what? Here we sit, our futures uncertain.

The grind of metal on metal caught both their attention and they quickly moved to the front of their cells. The time wasn't right for a meal. The lights began to raise casting their jail in more of a hazy glow, solid stone walls. No windows. Bars, a cool stone floor. Nothing but hard surfaces and the stench of waste. Kaimi took in their dire situation with the dark. They imagined hope, but seeing the four walls of solid stone.

There is no hope.

As the door ached open, a harsh white light cut through the grow-ing cold hues. Kaimi held a hand to his eyes, they needed time to adjust. Moisture filled his eyes, as he wasn't used to all the brightness.

Broad shoulders, perfect posture, and a trim waist, the outline of the captor blocked out the light standing there for a rare visit.

This isn't good.

"This is no place for either of you." The hard voice commented as he stepped into the jail. Giving both Kaimi and Nohealani a good look at him. He waved a hand triggering the sensor on the wall to close the door behind him, but his actions weren't what caught Kaimi's eye, the man carried something in the other hand...what?

A solid case.

"And how are we today?" Their jailer asked, his tone neutral. "Kai-mi, you are looking a little thin. Are you getting enough to eat? I will instruct the others to increase your rations." He strolled over, peeking at Nohealani. "And what of you, Nohealani? Is there anything I can get you? I'm limited, but I will see what I can do. What about—"

"What do you want?" Nohealani spat at him.

"I've got some news." His gaze dropped and his lips lightened. The expression of concern changed.

The fresh scent of ocean mist caught Kaimi's attention. Memories of freedom rushed through his body, crashing on the solid bars sur-rounding him. Kaimi wasn't sure what was worse, being locked up or running and hiding. He supposed today was worse as no good came when Koa visited. Things must not be going well for the others.

"Tell us what you will, afterwards leave." Nohealani growled at him.

"No time for pleasantries... so be it." Koa shrugged. He knelt down and placed the case on the floor in front of them. His hands moved over the latches and with a loud click, the case opened. He glanced at both of them and inhaled deeply.

As much as Kaimi didn't want to move closer to the bars, he did. Nohealani followed.

Koa pulled out a pad and tapped. Without words, he turned the device to them, allowing them to view what he wanted them to see.

Nohealani moaned as tears streamed from her eyes. Kaimi reached for her through the cage touching her arm with his shaking fingers. He wasn't sure who trembled more, his sister or him. The video continued to play.

"He put up a fight, protecting your children, but in the end." Koa sighed, lowering the screen.

"Why!" Nohealani yelled. "Malo was nothing but kind to you. He treated you like a brother."

"True, but he, like you, and the rest of your family, were on the wrong side of things. The people above will come here and destroy our home. The queen and king never wanted to see this certainty and you..." Koa pointed at Nohealani and Kaimi. "Were willing to help them. Support them."

"How can you say such things?" Kaimi yelped. "You know we never found out who sent the pulse. But, maybe now we need to reach out. Their technology isn't far behind ours any longer. Maybe now is the time we sail the seas and meet them. We can't hide from them forever."

"I never said we should hide, but we can't open our doors to them. They have no redeeming qualities. They've all but destroyed the planet and do nothing to make changes. They keep exploiting our world and they will do the same to us." He moved closer. "I want to keep us safe, and now I'm going to accomplish this task. Do you have any idea what they will do with what we know, how they will use our technology and all we've learned about the oceans? No."

Nohealani only cried, any strength in her now gone. Kaimi doubted his sister would have a level head in that moment. She needed to grieve. Koa may have broken her spirit finally.

Let her grieve. The tears and sorrow will make her stronger...I hope.

"There is something you need to see as well, Kaimi." Koa tapped the pad and held the crystal device up. "We found him near the Mouth of the Gods."

Kaimi watched the video play; voices called out yelling, fighting, energy shots of blue and red, finally silence. "You're a monster."

"Am I." Koa crossed over to Kaimi, glaring at him. "Am I really? You and our sister tried to kill me. After Mother and Father were murdered, you assumed I killed them." He shook his head. "I loved them. I would never hurt them and yet you thought the worst, but you were wrong. Like those who followed you. You caused the rebellion. I loved you. You were everything to me. I may not have shown my love and emotions as you do, as both you do, but that doesn't mean I didn't have them. I was never the monster you made me out to be. I may be the monster now, but you... you made me the monster long before I became one." He turned and made his way to the door. "As you can gather, neither Malo nor Makani survived. We gave them a chance to surrender, but..."

"No!" Nohealani collapsed.

"Not to worry sister, I'm taking excellent care of my niece and nephew."

"Please. My children... don't... don't harm them."

"I told you." He stopped. "I'm not the monster you made me out to be. No harm will come to them. I will care for them. They are family, after all."

"Koa, brother, please." Kaimi found himself pleading as his hands reached out between the bars. "We can fix this. We still need to find who murdered Mother and Father and who sent out the pulse originally. If you didn't trigger these events and clearly we didn't authorize the attack, then who? You can't—"

"You don't get to play the victim." Koa didn't turn from the door. "You would have killed me if you had the chance, both of you. The only ones to believe me were Ulani and Kai, which is why they are not here with you."

"Please, I'm sorry. Please." Nohealani pleaded, her voice cracking more with each word.

Kaimi never discerned his sister was capable of such a thing.

"Tell me you're wrong," Nohealani continued. "Makani lives. That this is a cruel joke, and you did not let him die in such a manner."

Koa turned with tears dancing around his eyes. "Makani loved you with his very soul and would have killed to save you. He fought like no other, he was my friend, but in battle we have no friends and during war there is only ugliness. I wanted him and Malo alive, they were never meant to be killed, but a miscalculation...the gods were not kind, instead of wounding." Koa swiped at his eyes. "I would have saved him if the healers..."

"He's dead." Kaimi's voice trembled, the shuddering moving quickly to the rest of his body. "The images aren't a fabrication." Bile raised again and his legs began to give out. He found the cot before he hit the floor.

"I will have both their remains collected and moved to the family vault to be with Mother and Father." Koa's tone fell soft through the space. "If you would have believed in me."

Kaimi nodded his head, but couldn't speak.

"Kai had a vision, but they are...well they are Kai." Koa's voice fell flat. "They said the vision will affect us all, but continued saying they would need to pray on the matter before explaining." His voice was softer, gentler. "Perhaps now that the last of the rebellion has been put down, I can return you to your chambers and we can get past this... somehow."

How can we get past this? You have broken us.

Kaimi remained quiet as the grinding metal door closed. A symphony of tears from Nohealani filled his ears, her sobs crashing into his own. His heart shattered, his muscles falling limp as sorrow rushed through his veins. He welcomed the darkness coming to overtake him.

~ Chapter Six ~

Karen brought her vehicle to a halt at the security booth and pulled out her identification information for the guard. Since the Pulse and the devastation caused by the waves of both trash and water, the San Francisco Bay shoreline had changed as had the bay itself, but nothing like what happened along the coast. This part of the Bay Area got off easy. Everything along the west coast was a mess, and some areas, like Baja California, much of the Mexican Riviera and the Strait of Juan de Fuca, were still recovering.

At least Vancouver Island and the Olympic Peninsula came out okay, and much like here, Victoria, La Paz, and Seattle appear as though nothing happened... well, except for the shifts in the shore.

"Dr. Linn, good to see you again." The female guard with the pulled back brown hair greeted her. "You are cleared to proceed."

"Thank you." Karen put away her identification and slowly drove her old ford Taurus forward, following the road to the new piers where she would find her sub. Thankfully the pier wasn't too far from her new office. Moffett Field had both changed and benefited after the Pulse. The water levels shifted and dredged out a lot of the shore, making the southern point of the San Francisco Bay the perfect location for the Explorer Pontus and some of NOAA's new ships and equipment. NASA had to learn to share the space, but the old base gave the government an excuse to spend a lot of money in the area, upgrading the location, making the local politicians happy for the influx of cash and jobs. So, she couldn't and wouldn't complain.

"And the hefty chunk of change Michael is paying to lease the pier, and the offices didn't hurt, either." She commented to the empty car as she continued to drive.

She found her parking space and checked her reflection in the rearview mirror, knowing she would have to ensure her appearance was top-notch, not only now, but for the media event. Massaging her lips together, she would forgo another layer on her lips for the moment. She hated society's importance on how she presented herself, but one's clothes, hair and overall looks did, in fact, have a big impact on how people perceived you. For now, she would be inspecting the sub, the sub crew, and her team.

All handpicked by me.

She couldn't wait to get into the sub and be a part of the craft's final testing. Not having Michael here was a shame, but he would be joining her, and the others, once everything was good to go. Not having Michael underfoot while she created her team helped and made the move and the process all the easier; sure, he had input, but mostly he worried about security and ensured none of the team, her team, well, their team, were going to be a problem.

I can't blame him for being so careful; people are assholes.

Stepping out into the sun, she glanced in the direction of the pier. She snatched up her bag and pulled out a pair of sunglasses and some of her lip balm. "Better." She pressed her lips together, dropping the balm into her bag.

Off to the side and ahead of her sat the Explorer Pontus. The sub didn't seem like anything special, with the crew rushing about, but what mattered most lay inside the hull. All their equipment and all their changes and upgrades. The French Admiral, her father's buddy from the war, promised her this sub was as good as any in the French fleet or the US fleet for that matter. Originally called the P301 Pontus, the sub was a prototype deep ocean sub which they mothballed when funding ran dry. The sub had been built not only for deep waters but to be a swift attack sub capable of full stealth drive and attack. The craft was meant to be the latest and most deadly ship in the French fleet, able to counter the newest threats to face France and her allies. But that was fifteen years ago. The sub was older, sure, but there was nothing wrong with having a few years under your belt.

And I'm glad to have given the old girl a new life and purpose with years of work and research ahead of her.

Seagulls called out from overhead, getting her to glance up to the sky before looking out to the Bay. Hints of salt water found her nose.

From here the sub looks all dark and black, probably something to do with the stealth mode, assuming the tech still worked.

"No use crying over what's gone." She glanced around, turning toward the building with her office. "Especially since we're finally going to have answers."

A few more weeks. Just a few more weeks.

Karen peeked one more time over her shoulder at the sub, lowering her sunglasses and filling her lungs with the air of satisfaction, she made her way to her office.

*****

"Captain Abbas, welcome." Karen stood and walked around her desk. Her office didn't look any better than at the last location. The only difference was this office was huge and gave plenty of room for her and her team of fourteen. "You didn't have to come over here, I'd have come to the Pontus."

"I'm happy to stretch and get out of the sub. Despite all the upgrades, we're still in a sub." Abbas took off her dark blue hat, showing her short hair. Her uniform was a riff off the US Navy's uniform, the color scheme a dark blue with gold accents and piping. The design was sharp and clean.

"Something we're all going to need to get used to." Karen inhaled. The idea of being in confined spaces didn't bother her, but being in tight spaces underwater, well, that was a tougher pill to swallow.

I'll be fine.

There was a crash from down the hall and Karen winced.

"Should you go check?"

Karen shook her head.

These interns are going to be the death of me.

"Sorry Dr. Linn." A male voice called out. "That wasn't any of the equipment...well a laptop, but nothing broke..." There were some additional mumbles Karen couldn't quite make out. with all the new staff in house working on getting everything ready for the trip, things were bound to get dropped and even broken, but still they all needed to be careful. Michael wasn't made of money and some of the equipment cost more than her car.

"Please be careful, Jayden." Karen responded, her tone neutral, or hopefully so.

"That wasn't me, Dr. Linn, it was Dinh."

Karen huffed. "All of you, please be careful." She glanced over at the captain. "I'll have to work on remembering all their names." Her voice lowered as she spoke, watching the captain, who appeared to have a sort of amused look on her lips and in her eyes.

Captain Abbas nodded. "A new crew always takes some time to get used to, as does being their boss."

Karen nodded her agreement. "So, what can I help you with?"

"Speaking of getting to know people, I figured I would take you to meet the officers and the crew of the Explorer Pontus..." Abbas stood tall, her hat under her arm. "Assuming you have the time."

There was another crash from down the hall, as if on cue from the captain.

Karen shut her eyes, "Now is as good a time as any." She inhaled deeply, keeping as calm as possible.

We'll get there. We'll get used to each other.

"Some old boxes this time." An older female voice sang out.

"Thank you, Dr. Chen." Karen responded. "You're in charge; I'm going with Captain Abbas to the Pontus."

Excited mumbles and murmurs came from the hall.

"Come on Captain, I don't want any tagalongs." Karen and the captain made their way to the door and out of the office before anyone decided to come to ask to join them.

Outside the office, the air was crisp and the smell of the sea filled Karen's nose. There were a few clouds in the sky, but nothing to worry about. The weather was perfect and would be flawless for the last of the sea trials. Light hit the dark exterior of the Explorer Pontus, causing the sub to gleam in the morning light. From all the reports, everything appeared to check out and she couldn't wait to get going.

"How long have you been in the navy?" Karen asked as they made their way from the office.

"Oh, twenty-five years or so." Abbas answered as they walked toward the pier. "How long have you been studying..." Abbas waved her hand in front of her, "all this."

Karen laughed. "Long enough to know not to answer that question."

Abbas smiled and adjusted her hat to block out the sunshine from hitting her eyes.

"I'm thrilled to have you involved with this mission and the sub; I understand you were the captain when the sub was under construction before they discontinued the program." Karen held up a hand to her eyes as she spoke, her eyes adjusting slowly to the light.

Should have grabbed my shades.

"I know every part of the sub, probably as well as my chief engineer, but don't tell him, plus taking this command's not a bad way to lead into my retirement." Abbas stopped. "May I speak freely?"

Karen paused and faced the captain, the sun now behind her. "I would expect nothing less; the mission is mine, but you are the captain."

"Some of the crew, myself included, wonder what you expect to find out there." Abbas's gaze met Karen's. "Please don't be insulted, the idea of a lost city seems..."

"Crazy." Karen nodded. She had grown used to this and all the questions. "I know. Trust me, you and your crew are not the first to question this quest of mine or my sanity." She sighed. "I understand believing in something like Mu, which has next to no proof of existing, is a challenge. We may find nothing. Maybe we'll find ruins of some ancient civilization. We might even come face-to-face with merpeople." She chuckled.

Abbas's shoulders stiffened and her face gave nothing away.

She'd be a scary good poker player.

"Something caused the Pulse, Susan, may I call you Susan..."

Captain Abbas offered a stiff nod.

"No one has been able to figure out what." Karen pointed to the water's edge. "Five years ago, the Pacific Ocean did something never done before. The ocean spewed all the crap we've been dumping in her back at us. And in the process, the event knocked out everything electronic from Alaska to Panama. The Pulse affected eight countries, altering the landscape of the western coasts, causing hundreds of thousands of deaths, and costing billions of dollars. Today we're no closer to learning what caused the Pacific Pulse than we were the day after the event." She glanced at the captain. "I want to know what did cause the Pulse and how."

"And you think the answer lies in Mu?" Abbas asked.

"I believe a civilization once existed out there, probably during the last ice age when sea levels were lower. That society may have been so advanced they had some technology we don't understand; this tech laid dormant for thousands of years until something caused the system or the technology to activate..." Karen deliberated a moment. "An undersea quake, volcanic venting, something. But we won't find out until we go there."

"And you think you can find out what happened?"

"I'm sure going to try." Karen straightened her shoulders and raised her chin.

The governments all appeared to give up on what happened, instead focusing on cleaning up and rebuilding. Yes, that's important, but so's finding the cause. How were they so sure what happened was a one-off and wouldn't happen again?

"Good." Abbas's head slowly moved up and down.

"Good?" Karen questioned.

"My wife was in Cabo when the wave hit; they never found her body." Abbas's tone was hard, but the pain was visible on her face and in her eyes.

"I'm sorry."

"All my officers lost people that day, which is why I picked them." Abbas continued. "I may not fully buy into your theory, but something caused the Pacific Pulse and I wouldn't mind having answers.

None of us would, and you seem like the only one interested in finding out."

"We'll find out what happened. I have to believe that."

"Are you ready to meet the rest of my...your crew?"

"Lead the way." Karen pointed as she followed Captain Abbas up the pier and to the Pontus.

*****

The air was warm and a bit stale, but being inside the Pontus and seeing her move and maneuver was impressive. Despite being in the sub with the surroundings tighter than Karen preferred, she felt fine. Excited even.

"Lieutenant Renard, watch the depth markers."

"Aye, Captain." Renard responded from the first pilot's seat. Her French accent a bit heavy to Karen's ear, but nothing she wouldn't get used to.

"Morin, make sure you stay on the helm. I don't want to pin the needle with the Dumbarton Bridge. We may have some new depths here, but we're still shallow."

"I'm on it, Captain." Morin responded. "Aiming right down the middle."

He was from Montréal according to Captain Abbas, and older then Lieutenant Renard, but held a lower position on the sub which struck her as odd, but good for Renard on getting to the chair first.

"Ensign, do you have our course set?"

"Yes, Captain." Bianchi responded from his station to the left of the pilot's seats. "Waiting on Commander Kaya's approval for our course."

"Commander, if you please." Captain Abbas instructed.

Commander Derek Kaya moved to Bianchi's station and reviewed the navigation equipment. He wasn't as tall as Karen had pictured, but he was solidly built with a large chest. His dark eyes matched his brown receding hair and his round face was clean shaven. Commander Kaya was the image of the perfect First Officer... at least Karen thought so.

The Commander scanned the monitors and tapped at several of the controls in front of him and the young ensign.

There were a lot of pieces of equipment Karen wasn't familiar with or understood here in the control room, but watching the crew work under the guides of Captain Abbas was impressive; she understood every part of the Pontus and ensured everyone here did too.

"Once we get past the San Mateo-Hayward Bridge we will be clear of our biggest challenges, the Bay Bridge and the Golden Gate will be easy in comparison."

Karen nodded. "What are the depths like here?"

"Since the Pulse," Kaya, the First Officer checked the screen. "Forty at the shallowest where we are now, but the bottom drops to seventy past the Dumbarton Bridge; the Pulse deepened the water here..."

"Still, the channel is narrow, so we have to keep this big girl nice and steady, right, pilots?"

"Aye," the two pilots responded.

"Well, I've got to say, seeing all this and being here today with you is amazing." Karen commented as she glanced around the bridge. Every console and piece of machinery here was meant to run the Pontus and ensure the safety of everyone on board. She understood there were some redundancies in engineering, but she hadn't been down there yet. From the bridge you went up to communication and the observation area. This is also where you departed the sub. The ladder was a bit much, but nothing Karen couldn't handle. The observation area was worth the climb. The bridge sat midship, and you reached the rest of the sub from here. The layout felt odd having the nerve center of the sub also be the main entry point. However, the bridge could be secured by the water-tight doors, so from a safety standpoint she guessed the design made sense.

"Coming up on the San Mateo-Hayward Bridge now, Captain." Renard called out.

Abbas picked up the phone next to her, "Comms, contact our escort and let them know we will increase speed once we clear the bridge; no point in driving like we're going to church on a Sunday."

"Should we do that?" Karen asked as she glanced around at the crew rushing about. "I mean, don't we need to be careful?"

Abbas's lips raised in a smile. "Once we're past the bridge, the floor drops to a hundred feet, and the channel opens up as well. A little extra juice won't hurt anything. The push is good to assist this lady in stretching her legs."

There was a buzz and Commander Kaya answered the phone. "Cleared for increased speed, Captain."

Abbas winked at Karen.

Karen exhaled, not realizing she was holding her breath this whole time. "I'm not ashamed to admit I've never been... well, here before."

"Give yourself some time to get used to the surroundings and the noise." Captain Abbas offered. "But we'll take good care of you, your team, and the others."

"We've increased speed, Captain." Morin announced.

"We should be in the big blue in about ten minutes." Bianchi announced from navigation.

The sub continued smoothly along their course, making their way past Oakland and San Francisco, if the displays were to be believed.

"There she is." Renard beamed at the sight. "What a beauty."

"I'm glad she was strong enough to withstand the wave and all the debris." Kaya offered.

"They sure understood how to build a bridge in those days." Abbas remarked.

"Well, at least that one." Karen smiled as she watched the monitors, seeing them go under the Golden Gate Bridge.

Another buzz from the phone next to Abbas and the First Officer. Kaya picked up the phone. "Our escort is heading off. We're cleared to go."

"Well ladies and gentlemen, we're on our own." Abbas declared before taking the phone from Kaya and pushing a few buttons, "Bridge to Pontus, I'm pleased to announce we cleared the Golden Gate Bridge and we're on our own. Congratulations to you all, but let's not celebrate yet. Let's kick this lady into gear and find out what she can do. All hands prepare for depths." She put the phone down. "Navigation, let's head to the Farallon Islands and set our depths at... one hundred and fifty meters and we'll go from there. I want checks of all systems. Kaya, I want you down with Tomas in engineering."

"Aye." Commander Kaya responded and headed off through one of the hatches.

"Well Karen, once we do our tests, you should have your sub and crew ready to go."

"How deep you planning on taking us today?" Karen took a step closer to the captain, filling the space the commander had vacated.

"Depending on how things go, and if we run into no issues, the water around the Farallon Islands drops to about six thousand feet—"

"Can we..."

Abbas held up her hand.

"Today we'll go to a max of four hundred meters. I want to break in the Pontus slowly. Over the next few days, we'll keep increasing the depth and see how she does."

Karen fanned her face. "I see."

"Why don't you go up to the observation area and enjoy the view?" Abbas offered. "We'll be doing routine checks on the systems down here so you won't miss anything exciting."

Karen's eyebrows raised as she glanced toward the captain.

"You have my word." Abbas raised her right hand. "Morin, turn on the exterior lights and see what we can attract. Give Dr. Linn a chance to enjoy the sea life."

"You got it Captain." Morin responded and flipped five switches at his workstation.

~ Chapter Seven ~

Michael pulled out the knot of his tie and frowned at his reflection in the mirror. His cheeks were rosy and there were beads of sweat on his forehead. "Why am I so nervous?" He redid the knot of his tie for the third time. "This is stupid." Allowing the ends of the tie to drop from his hands, Michael shook out his hands and wrists and inhaled a deep, cleansing breath, catching the scent of his cologne. The notes of cedarwood and geranium caught his nose. A chuckle escaped his lips.

"I've seen the guy fully naked with a boner, having sex multiple times with multiple partners. He's been a performer for a couple years, so there is nothing I haven't seen of him." Michael moved to the mirror, taking his tie in both hands, and made the knot. Images of Tom helping him tie a tie for the first time filled his memories. Tom standing behind him lecturing him on the importance of the act. Michael closed his eyes and he was there with Tom as his hands made the movements. He opened his eyes. "Finally."

The dark blue suit offset by a lighter blue shirt and the bothersome complimentary tie. The tone on tone look was something he liked and people told him, at least Sharon, something he could pull off. He picked up his suit brush from the dresser and brushed at his lapels and the front of his jacket. Giving his reflection a satisfied nod, he checked his watch.

Right on time.

Making a final check for everything else he needed for the night's event, he headed out of his bedroom and down to the garage to his Tesla.

The drive to the eastside was uneventful and, luckily, traffic a breeze, still he never took anything to chance with how people drove these days. People drove faster and with much less caution. Glancing around, he found a spot to park in front of Alister's home. He checked the navigation to ensure he was at the right location and tapped the screen, "Call Alister."

"Calling Alister." The computer voice responded.

After a moment or two. "Wow, right on time." The man's voice sounded out from the speakers of the car. "I'm on my way."

"I have my silver Tesla."

"Oh, fancy." Alister quipped. "See you in a couple."

The phone clicked off and Michael released the air in his lungs. "This isn't a date. Tonight is a work event, and he's my guest."

Michael glanced around the neighborhood. This part of San Jose wasn't anything special, Simple middle class living. At least this part of the city wasn't affected by the Pacific Pulse, which was a good thing, especially for the property values. Still, most of the houses were small, clearly having more than one family living per home, if all the cars on the street and in the driveways were any indication.

The housing problem here wasn't helped by the Pacific Pulse.

There was a tap on his car's window.

Michael startled and quickly jumped out of the car, "I'm sorry, I was lost in thought."

Alister beamed ear-to-ear. "Sorry about that. Didn't mean to scare you."

Michael shook his head, moved to the passenger side of the car and opened the door.

"Wow, thank you." Alister glanced Michael up and down. "Sharon mentioned we were going to a charity event... but now this evening feels a bit like a date." He chuckled. "Plus, you look amazing."

Michael coughed. "Thanks. You do too." He watched Alister get into the car. His cream suit looked impeccable and the slightly darker sweater under his jacket complimented his skin tone perfectly. The layers under his jacket helped to give Alister a more bulked up appearance, not that he needed any enhancements, and with how form fitted his clothes were he still showed off his flawlessly firm body.

He's the whole package.

Michael made his way to the driver's side of the car, inhaled deeply and got in. Alister's gaze watching him as he got situated.

"You know, if this is a date, I don't mind... if you don't."

Michael turned and faced Alister. His dark almond eyes, black hair, and high cheekbones made him appear delicious and completely too young for Michael. The idea, however, made his heart flutter and his pulse quicken. "And what about Rowan? His name is Rowan—"

"That ended months ago." Alister cut him off. "I assumed you had found out." His gaze dropped and his lips pulled away in a frown. "I figured that's why you invited me tonight." He adjusted how he sat and put on his seatbelt.

"I'm sorry."

Alister shook his head. "I should have known better. Once he realized what I did, he couldn't handle... all this." He waved his hand as if swatting at the words and the memory. "He bailed."

Michael huffed and started the engine. "Unfortunately, that happens to us all." He bit his lower lip. "An occupational hazard... I guess."

"I wish people weren't so judgmental. I like what I do. I like performing. I enjoy being part of people's fantasies." Alister laughed. "I mean, I understand I can't do this forever, but for now, why not?"

"And what do you want to do when you age out?"

"I wouldn't mind doing what you do, or learn more about investing, become a day-trader or something in the financial industry."

"There are classes you can take."

"Yep," Alister acknowledged. "I've been looking into them. I've already got a small portfolio, nothing fancy right now, about forty-grand."

"Not a bad start."

"Thanks." Alister ran a hand over the dash. "This's a great car."

"Maybe I can help you," Michael brushed off the comment about the car. "We might spend time talking. I could have you work in the office a couple days a week. Learn more about the business end of our industry. Sharon's been on me to get her more help." He pulled away from the curb and started driving. "There would be no strings attached and you wouldn't have to do anything..."

Alister grinned, showing off his perfectly white straight teeth. "I didn't think you'd be like that. The whole *quid pro quo* doesn't seem to be your style. You've got a good rep around the studio; everyone likes you and respects you. And we all know how well you take care of us, not like some of the places where they treat you like a piece of meat."

"Trust me, being respectful doesn't always mean anything." Michael countered. "There are a lot of times when you're expected to give private shows..." he shuddered.

At least Tom wasn't like that, thank god. He was definitely a good guy.

"Yea, you're right, there are a lot of assholes out there." Alister glanced out the car window. "We'll see how you behave before I jump into anything." Alister faced Michael and smirked.

Michael nodded.

Yep, he has a good head on his shoulders. He's exactly what he appears to be. Not at all like me at the start.

*****

The GlassHouse was filled with cocktail tables, decked out with gold and silver coverings, accented with what appeared to be crystal vases filled with orchids, roses and greens. More flowers, up lighting, and plants clustered around the event space, filling the area's dead space, giving the room the feel of the outdoors. The scents of spices, herbs, cooked meats and fresh flowers permeated the entire room, not in a bad way, but in a way enabling Michael's body to release any tension still held over from the day. For a non-profit affair, they sure had gone all out. The Silicon Valley Council of Non-Profits managed to put on an event when they wanted, and clearly tonight they wanted to go all out. No wonder the tickets were expensive and why his foundation had been asked for such a large donation. He peeked around.

If they only knew.

"This is fancy." Alister held a glass of white wine in his hand as he took in the scenery.

"Always is. Every year they put on this big event to honor some of the local non-profits. The Lumière d'espoir Foundation in Los Altos sponsors a big chunk of the event, but I don't see the Executive Director, which is odd, considering they always send someone." Michael shrugged.

"How do you fit into all this?" Alister asked, his shoulders tensed. The relaxed man who was in the car appeared quieter and more reserved.

"I don't, well, not really." Michael continued to glance around the room. "I have a charity, well I fund a charity, the Reed Family Foundation, named in honor of my mentor, who passed away quite a few years ago."

"I'm sorry."

"Cancer's a bitch." Michael sneered. "The foundation provides a lot of investment to several local non-profits in the area. We support everything from youth activities to senior housing and nutrition, as well as substance abuse and victim support services."

"You do all that?" Alister's eyes appeared larger and his mouth slightly agape.

"Not me, the foundation. The non-profits not technically connected to me or my businesses. I keep the two separate, or all these wonderfully good-hearted people will turn into one of the loudest and ugliest group of hypocrites the valley has ever seen." Michael chuckled. "I once had Sharon try to set up a meeting with the former Executive Director of SVCN... I can tell you the meeting did not go well, still, they were happy to take my money as long as I would agree to being listed as anonymous." He inhaled and took a sip of wine, holding the glass harder in his hand than needed.

Exactly what Tom warned me of. But I thought...

Michael shook his head.

"So, they have no idea." Alister asked.

"Nope. They don't know and I don't offer the information. The foundation employs an Executive Director, David Vargus, who is respectable and beyond reproach. He and his wife will be here tonight to represent the foundation...I'll introduce you." Michael smiled. "He's a good man and doesn't care about what we do or where the money comes from, and he knows how to play the game."

"I don't know why you bother; these people seem like assholes." Alister's smile vanished from his face.

"I bother because helping people is important, leaving the world in a better way is vital. If the Pulse taught me, well, us, one thing, it's that we cannot take the planet for granted; Mother Earth always has a way of putting us in our place when she needs to."

"I suppose, but these people should be more respectful of everyone. And more tolerant."

Michael shrugged. Alister was correct, but these were different times and humans appeared to be getting worse with each passing year.

Maybe we'll get better. Hopefully.

"How did you get tickets for this event?" Alister continued watching the room, his gaze bouncing from person to person. "Aren't you worried about someone recognizing you... or me?"

"No, not really." Michael leaned in, his voice growing softer. "Who would say they recognized us, without bringing potential judgmental eyes on themselves?"

Alister chuckled. "So, we have a game of standoff."

"Pretty much." Michael pointed, "Ah, there's David; we should say hello."

Alister glanced to where Michael was looking. "He provided you with tickets?"

"No, I bought the tickets and made an anonymous donation to attend the event. Which is why the person at registration had trouble finding our names, also why I had the digital copies of the tickets, in case."

"All this song and dance, for a bunch of people who don't deserve your time or money."

"These people may not deserve any of what I provide, but they help a lot of people here in the valley, and don't get me wrong, a majority of these people couldn't care less about who we are, or what we do, as long as we give, but there are those." Michael put down his finished glass of wine. "Come on, let's go say hello to David."

"Lead the way, you're the boss." Alister finished off his wine and placed the empty glass near Michael's. "You should give your money to people who don't care, though. You really should."

Michael glanced at Alister. "What are you doing tomorrow?"

"Um... nothing yet. Why?"

"You wanna see where a big chunk of my money is going? Where I don't have to hide, plus, if all goes well, we might find out what caused the Pacific Pulse."

"Seriously?" Alister's eyes lit up.

Michael nodded and rested a hand on the small of Alister's back. "We can talk more later. I'd like to catch David before we go in, or before he gets inundated."

*****

"I brought you a coffee." Michael pointed to the cup of coffee in the cup holder. "I wasn't sure how you liked your drink, so I hope regular is okay. There is cream and sugar in the bag."

"I should have spent the night with you last night." Alister adjusted his green crew cut sweater as he sat down. "If I would have known you were going to get me up this early." He fastened his seatbelt, picking up the coffee. "Thanks for this, black is fine. And thank you for last night. The party was fun and everyone seemed nice."

"You're welcome on both accounts." Michael started the car and headed off toward Moffett Field. "I figured the coffee was the least I could do for you, after keeping you out so late last night."

"Well, one way, I can think of a few others."

Michael cleared his throat as his cheeks warmed.

"Especially considering I had to play nice last night." He sipped his hot coffee. "Still, the event actually wasn't too bad, especially the food, and I'm glad to see your foundation recognized for all the work and services you provided."

"I'm pleased for David, he does quite well. Luckily, I don't have to be involved in the day-to-day, which is a godsend."

Alister sipped the coffee. "I liked his comment about how he's grateful to all those who help to alleviate the ills of the world, no matter who they are or where their money comes from."

Michael's cheeks pulled up into a grin, and he couldn't help but laugh.

"No coffee for you?" Alister asked, resting the cup on his jean clad leg.

"Love the smell, but I can't stand the taste; coffee always tastes like *burn* to me."

"I need coffee to function." Alister took another sip and closed his eyes, a smile crossing over his lips. "So, where're we going?"

"You'll see." Michael glanced over at Alister, and what he assumed to be a smile bloomed across his lips and cheeks.

They made their way onto the freeway and continued onto the 101 in silence. Alister enjoyed his coffee and Michael appreciated the quiet. Sometimes being allowed to sit, and enjoy company in comfortable silence was a blessing. He didn't feel the need to make idle chit-chat with Alister, so by the time they got to the security gate, Michael had almost forgotten Alister was with him.

"What do you have happening at Moffett Field?" Alister returned the empty coffee to the center cup holder.

"A surprise, you'll see," Michael teased, deciding he would let Karen and the sub speak for him. He rolled down the window and handed over his clearance to the guard.

"Good morning Mister Donovan, may I get the name of your guest, please?"

"Alister Nguyen." Michael responded with a wave of his hand towards Alister.

The guard tapped on his pad. "Thank you, you are cleared to proceed. Have a good day."

Michael nodded and continued on course, raising the window.

"Kind of creepy." Alister glanced out the window. "I haven't seen any of this up close. I didn't realize so much had changed; check out the sub and those boats."

"The boats are for NOAA and the sub... well, she's the Explorer Pontus, part of why we're here today."

"No way, seriously?"

"You said you wanted to see another of my passion projects, where I don't hide anything, well here we are." Michael found a parking spot and glanced to the building with the offices where they would find Karen and her team. Stopping the car, he pointed to the building. "Shall we go meet everyone?"

"This I've got to see." Alister unbuckled his seatbelt and opened the door.

The two men made their way to the office door and Michael stopped. "I should warn you, Karen... is... well... Karen."

Alister nodded.

Michael pulled out his fob and the door opened. He held the door for Alister to walk through, then he followed, only taking a quick glance of Alister's backside. There at the front desk sat a guy in his mid-twenties banging away on his keyboard, focused on the screen.

"Doctor Linn, there're a couple of people here for you." The guy didn't bother looking up and he continued to type.

Karen popped her head down the hall. "Did you ask who they were?"

"What?" the guy responded with next to no movement or emotion in his words.

"Karen, it's Michael." Michael called down the hall, deciding to bypass the guy at the desk, but not willing to walk in and act like he owned the place, even though, technically, he kind of did.

"Oh. Right." Karen replied with a laugh, "Why don't you come down this way? I can introduce you to the team. The charming fellow at that desk is Ezekiel." She pointed.

"Hey." He continued to focus on the computer.

Alister glanced at Michael before peering down the hall. "Team?"

Michael nodded. "A pleasure to meet you, Ezekiel."

"Yep.". Ezekiel barely responded.

Michael and Alister made their way down the hall without another word from Ezekiel. Once they reached the end of the bare hall, Karen stood ready to greet them, rushing a hand through her hair. The tan pants covering her showed wrinkles marching up and down her legs. The dark-blue long sleeve shirt matched the creases in her pants and hung partially caught, crumpled around the waist of her pants. Her hair pushed off her face in a short cut, and when done up, always complimented her appearance; today she looked more disheveled and rushed then in the past. Even her typically glistening lips appeared dry.

"Sorry about Ezekiel, he's a good kid, just not the social type." She reached out her hand to shake with Michael. "I can't wait for you to see the sub. She's a beaut."

"Karen, I'd like to introduce Alister; he's joining me today, seeing what I do when I'm not working and how I'm trying to make a better tomorrow." He laughed.

Karen glanced between Alister and Michael, subsequently reaching out her hand. "Pleasure to meet you."

"And you." Alister offered his hand in return. "So, what's all this?"

Karen laughed. "Didn't he tell you?"

Alister shook his head.

"I figured I'd let you explain." Michael responded, stuffing his hands in his pocket.

"We're going to find the lost city of Mu in the Pacific Ocean—"

"What?" Alister started to laugh.

"And we're going to see what caused the Pacific Pulse." Karen continued, clearly used to people laughing at her.

Alister scanned between Michael and Karen, Michael's gaze never faltering. "You're both serious?"

Michael nodded as Karen spoke. "Why don't I give you the tour? We can meet the rest of the team, and you can see how crazy or not crazy I... well we... are." Karen pulled Alister by the arm and Michael followed as she started to explain everything going on, and who all those were involved.

By the time they were finished, Michael and even Alister had an excellent understanding of what they were trying to accomplish. Karen had assembled quite a team. There was Karen, of course, and there were two oceanographers, Doctor Chen, who specialized in geophysical fluid dynamics and plate tectonics, and Doctor Sanchez, whose field was the geology of the sea floor. They were assisted by two grad students, Mason and Isabel. Dr. Dubois and her grad student Lucas were the resident geologists. And Karen managed to find two climatologist doctors, Jenner and Samuels. Both, from all accounts, had a greater understanding of the climate than Michael ever hoped to understand. And supporting all their efforts were six interns: Bo, Mila, Dinh, Hanh, Amanda and, of course, Ezekiel.

Michael wasn't sure how he would keep all of them straight in his head, but he would have to try.

"Still think we're out there?" Karen faced Alister. "And you still haven't seen the sub yet."

"This is... I mean... wow... do you honestly think there is something out there?"

"That's what we're going to find out."

"Given how much the seas have risen since the last ice age, a lost city or some kind of ancient ruins are highly likely, proving some ancient civilization existed there once," Doctor Jenner stated. "As for their level of technology and if their technology might have caused the Pulse remains to be seen."

"Which is why we're going to search." Karen added with a firm shake of her head.

"And you're funding all this?" Alister glanced over at Michael.

"Pretty much." Michael acknowledged. "There have been a few grants and the French government provided the sub. The UN offered some financial support, as did the US government, Japan, and Mexico even kicked in some money, but not near enough."

"Wow."

"You want wow, let's head to the sub." Karen pointed down the hall to the entry of the office; she reached into her pocket and pulled out her lip balm, giving her lips a refresh, stuffing the balm into her pocket. "After all, that's what this visit and research is all about. And whoever declared size doesn't matter hasn't seen this sub." She roped her arms in between both Michael and Alister, leading them through the office and down the path to the pier where the Pontus sat.

The morning haze put the surroundings in shadow with the hills and mountains a grey outline devoid of color. Walking up the pier, Karen rushed ahead to give the crew a heads up about their soon to be guests. Michael took this opportunity to stop and take Alister by the arm. "I know this sounds crazy. I can't possibly imagine what's going through your head right now, but if there is any chance of us finding out what caused the Pacific Pulse, I'm happy to pay any price."

"And you believe Doctor Linn can figure all this out."

"I hope so."

"I'm not going to pretend I understand any of this," Alister began. "But we all know what the Pulse did and how many people we lost, so if this will get us answers, why not?" His nostrils expanded as he deeply inhaled the salty air through his nose.

"Thank you." Michael's shoulders lifted and his neck relaxed.

"Plus, I've got to see that sub." He pointed to the Pontus.

Karen stood waving. She stayed with another person in some kind of uniform and hat. "Looks like we're up." Michael waved. "She's Captain Abbas. I met her once, a few months ago. I like her."

"Nice." Alister continued to glance around the research area, taking in the boats, pier and other personnel rushing about.

They made their way to the Pontus and after introductions and a brief overview of the exterior of the sub, the four made their way into the vessel. The damp, cool morning air was replaced with dry, processed warmth holding undertones of mechanics and oil.

"Welcome Michael and Alister," Captain Abbas greeted as the corners of her mouth pulled up, her tone remaining polite but restrained. "This is our communications, main hatch and small observation area." The captain pointed. "This space isn't an overly large area, but the observation section is quite impressive when the shielding is open and the lighting engaged."

Michael glanced around the space. "The area is bigger than I imagined." He examined the built-in lounge and the covered windows. "How many crew on board?"

"Forty." Captain Abbas responded with a stiff nod of her head, "Ten officers and thirty crew."

"With the forty crew and my research team, we have space for fifteen guests." Karen took a seat on the sofa.

"This sub can hold seventy people?" Alister asked, glancing around the lounge.

"We didn't want to cram people in, but if the sub were outfitted as originally planned, we would have had a compliment of one-hundred and forty." Abbas commented. "But the sub doesn't need all those hands, and we still have three shifts, but trust me when I say this is a luxury liner compared to some of the subs I've been on..."

"Wow."

"Captain, you're needed in engineering." The communication person stated with a glance to Captain Abbas.

"Will you excuse me?" Abbas put on her hat and adjusted her jacket uniform. "Inform Commander Tomas I'm on my way."

The communication officer nodded.

"Karen, you'll have to take over the tour." Abbas moved to Michael and Alister. "Mr. Donovan, good to see you again. Mr. Nguyen, a pleasure meeting you."

Michael watched as the captain went down the ladder. He walked around the space again, running a hand over the seating and the smooth walls. Taking in the mix of form and function, where the communications officer sat, all the monitors showed different images of the sub's interior and exterior. The young crew man wore a headset to block out the noise of the area and had a firm but comfortable voice. Michael inhaled, his nose hit with both metallic and antiseptic notes. "Wow, this part of the sub looked so different on the computer."

"You haven't seen anything yet." Karen gestured in the direction of where the captain vanished too. "Shall we?"

"Lead the way." Michael glanced over at Alister. "You ready for this?"

Alister nodded, his eyes ever wider as he continued to scan the space.

The three made their way down the ladder and onto the bridge; Karen introduced Michael and Alister to the crew and the officers who were on duty before moving them forward. Level two housed a majority of the ship's command, including the weapons command area. Forward of the bridge were the galley with officer and guest dining, a mix use conference/reception space doubling as a guest and officer lounge. Past the functional space, they moved down a hall with guest quarters on either side, ending at a door leading to the largest cabin on the sub, which was Michael's since he funded the research. As they moved through the bridge again, they headed down the main corridor housing the captain's quarters, officer's quarters, more guest quarters and near the rear of the sub, the main lab, additional small meeting rooms and medical facility. They peeked into medical and made introductions with Doctor Mia Rizzo and her medical team. The doctor's Italian, maybe Sicilian, accent was not something Michael was used to hearing, especially here in the Bay Area. Michael wasn't sure what he expected from the subs medical facility but Doctor Rizzo assured him her and her team would be able handle anything.

At both the forward and aft of the sub were ladders taking crew and passengers down to the next level. There was also a ladder running the full height of the sub right off the bridge. All the egress and ingress points had watertight hatches, so if needed, they could be sealed off in the event of an emergency. Another visible safety feature of the sub.

Michael couldn't help but be impressed with the layout of the sub. Parts of the sub reminded him of a smaller cruise ship, or maybe a better image would be a river cruise ship. He expected to feel cramped, and the space was tight to be certain, but he had space to move and the headroom wasn't as bad as he had assumed. On this main level, the design team did a good job of hiding much of the exposed conduit and sub workings, which he appreciated.

The three made their way down to level three. This part of the sub housed labs one through five, and a huge observation lab, similar to the observation lounge, featuring a large window, which if needed, could be secured by an outer and inner watertight door. Also housed on this level were the crew dining area (cleverly connected to the main galley above via a dumbwaiter and ladder) research team and crew quarters, a large recreational space and gym with an impressive showing of machines and free weights. There was even a small hot tub, steam room, and sauna.

As with level two, all efforts were made to ensure this space had a clean, sleek feel, keeping much of the sub's inner workings out of sight, and out of the way of the people who worked on this level.

They descended down to the bottom level, which they found to be a more utilitarian area. There were several access panels, and above them were pipes and conduits running the length of the sub. If the bridge was the brain of the sub, this level housed everything else. There was no need for any of the fancy trappings as above; this space was the heart of the sub where all the real work was done.

In these main arteries of the sub, crew rushed about passing Michael, Alister and Karen as they went about their duties. On the upper levels, they only met crew in the galley, medical facilities and the recreation room and gym. Michael noticed this area had been built solely for function, whereas the other levels were set up for guests, officers and the researchers. It was built to run the sub. They found the armory, drone command, and the back-up weapons command; all stations were manned and crew members were running their checks.

Karen moved Michael and Alister through quickly so they didn't get in the way.

The group moved to the rear of the sub. This space was nothing like the others; a lot of open area with the noises and the vibrations from the engines. None of the engine room was what Michael had expected. He was glad he didn't have to work in this area. The scent of oil and mechanical fluids was all around him. He remembered a movie he was in, *All the Captain's Seamen*. The story, if there was one, had been located on a sub. He had a rather spicy scene with the 'chief' engineer, in the engine room. The set was nothing like this.

We weren't even close with the actual look or feel.

Michael pushed the memory from his mind as Karen took them to the forward of the sub, away from the vibration and noise, through multiple water-tight doors, and into the wet lab with dive hatch and mini sub launch. The smell of sea water was everywhere.

"That's Bob." Karen laughed with a nod of her head toward the craft. "He'll take six people down deeper than the Pontus can go, and get us into any of those tight places this big girl..." She clapped the side of the sub with her hand. "can't. And if we need something smaller, well, we passed the drone control room. Bob can also serve as a lifeboat should we have to leave the Pontus during an emergency." She grinned. "You know, in case we get attacked by a giant squid."

"Incredible." Michael glanced around the space with large eyes.

"How did you afford all this?" Alister commented and glanced between Michael and Karen.

"I know people," Karen responded. "People who like me." She added with a firm nod.

"And we got a lot of the equipment used, from scrapped subs and research ships." Michael added.

"That too." She followed up as she stuffed her hands in her pocket. "Still, this sub is an investment. California State University, Monterey Bay have already been in contact, wanting to rent time and space on this bad girl, but that's something for later. Once we're out there and this baby proves herself, there will be more. Current estimates and financial projections show we'll break even in five years, but those numbers can jump to seven years depending on what we need to do and how we want to use this baby."

"I thought subs only had a couple of levels. This seems huge." Alister waved a hand around.

"Keep in mind," Karen started, as the smile on her face brightened. Even how she stood shifted, as if about ready to give a lecture to a class full of students. "This sub wasn't built for war. The Pontus's been built for research and exploration, with her naval functions coming in second, so a lot about this sub is different."

"Which is why the Pontus never saw any use, until now," Michael added.

"The French navy didn't want to pump any more money into the project as the program ballooned over budget, so I called in a few favors and now this lovely lady is here." She again tapped the bulkhead, pride radiating out of her every motion.

"This is fantastic." Alister's gaze bounced around the interior, taking in the sub and the equipment. "And you don't care about all this being paid for with money from…" Alister peeked at Michael.

"I don't care what you and Michael do, or how he makes his money, as long as it's legal." Karen chuckled and shook her head. "The way I view all this silliness is, people get way too hung up on sex and sexuality. Don't we have anything more important to worry about?" she gestured a hand in front of her, waving off her own comments. "You know the biggest consumers of porn come from the bible belt and from all those ultra conservative countries. They are so full of shit, especially that prick in Florida. Preach one thing, but when they are home alone, they all whip their dongs out, and have a jolly good time watching the movies you make while playing with the toys they've bought from you."

Michael chuckled. "She's not wrong."

"Well this is amazing." Alister's eyes continued to be the size of saucers as he scanned the facility.

"You should come with us, if your boss'll let you." Karen offered again, pulling out her lip balm and giving her lips another layer. "There is a lot we're going to do and accomplish. Plus, we have the space, or you two can share Michael's cabin." She smiled. "Anyway, we don't leave for a couple more weeks, so you can figure your schedule out, assuming you even want to join us."

A whistle came from the speakers.

"Doctor Linn, please contact communications, Doctors Chen and Dubois are asking for you. Doctor Linn, please contact communications." The male communications crew member's voice called out over the speakers.

"This is why I didn't want all the help before." Karen pointed at Michael, but there was a bright smile on her face. "I swear, they are all brilliant but..."

"That's what happens when you're in charge." Michael grinned, taking a final look around the wet lab and seeing where the mini sub was secured. "We should head up. I wouldn't mind taking a closer look at my quarters."

~ Chapter Eight ~

Current.

The palace hadn't changed, not one bit, since Kaimi had been here last. Well, his memories now seemed clouded. The last time they saw the palace, flames burned through the crystal windows and much of the beautiful architecture seemed lost to the ages, but five years had passed. Now the grand hall appeared as he remembered. In fact, if he were to be honest, the space felt lighter. Maybe the lightness had to do with him being locked up for so long, or maybe the change had to do with the weight of his parents and potentially ruling the kingdom now off his shoulders. He wouldn't admit this to anyone, but since their murder and his subsequent imprisonment, the idea had crossed his mind. Especially with Koa now running things and with him having nothing to do but wallow in self-doubt and reflect on the death of Makani.

I let all that happen? Everything up to this point is my fault. Now look around. Nothing I did made a difference.

"Makani," Kaimi whispered as he moved toward the throne where Kao and the rest of their family already sat. Well, everyone except him and Kai Malina. They would be coming in once everyone was settled. According to Koa they had been in solitude meditating for weeks, only breaking for meals and the occasional stroll in the gardens and walks by the ponds. Clearly this vision wasn't as unambiguous as Koa made their precognition out to be when they were first told about this new prophecy.

Well their first divination. More came. Another prediction. All these revelations, clearly Kai Malina and Mana Lani have been keeping them all on the turbulent seas for too long.

"With the gods' grace perhaps we'll finally get answers." Kaimi approached the king, Kao, and bowed.

"If I've learned one thing, brother, Kai and Mana cannot, and will not, be rushed," Koa replied with hints of a frown dancing at his lips.

"And the gods are often too vague to interpret," Nohealani added, the bite in her words not lost on him, or their brother if the muscle twitching in Koa's neck gave any indication.

"No truer words have been spoken," Ulani chimed in, a bright smile on her face. "I'm so glad we are all here again and together. I know these last years have not been easy, but having us all together...Mother and Father would have wanted us acting as one."

She's always been the most positive of us.

"Not all of us are here." The ridges around Nohealani's eyes and mouth deepened, her youthful appearance gone, replaced with the appearance of a woman who had suffered a great loss.

At least she has Allyn and Palani in her care, which offered her some peace.

Ulani's lips pinched together and her gaze dropped. A slight whisper of, "I'm sorry," reached his ears as she turned to the assembly hall.

Kaimi found his seat. Glanced out at those who have been assembled. The council members and those holding higher offices in the kingdom, as well as invited guests, and those who would spread the word, once spoken, were given space in the gallery so they may witness and hear with ease. He leaned closer to Koa. "Have they anything on who killed Mother and Father? What of the pulse?"

Koa shook his head.

"What's the point?" Kaimi's level of snark and frustration was kept to a minimum. They were supposed to see and know all. This is why he held little faith in this ancient ritual, but tradition was important to his parents and, as he learned, important to their people. He shifted on his seat, adjusting his white ceremonial sarong.

"You always questioned the gods too much," Koa countered, his voice equally as low. "We will learn what we learn, when the gods are ready."

Kaimi huffed as he shifted how he sat. The tension in his neck and shoulders building similarly to how pressure builds in a kettle.

"Regardless, I'm pleased to have you here with us, both of you." Koa glanced at Nohealani, offering her a soft smile. "As Ulani stated, Mother and Father would be pleased." He adjusted his coral and gold crown, the one their father wore when he was alive.

Kaimi was sure their mother's crown was secured and put away, waiting for Koa to take a mate. The ornamentation would be altered for them once bonded. He figured Koa would have already had the necessary adjustment made to the crown for him, and he was not wrong, as the crown fit him perfectly, as did the additional ceremonial garments.

He makes for a strong king.

"I hope you are right." Nohealani pulled Kaimi from his thoughts, her eyes glancing out at the gallery of people slowly filling in the chamber, the level of noise increasing as they assembled.

Koa glanced off to the side entry, Kaimi following his gaze. A guard nodded.

"The time has come." Koa announced, standing to welcome the council and the others in attendance. He had assembled a mix of young and old, of all genders. Koa had kept to their mother's wishes, having as much representation from the community as possible.

Within moments of Koa standing and speaking the room reacted to him, the lights dimmed and the traditional ceremonial torches lit. The room filled with a warm glow and off to the side, a group of musicians began. The music started off soft to gain the attention of those attending. As more of the people settled in their spots, the pahus grew louder as the ukuleles and Ka'eke'ekes joined in.

Kai and Mana always did enjoy the pageantry. I'm surprised there are no dancers.

The image was barely in his head, before the first fire dancers appeared. Kaimi bit back his disapproval as everyone paraded around. Despite his discontentment, the dancers were impressive, the same as the music. An ache pulled at his heart as he watched the performers as they waited for their sibling and the family Māhū. The warm oranges, reds, and yellows glistened off the dancer's bare chests and legs as they continued to fill the space with their movements. Makani loved these dances and the music. When they were wed, he had to sit through an eternity of performances, but those moments were worth seeing the reaction from Makani; the fire performers, dancers and tumblers made Makani happy and the memories he holds are good ones, if not a bit painful.

Makani would have approved, if not tried to join.

The music and dance stopped as Koa outstretched his arms to call everyone together. "Bring forth Mana Lani and Kai Malina." His words reverberated through the hall. As much as Kaimi questioned his brother being the king, he had to admit Koa represented their parents and the family well. Especially now.

He is also, possibly, more forgiving of them than I would have been.

Kaimi watched as the two Māhū appeared from between a row of lighted torches. The smoke and fire danced around them, giving them an otherworldly appearance. The two were covered in white cloth and wore carved masks to cover their faces and to represent the gods they would be speaking for. Murmurs filled the space as they continued to make their way forward into the center of the chamber. They stopped and stood before Koa.

The God of War and the God of the Ocean. None have spoken for Ku in...well a long time.

The pit of Kaimi's stomach dropped. There was no worse combination of gods to be speaking to them than Ku and Kanaloa. He had heard stories from his mother from when her grandmother was a child: Ku and Kanaloa appeared and when they left the Mouth of the Gods was sealed and Faga Bay formed. The Gods' appearance was also the time when the Manō hae first appeared in the bay.

Koa reached out his arms again, his staff firmly rested in his left hand. "Please settle, let us hear what the Gods of War and Ocean have to say."

Kaimi knew his brother well and the projection of calm and strength covered his worry. What were Mana and Kai playing at? He inhaled and glanced at the rest of his family. Everyone had their masks of calm firmly in place. Hopefully, he did as well. Even though he didn't fully believe in the mystical powers of the family Māhū, several people did, and he learned all too late the power of the gods was not to be trifled with.

Mana came forward. They wore the mask of Ku, God of War. "Prepare as the outsiders come for you. They will rain down pain and death upon you. Perhaps even destroy this world we created for you." Their words screamed across the hall, each syllable clear and concise. There would be no misinterpretation. "Have no doubt they bring a warship to you, one that can travel the ocean and reach this haven. You are no longer safe."

Koa stood glancing between the harbingers of doom, not speaking. There was nothing to say at this point, but Kaimi was sure Koa would have plenty of questions when the time was right.

Kai stepped next to them. "My waters can not hold them at bay as their ship does not sail on the surface but from below." The mask covering Kai's face moved with each gesture, as did their hands. The motion was almost a dance of storytelling. "Take this warning and prepare, as I am unable to stop them in their mechanized whale of death."

"You have little time to prepare," Mana spoke, this time their movements and their mask echoed the same motions as Kai. "They will be here by the next receding of Faga Bay, where they will find entry as the Manō hae will be off for their spawning."

"Tell us, Ku." Koa stood tall but lowered his staff, showing his reverence for the power of the gods before him. "How do we protect ourselves? How do we keep our world safe?" he asked, his arms outstretched and his head lowered to show respect.

"I have given your scientist the tools to leave Mu," Mana spoke. The mask of Ku continued to move. "These new tools will allow you to swim through my water's depths like a dolphin or whale. Your warriors must go and meet them," Mana demanded, as they continued to speak for Ku. "Once in the depths—"

"I will send my children to these waters to fight with you." Kai continued to speak for Kanaloa. "They may only provide minimal assistance, but they will be there for you."

Koa took a step forward, moving closer to their, to his, Māhū. "What more can we do? What of the other gods? Will they not assist us?"

Kaimi was impressed with how his tone remained so level. He sounded so much like their mother at this moment. She never appeared rattled even when dire news came. This was a trait he wished he had inherited.

"The gods have not forsaken you or your people entirely," Kanaloa continued through their sibling Kai. "They will help if needed, but they are tasking you with the protection of Mu. As the new ruler, you must face this challenge on your own before our brothers and sisters will aid you, should you require their assistance," Kai continued, the mask of Kanaloa moved as they spoke.

"We will send out a new pulse." Koa spoke. "To stop them and keep them from coming here."

"No!" Kanaloa shouted through Kai. "You will not use my waters in such a way again. You angered both Hikule'o and Tāne Mahuta with the damage you caused her lands and his forests. They will not tolerate such action again. To do so would be to bring on their wrath."

"They have forsaken us. The Goddess of Earth and the God of the Harvest" Nohealani spoke, perhaps only a whisper, but Kaimi glanced at her and observed the worry dancing around her eyes, despite her composed face.

"Will the gods grace us again when the threat is gone?" Koa's voice shook for the first time with a slight tremble, only noticeable to those who were close to him. Perhaps a few others caught the shift in his voice. Either way, Kaimi recognized the change, no matter how subtle.

"Ensure Mu's survival and the people she houses, and the gods will reward all." Ku bellowed through Mana, their mask bouncing and moving as their head moved. "Now we leave you. The rest is up to you."

And with that, Mana and Kai headed to the exit.

Voices raised as each person present jockeyed to be heard. Gazes turned to Koa, waiting to hear what the young ruler would say and do next. Even Kaimi found himself looking to his brother for guidance, if Mana and Kai's prediction came to pass, the outside world would find a way here, and given they still had no idea who caused the pulse, what would these people do to retaliate? Would they attack as foreshadowed by Ku and Kanaloa, or would these intruders do something worse? Would they come here and destroy Mu, their home?

~ Chapter Nine ~

Karen sat with her hands tightly clasped as she listened to Dr. Rochelle Farmin Director of the White House Office of Science and Technology, and The Honorable Vincent Parkman from the United States Secretary of Energy. The conference room smelled of cheap cologne and even cheaper perfume. She had no interest in being trapped with these two people for this long, but here she was. The two had Michael and her tied up for hours about the proposed mission to find out the cause of the Pacific Pulse Event and the lost continent.

"So, you can see our point. Since the event and the influence the Pacific Pulse had on our local environment, we are interested in what's out there, and we can't..." Dr. Farmin finally took a breath.

"I see what you think is your point..." Michael started, "and I completely disagree." Tinges of red danced around his neck and his ears. His voice was level, but there was anger bubbling under the surface. "What I see—"

Karen cut off Michael before he uttered anything that might get them into trouble. To date, the US Government and the Office of Science and Technology had steered clear of Karen and her research. Until now, especially with what the potential ramifications meant when she proved her theories right. "What we see..." Karen began, her voice much firmer and harder than she planned, but the shift as present as the nose on her face. "is an opportunity for the United States Government to send a representative or two to join us."

"Karen." Michael's head snapped in her direction.

"You see," Karen continued, resting her hands on the table, ignoring the artificial floral scent assaulting her nose since these two stalked into the office. "I've been waiting for this opportunity to have you finally come to the table. I'm sorry you've taken so long to step forward."

"Well, that wasn't…" Secretary Parkman began.

Karen waved him off and continued. "I know full well Vinny here and you, Dr. Farmin…" she pointed between them. "well. You don't think much of my research or my business partner, but now with the project ready to launch, the US government doesn't want to appear complacent when we find out what happened five years ago. Especially with the CIA releasing Dr. Chan Thomas's book and the additional fallout from his prediction of a mass extinction event."

Both the Secretary of Energy and Dr. Farmin remained silent, but the flush of pink dancing around their cheeks and collars gave Karen all she needed. She leaned forward. "How awful would the missed opportunity look for the President to have squandered this potential discovery? Bearing in mind, Chan's predictions are on an 11,500-year clock and we are well overdue. Aren't we? Or are we…considering the Pacific Pulse?"

Farmin and Parkman shared a look.

"Why, she would lose her bid for reelection in two years," Karen started. "And all the environmental groups would come after her, especially since she's their champion." She laughed as she pulled out her lip balm and played with the tube in her hands. "Her opponent would eat her alive and I can't see the people, all our people being too happy with her, especially since this whole thing happened on her watch. No, I see all too well. We both do."

"You misunderstand, she doesn't…"

Michael cut off the Doctor, composing himself and seeing where Karen was going with all this. "Imagine what the media would say? I can see the headlines now; disgraced scientist and adult industry mogul solve the biggest environmental mystery to strike the Pacific West Coast in history, while the President sits in Washington battling with Congress." He shook his head. "The whole fiasco would be a PR nightmare no amount of Washington spin would ever fix."

Karen added, leaving the tube in front of her. "You see. We understand perfectly well what is going on here."

The conference room fell silent. The only noise was the four breaths and four hearts beating. Even the stink of the floral fragrance took a back seat to the pounding of their collective hearts. Karen leaned in her chair, waiting, lightly rubbing her lips together. Hoping to get clear of the scent and to see what they had to say now. Her thoughts fell on their first meeting with these two and how they mocked her and her research. They told her her theories were a joke, and she was wasting their *valuable* time. Now whose time was being wasted? She still had data to analyze and there were still reports to go over from the Pontus; they only had a short time before they set off and they still had the official media announcement, press conference, as well and the pre-launch reception.

"What do you need us to say or do?"

Ha! They blinked first. Good. We got 'um.

Karen spared a glance over at Michael, the grin on his face growing. She picked up the balm and returned the tube to her pocket.

"For starters, as I said." The muscles in her neck and shoulders relaxed. "We will be happy to have two of your Scientists join our expedition if you'd like; however, I'm in charge, they are my guests. They will not try and bogart my work or my team, no last minute pulling out a document from the President granting them authority or whatever trick you might try planning. The crew and the research team report to me and since they are all foreign nationals, my authority is guaranteed along with Mr. Donovan. If something happens to me, all power and authority goes to him." She peeked at Michael. His head offered a slight gesture of support, so she continued. "I won't have any of your nonsense and there will be no military presence. This is a research ship, not a navy play thing."

"Agreed." The Honorable Vincent Parkman responded. "Anything else?"

Karen contemplated a moment.

This is too simple. They are agreeing way too easily. Maybe I do have them. Maybe they need me and are worried. I like this.

"Also," she inhaled, smelling the government issued scent off them. "Since we're going to be under the sea, no strong fragrances on the sub, the air filtration system is good, but I don't want to smell whatever smells you're wearing again. Not on my sub."

Michael bit back a laugh.

Dr. Farmin's eyes narrowed and Secretary Parkman frowned.

Maybe I do have the upper hand. Have I, well, we, bested the US Government? No. Still, perhaps.

"I'm quite serious." Karen continued. "None of the crew or my team will be wearing scents, except for deodorant, so please keep your perfumes and colognes at home."

Secretary Parkman nodded. "Understood."

Michael cleared his throat. "I'll have my lawyers draft up an agreement and NDAs. The President or whomever they designate will need to sign off. Agreeing to our terms and conditions. Everything we do will be above board and you will not do anything counter to what we agree to, and if you or the President decide to break the contract in any form, my lawyers will have a field day, I didn't get where I am today by getting screwed over by the likes of you. I know how you people see me... see us..." He pointed to Karen and himself. "And remind your team who won, not once, but three times in front of the Supreme Court." Michael stood up and buttoned his suit jacket. "I believe we're done here." He glanced over at Karen, who stood next to him.

"I and one of my lead research specialists will join your mission." Dr. Farmin offered a curt nod. "You won't have any issues from either of us." She stood, adjusting her suit jacket. "However, I would like to ask if you find anything we all share in the credit."

"Well, that depends." Karen crossed her arms over her chest, her gaze narrowing on both government officials before her.

"On?" Secretary Parkman asked.

"We want the full endorsement of the United States Government and a token contribution to the research to be announced at the press conference. Where copies of the signed agreement will be distributed to the media."

"What?" the Secretary glanced between Karen and Michael.

Michael beamed. "I don't believe Dr. Linn stuttered."

"You see, I want to be protected, on the off-chance things don't go to plan." Karen's tone held firm and she suddenly felt like she towered over everyone in the room. "Since the President wants to share in the glory, she will have to share in the risk."

"We'll see what we can do." Secretary Parkman commented, but the look of worry in his eyes told Karen all she needed to know.

I won.

"Remember, the clock is ticking, and if everything isn't signed and dated by the launch, Dr. Farmin and her guest will be left on the dock."

Karen moved to the conference room door. "Now I believe you can show yourselves out."

Without any additional comments, Dr. Farmin and Secretary Parkman vanished through the door and out of the office. Karen shut the conference door and faced Michael. "Wow, we got 'em." She laughed.

Michael nodded.

"I figured you were going to lose your cool." Karen reached out and rested a hand on his arm.

"I was." Michael exhaled hard. "Who the hell do they think they are coming in here and making those kinds of demands?" He gulped in several lungs full of air. "I noticed you didn't hold back on the perfume comment. Granted, the scent was awful. Who wears that type of scent these days?"

"The dead." Karen crinkled her nose. "Their cologne or perfume…" she shook her head. "I refuse to be assaulted by those scents of death again. Not on our sub."

"Well good. Plus, I paid for this expedition, not them. And this is all your work. They had no right coming in here like they were in charge. We pay our taxes, we've filled out all the paperwork, and we even had to go outside the US to get the vehicle, plus where we're going is in international waters, so they have zero claim."

"And that is why we won the game of Russian Roulette." Karen dropped to the chair closest to her and shook her head. The weight of the afternoon and the meeting catching up with her. "They assumed they could come in and bully us, throw the US Government and the President in our face. Thank goodness you aren't only a pretty face."

Michael laughed. "Doing what I do, you have to be tough, and have excellent lawyers behind you. The government isn't to be played with. They are no joke. And I have a feeling we still can't trust them, even with all this. They will try something, they always do."

Karen nodded. "I know. We have to make sure everything is signed, sealed, and delivered before we launch or they aren't coming. I won't risk this mission. I can't. This is too important."

"Will our gambit work?" Michael questioned.

"Oh yes." Karen rested her head on her clasped hands before her. "They will make sure the President is protected, and they will be sure to be able to spin both our success and our failure to her favor. We are smart, but I'm afraid they are shrewder and slimier than either of us."

Michael laughed. "You know, I've been screwed before, but never like this. I'm worried."

"Don't be." Karen smiled up at him. "I've worked with their sort before. They think there is something in the Pacific Ocean, or have a feeling at least I'm right and we'll find something. Our research being this far along and us having the Pontus is why they are giving in to us. They don't want to risk being left out."

The crack of Michael's knuckles echoed around the room. "We have to be ready for them to screw us over."

"We will be." Karen pulled out her lip balm, giving her lips another swipe. "I have records of everything. We can make copies and give the documents to your legal people and I'll give copies of everything to my legal folks."

"Are we wrong having so little faith in our government?"

"You're probably too young, but President Reagan once proclaimed, 'trust but verify', that's what we need to do." Karen adjusted the glasses on her face. "Enough about them. Have you decided if you're going to bring Alister with us? He's a cutie, and the two of you make an adorable couple."

The flush on Michael's neck moved to his cheeks. "He's sexy for sure, and I enjoy his company, plus he's brilliant, so smart. I don't know."

Karen laughed and stood up, tucking the chair in. "Look, we don't get a lot of chances for love in our lives. The paths we both follow make opportunities even less likely, so if bringing him along leads to bigger and better things for the two of you, bring him. What's the worst that can happen?"

"Never tempt fate." Michael sucked air in through clenched teeth. "We'll be stuck in a research sub with a bunch of scientists, a government monitor, and we're looking for your lost city and the potential cause of the Pulse. A lot can go wrong, and I think we both know there is a lot that can happen."

Karen nodded. "Well, having some eye candy on the sub always helps with morale."

"Why Dr. Linn, do you have a crush on one of my employees?"

"I may be old, and I may be a crack-pot scientist, but I still have my sight." She winked. "Alister is a cutie with a nice tushy."

They both laughed as Michael headed to the conference room door. "Should we go and get things ready?" He opened the door and gestured to the hall.

"Sounds good to me." She reached out and took Michael's arm. "I'm serious about Alister. Bring him, you never know where things might lead."

*****

Michael glanced through the final documents from the Office of the US Secretary of Energy and from the White House Office of Science and Technology. He didn't understand politics. When important issues faced the country that politicians didn't want to deal with, these matters took years or decades before anything moved, but when the issue was something they wanted, paperwork got rushed through in days. His legal team had reviewed everything, suggesting neither he nor Karen cash the million dollar grant award the federal government awarded them. Without the money, the government had less power over them if things went south. Otherwise, everything appeared in order, and he and Karen were able to sign off on the documents, granting Dr. Farmin and her lead researcher Dr. Wayne May-Jordan clearance so they would be able to join the team.

Leaving Alister. He had been toying with officially inviting him to come along, and if the choice had been Karen's, he would be front and center, probably dressed in a super gay version of a sailor's uniform. He chuckled. If memory served, Alister had been in a film wearing said sailor uniform already. He shook the image from his head. The cell phone on his desk mocked him. He sighed and picked the device up and tapped out a message:

You still interested in going under the sea and seeing if we can find out what happened?

He waited a moment, toyed with deleting the message, but finally hit send. Before he put down his mechanical leash, there was a chirp:

Are you serious?

Yes.

Came the answer and Michael smiled. There was another ding.

Do I get my own cabin, or are we going to share?

Alister added a winky face emoji at the end of the sentence. And Michael quickly responded:

You'll have your own cabin.

Michael typed out with a bit of a frown. Sure, sharing his cabin and his bed with Alister would have been amazing. Karen was right about love and relationships. They didn't happen much in his industry, so why rush? Why not explore the possibilities and see what happened between them? They didn't need to dive into bed. Despite how much fun sex would be; especially knowing he and Alister would be completely compatible.

He huffed, and another ding found his ears:

Probably for the best. Thanks for the invite. I can't wait.

Michael put down his phone and focused on the work before him; he had a speech to write and now a wardrobe to plan out for the trip. The trip was planned for fourteen days and they were going to be under the ocean, so he didn't have to plan for much, but still with Alister there, he wanted to make sure he looked good.

"Hey Sharon." Michael called out.

"Yep." Sharon responded.

"Can you make me an appointment over at the Los Altos Beaux Vêtements. I want to pick up a few things."

Laughter echoed from Sharon's office. "You decided to bring Alister on the research trip, didn't you?"

"No. Well, yes, but I still... you know what, call Fredrick and get me an appointment tonight or tomorrow, please."

"Sure thing." Sharon responded and continued to giggle.

Michael shook his head. He found himself both amused and annoyed that she understood him this well. He wondered, briefly, if this is what having a mother would have been like. Not that he imagined Sharon as a mom, but there were times in their relationship he found himself thinking this thought.

~ Chapter Ten ~

The following days had been a circus of details and planning. Michael had his team involved in every detail, leaving as little as possible to chance. This wasn't their typical product launch or speaking event at the Adult Expo, where boundaries were easily pushed and they were allowed to be as avant garde as they wanted. No, this was for the *respected* media and leaders in local, state, and federal government. This was a big deal, and every fleck of sand in regard to the trip weighed his shoulders down. He witnessed the same worry, not in his team's faces, but in their shoulders, how they stood, and how tempers flared. Even Sharon held worry in the deepening of the wrinkles on her face and the darkness under her eyes. Typically, nothing appeared to phase her, but today, and this media event had wormed unease into her.

"We've confirmed all the media and their passes." Sharon peeked up from her tablet. "I wasn't sure they were all going to be there, but..." she trailed off.

"And what about our other guests? Michael asked from where he sat in Karen's office conference room.

"Everyone is going to be here."

Michael nodded.

"Michael..." she paused.

He snorted and leaned in.

"You don't think they are setting you up, do you?" The words dropped from her mouth like bone china plummeting to the floor. "This all seems too easy, and everyone has been too nice, well niceish."

Michael sat in silence. His mind had been playing out various scenarios the past few days. Everything from townspeople with pitchforks and torches, to the press crucifying him, to the military coming and seizing all their equipment and the sub. He had pictured a million and one ways this might all go wrong.

Why am I worrying over this?

"Sharon." Michael pulled his focus together. "We'll be fine." Was he saying this for her or for him? He wasn't sure. "Everyone has done their part. Our legal folks have gone over every contract, every NDA, everything. The marketing and PR team have done all the legwork, now all Karen and I have to do is get out there and talk to folks, announce the agreement with the government, introduce the good Doctors Farmin and May-Jordan and answer the questions from the media."

"But you've never done anything like this before."

Michael's eyebrows raised as he watched her.

"The AVN is a lot different from CNN or Fox or MSNBC."

"You forget, I've been interviewed by all of them before."

"Not like this." Sharon tapped her fingers on the conference table. "I'm worried about you. I want them to take this seriously and to take you seriously. Maybe you should have Candace or Daniel speak with them. They know how to bite back and deal with the media when they get out of hand."

Candace or Daniel handled the media and fielded questions like a baseball player fielding the ball, which is why they were in their respective positions, VP of Marketing and PR and VP of Communications. The two would be there, but he needed to do this. He needed to show the world he wasn't a big dick and a great pair of balls. He wasn't a former model and a porn mogul. "Sharon, I can handle myself. I know what I'm in for. So is Dr. Linn. Dan and Candace have drilled us for days."

She sighed. "Well, at least Alister will be there. I like him. He's good people."

Michael laughed. "I'm glad he's been helpful and learning. I figured you deserved to get some extra hands."

"Some extra hands you're taking with you on this little four-teen-day trip under the sea." She pursed her lips. "How is him being gone two weeks supposed to help me again?"

"Ah." Michael felt the heat in his neck and cheeks.

"Exactly." She stood up. "So, I'll be off in the wings and if these media types or anyone gets out of hand, I'm going to kick some ass."

Michael chuckled.

"I'm not kidding Michael," Sharon's voice deadlier than he had ever heard before. "I won't have them mocking you."

"Thank you." Michael couldn't help the swelling of pride in his chest as it warmed his core.

She really is a great friend...assuming I can call her a friend as well as an employee.

Sharon nodded. "Now, let's get out there and get this over with. I'm going to need a big glass of wine when this is finished."

"You and me both." Michael stood and buttoned up his suit jacket.
*****

Karen paced back and forth in her office. They had been practicing with Michael's team for days, and she wasn't sure if the constant practice is why her nerves were on end, or if in a few minutes she would have to stand in front of the whole world and tell them everything. Tell them what she planned and what they were going to do. She had the science and the backing from the United States, and surprisingly from six of the eight other countries affected by the Pulse. These endorsements and all the additional research offered them extra legitimacy, but the added attention made them vulnerable. If this all went wrong, she and Michael would be on the hook. She would be finished. If that was even possible.

"No." She shook her head. "I'm right. I know I am." No one was there to hear her remarks as she took a frustrated mouthful of air. "They came to me, to us. They must think there is something out there as well. They had plenty of time to stop us, to pull the plug, but they didn't." She nodded.

Her office in this location was small, and Michael and his people were using the conference room. This was the one place she would be able to catch her breath and get ready. She needed to use the bathroom and check to ensure she looked her part.

Why does this matter? I'm a scientist, not a beauty queen.

She grabbed her blazer and purse and walked to the door, made her way down the hall to the bathroom and slipped in, locking the door. At the sink she pulled out her brush, lip balm, and her makeup. She didn't wear a lot of makeup, but a little coverup and powder, as well as something for her cheeks and lips that gave her a polished look she approved of. Making up her face and getting all fancy never bothered her, and she always reckoned she donned a suit of armor when she got all duded up. Plus, considering all the cameras and lights, she did want to look her best.

After fussing and using the bathroom she was ready, or as ready as she would ever be. Images of her team, of her research, all played around in her head. She wasn't the only one who put her neck out. Everyone else involved had something at risk, maybe that's what worried her most. All this was more than her. She handled the ridicule her whole life; she grew numb to comments and all the BS, but what about the interns, what about her fellow scientists, they had their whole lives ahead of them and the potential for a big black mark on their future, if things went badly.

A shudder forced her to reach out for the counter to steady herself.

"Enough Karen." Her voice raised to her reflection. "You've got this. You're ready." She gave herself a firm nod and opened the bathroom door. "Ready or not, here I come." She commented as she left for the media circus.

*****

The setting sun lit the area in front of the sub in a warm glow; the bright oranges, reds, and yellows all danced around the area and the people. *Golden Hour,* some of the interns called it, and now she could see why. The water in the bay lapped softly on the shore and the pier. Even the seagulls hovering off in the distance added to the beauty. The only things out of place were all the people and the media. Karen inhaled, seeing everyone there; they were waiting for her and Michael. She caught sight of her partner and walked over to him. "Are we ready to do this?"

Michael nodded at her. "As ready as we'll ever be. I have some of my folks smattered in and around, plus we have security in case."

"You don't think we'll have any issues?"

"Better to have the security and not need it, then to need security and not have it."

"I'll be honest, I wish we could skip this part and head to the party instead."

Michael laughed. "Me too, but let's get up there and show the world we are more then what they think."

"Works for me."

Karen and Michael made their way to the stage erected for them. They found the microphone and podium and off to the side were members of Michael's event team as well as Dr. Rochelle Farmin and Dr. Wayne May-Jordan, who would be joining their mission. Once they found their marks, Karen stepped forward and began to address the crowd. Michael and she agreed she would start to introduce them and the project. Afterwards he would come up and talk about the funding and introduce the folks from the various governments who would be joining them. They would take questions and depending on how the Q&A went, they would see how long to go for.

As she started to speak she noted Michael's people were there passing out the press kits with all the presentation materials. She was impressed with how well they were prepared; they had planned for things that never even crossed her mind, which made her appreciate Michael even more.

As she spoke, she grew more comfortable and assured of her work and her team, which she managed to introduce and point out. Finally, after explaining everything and indicating the Pontus several times, she would have loved to give them all a tour of the sub, but for safety and security reasons, a media tour was a nonstarter. They did provide everyone in attendance with an overview of the sub with some high-quality print worthy images, so the photos would have to do.

After several moments, she caught notice of Daniel off on the side giving her the sign to wrap up. She nodded at him. "Right. Well, I've hit my time limit. I would like to introduce you to Michael Donovan, who has graciously funded my research and everything you see before us. I couldn't have done this without him."

A smattering of applause filled the surrounding area, which Karen ignored as Michael's smile grew and he approached the mic.

*****

Michael inhaled. "Thank you, Dr. Linn. Working with you has been a pleasure. Being involved in such an endeavor has broadened my mind and I look forward to finding out what caused the Pacific Pulse and what else we might find out there." He glanced around at the cameras, ensuring he spoke to each one of them. Karen and he had agreed they would focus more on the Pulse and less on Mu; the event would be an easier sell to the public and the government; however, they would not steer clear of the topic of Mu. After all, Karen's research focused on Mu and he needed and wanted to respect all her years of study.

"As many of you already know, we have been in talks with the governments of the eight countries affected by the Pacific Pulse, and as of this afternoon, six have offered their support and their endorsement of Dr. Linn's research." Michael paused. "Their information has been provided in the media packet each of you should have. However, since the sub has limited space, we are only going to have a small outside delegation, and tonight I'm pleased to introduce you to Dr. Rochelle Farmin, Director of the White House Office of Science and Technology and Dr. Wayne May-Jordan, who will be joining us on this mission." He pointed to the side of the stage where both doctors were sitting. They stood and waved. The media zoomed in on each of the doctors and quickly returned to him. "You'll get a chance to talk more with the doctors and the rest of the team at the reception." He took several inhalations and glanced at Karen, who moved closer to him. "At this time I would like to take some of your questions."

Piranha around a bloody carcass moved with more grace and finesse than the reporters, who now called out and waved their hands, trying to get their attention. Michael nodded to the smartly dressed woman with blond hair. "Kathy Martin, CNN. Mr. Donovan, given your profession and your history in the adult entertainment industry, why would someone like you be interested in funding someone like Dr. Karen Linn?"

The sting of the words hit Michael like a slap on his cheek, but he had expected this question. "Well, even someone like me can see the Pacific Pulse did a number on the west coast and hurt a lot of people, so considering no one else was willing, at the time, to address the cause, when Dr. Linn contacted me, seeing a void in leadership, I stepped in."

"And the claims of a lost continent?" Ms. Martin followed up.

"Dr. Linn." Michael glanced at Karen and she nodded.

"Something caused the Pulse." Dr. Linn started. "We don't know what. There are a lot of theories out there, including mine, but we don't even know what we don't know yet, so I'm not willing to rule anything out."

"But seriously—"

"I'm not saying we're going to find *merpeople* or anything of the sort, but there may be something down there. Dr. Chan Thomas' book; *The Adam and Eve Story*, which was recently declassified from the CIA, offered details and theories that several people didn't take seriously until after the Pulse. We aim to search and explore the ocean's mysteries and if we find the lost city of Mu, proving the location actually did exist, all the better."

There were chuckles from the media.

"And you think following up on the theories of Dr. Thomas, Augustus Le Plongeon, and James Churchward, who by all accounts, were not the most reliable researches in this field, are going to lead you... you, Dr. Linn, to find out what caused the Pulse? Debbie Jefferson, ABC News." The dark-skinned reporter called out.

"Scientists build on one another's works." Karen glanced around the crowd. "None of us works in a vacuum. Dr. Thomas built his research on the shoulders of others, and I'm following suit."

"Didn't Plongeon believe his wife, Alice, to be a descended or reincarnated Queen of Mu?" Jefferson added the snark and mockery clear in her tone.

There were laughs from the crowd. Michael stepped forward, but Karen held up her hand.

"And Einstein was a Socialist. Benjamin Franklin owned slaves. And Steven Hawking is rumored to have had an affair with Elaine Mason, before divorcing his wife Jane." Karen paused. "I don't see your point. Scientists have always been known to be a bit eccentric, and not quite what society would have liked them to be, including me, I suppose."

There were more laughs from the crowd, but this time not at Karen or Michael, but with them. She even offered her own chuckle.

"And the government is going along with this *theory* of yours? Evan Green, Fox News."

"They wouldn't be here today if they didn't feel there was some merit in the research and the mission." Michael pointed to Dr. Farmin and Dr. May-Jordon, who were happy to avoid the Q&A for the time being.

"But Canada and Costa Rico have clearly stated they feel the money is a waste, and these funds might have been put to better use, so not all countries agree with your planned adventure." Mr. Green continued.

"Not many countries agree on everything." Michael countered. "However, as we've pointed out, six other countries have now offered their support including, Mexico and the United States, which considering the effects the Pulse had on these countries says a lot."

"And might I add," Karen interjected with a sharper tone, "we have also had support from France, which was the first country to support this research project. And not to forget Japan."

There were murmurs from the crowd.

"Dr. Linn." A reporter waved their hand, shouting over the others. "Dr. Linn, Carlos Fernandez, Mercury News, Bay Area News Group. Aren't you risking a great deal, reputation and career? Why put the added pressure of working with an unapologetic porn mogul? Are you worried about how people will respond to your findings, and additionally, aren't you worried any success from your research and mission will be soiled by where the funding comes from?"

Karen's eyes narrowed on the male reporter. Michael witnessed the red on her neck and forced calm through his body with each lungful of air.

Karen smiled and focused on the reporter. "No. Not in the least. Research is research, theories are either proven accurate or not, typically the scientific community isn't as judgmental as the general populations, including the media and reporters such as yourself."

"That isn't—"

Michael stepped up, "Mr. Fernandez." Karen saved him with the government. Now he needed to return the favor. Michael pushed forward as bright a smile as possible. "Dr. Linn did in fact go to many other sources including the United States Government for funding, but as we shared, no one was interested, for whatever reason, so when she came to me, I decided since no one else wanted to give her a chance or to fund her project, I would. That's all. My decision was simply to help. I stepped up when no one else was able. Yes, I'm aware our arrangement is unique, and most people who work in my industry tend to stay on the fringes of society, but that doesn't make us any less interested in making a better tomorrow for us and our families. I hope this common goal would outweigh any sour taste people have over how this wonderful scientist and this project have been funded."

Fernandez fell silent as another journalist jumped up. "Louise Scott, BBC. Despite this event being localized to the west coast of

North America, the effects of the Pulse were felt globally. What do you say to the people who lost family and friends? How do you justify not only wanting to find the cause of the Pulse, which is admirable, with the desire to prove your baseless theory about Mu, Dr. Linn?"

Karen nodded. "Finding the truth is not an easy task, I understand there are a lot of people who think the idea of this lost continent, or lost city is ridiculous, but everything is lost or a mystery until the unknown is found. In 1954 the lost city of Lothal—Gujarat was found and is arguably one of the most important excavated cities among the long-lost cities of the world, Lothal shows the brilliance of city-planning and organized structures during the times of the Indus Valley Civilization. This is among one of the most famous lost ancient cities in India. The city was found less than 100 years ago. So, just because we haven't found something yet, doesn't mean Mu's not there. And there are so many more; Machu Picchu, Mesa Verde, Petra, Taxila, so many. So, should those people who found these locations not have looked for them? What history would we have missed out on if people didn't bother?" Karen paused. "I understand there are those who might be upset with my research, and I hope in the end, no matter what we find, they will appreciate why we had to do this, especially now."

Michael got the signal from Dan to wrap up, "Well, that's all the time we have; however, we have a reception waiting and we invite you all to join us, you'll be able to talk to the rest of the team, including Dr. Farmin and Dr. May-Jordan. If you aren't able to stay, you have all the contact information, should you have follow-up questions."

~ Chapter Eleven ~

Kaimi watched as his brother, Koa, paced the chamber hall. His footsteps echoed off the stone floor and walls as the light from the crystals showed the worry on his face as well as his determination. Gathered too were the members of the High Council, as were he, Nohealani and Ulani. Mana Lani and Kai Malina were off to the side seated. Shadows always followed the Māhū no matter how bright the location. They had no say in the ruling of Mu, but as they were the representatives of the gods, they were welcomed to hear and to offer council as requested. Several servants and guards stood off at their various posts, close enough to respond if needed, but out of the line of sight to not be a distraction.

The chamber was set differently from when they all heard the vision and the warnings from Ku and Kanaloa. A large stone table sat in the center, with chairs placed around where everyone would be able to meet and talk. On the table lay maps of Mu and the surrounding area. A bank of screens had been lowered from the ceiling, allowing them to pull up whatever additional data they needed. The space typical for tradition and ceremony were now set for the planned invasion, or battle, or attack, or encounter, or visit. Kaimi wasn't sure what to call this new unknown.

I wish Mother and Father were here, they would know what to do. Or at least act like they did.

"Your Highness," One of the elders began. His face full and withered. His tattoos were fading, however, he still had strong shoulders and chest. "We have seen the images from their world, we know they are coming. We have even seen the vessel they are bringing. We must act to stop them."

"Many don't believe they can reach here," another elder spoke. She had long gray hair and reminded Kaimi of his grandmother, the kindness only offset by her determination. "They do not have the technology, and only in recent years with the development of our new Manō hae suits can we easily reach them and the above world." She glanced at the others assembled, ensuring to make eye contact with each of them. "I do not believe we have anything to fear."

"We've heard the gods, and we have seen the above worlders with our own eyes. They are coming." Koa stopped and glanced at the screens, pointing at the images they showed. "Or do you doubt the words of our gods? And your own eyes?"

Everyone fell silent as Koa played the images again, stepping clear so they were visible to all. An older woman and a man perhaps not too much older than him stood speaking, talking about their plans to find them. Yes, they still didn't know where to look, but they had a general idea and given how determined they looked, especially the woman, they would be found. At least that's what Kaimi believed, as did his brother from the looks of him. There were a few whispers, but nothing more. "The gods revealed they are coming in a ship sailing below the water, and we have seen their...submarine." The word played hard off of Koa's mouth and to Kaimi's ear.

"They've had the technology for hundreds of years." Kaimi finally spoke, surprising himself as well as the others. He hadn't felt the need to speak, plus given what he had been through, and his uncertainty, he believed speaking would be best left to his brother. The words continued to flow from Kaimi's mouth, "and with each new iteration of these vessels, they have gone deeper, come closer. Now, with this new vessel, they will be able to reach us. The above worlder's arrival is no longer a stretch to believe. The question is not if or when, but how to counter them and protect our home. Should we need to."

"You now believe they will come to invade or attack us?" Ulani questioned, the words surprising the room, as this was the first she had spoken since they were all seated around the table.

Nohealani faced him, her eyes narrowing and a frown growing around her lips.

She's unhappy with me and my words.

"I'm unsure." Kaimi admitted. He didn't want to believe the claims. However, he heard the comments made by the scientist and the man who funded her research, and this new undersea ship. They were coming to find out what caused the Pulse, they were coming to search them out. So, what would they do when they reached them?

What would we do if our roles were reversed? Perhaps that's what has me the most concerned.

"Brother, you are supposed to be the voice for them. You have always been their champion." Koa walked up next to Kaimi and placed a hand on his shoulder. "You wanted to reach out to them. What's changed?"

Kaimi shook his head, "Nothing. I'm not sure. I'm concerned for you and for all of us. We've suffered greatly the last several years and now this. Plus, I ask myself, what would we have done if we were them?"

Did he believe these scientists and researchers were coming to attack them? No, he didn't. They had warriors for such matters. Did he want to reach out to them and open a dialog? Doing so might be wise, but given all he knew now and all he had lost, human nature and wanting to take revenge on someone who hurt you plagued all his thoughts. He lost Makani for his ideals. At one point he wanted to kill Koa. The desire took years for the pain and the need to fade. Now here he sat asking to think through the motivations of people who they barely had anything in common with. If they weren't all human and from the same planet, they might as well be completely different beings.

"My team and I have been improving our manō hae suits." Noe chimed in, standing and walking to the screens and pulling up the details for the others to see. "We have a hundred ready for deployment, and our warriors have been training in them. With great success." Noe called out. "We can use them and meet their machine head on. We can use our energy weapons against them and neutralize their vessel."

"And then?" Nohealani asked, her tone stronger and louder than anyone at the table. "We start a war with them. We can't use the Pulse again. The gods forbade us. So what, we start fighting them, kill them, they bring another one of these ships, we've seen how they wage war, they will slaughter us. Who else has to die?"

"We cannot hide here," another of the Elders declared. He was quite possibly the youngest of the elders, barely Kaimi's age, maybe older. Half his proud face had been covered in his family's markings. "They will destroy us."

"We die." Nohealani countered, her voice strong, but Kaimi glimpsed past her words. She waited to greet death to rejoin her husband, Malo. She couldn't think like this. She still had Allyn and Palani to think about.

She has to remember we do this for not only our people now, but for all who come later. She has to remember her children and move past the sorrow and pain.

"You speak madness." One of the Elders banged their hands on the table. "Why are you even here? You and your brother tried to..."

Within seconds, everyone was talking, and the calm conversation turned into shouting and yelling. Fingers pointing, some standing and others banging their hands on the table to be heard or to emphasize their point. Is this what they were now? Is this who they had turned into over the last several years since the death of Kanani and Palani, queen and king.—*No.*— Kaimi watched as heat rose from his belly to his neck. This is not what his parents wanted. This isn't what he wanted. They were going to get nothing done.

We need to stop this. This needs to end.

Kaimi was about to stand and speak.

"Enough!" Koa shouted, calling their attention. "We will not start a war with the above world. What we will do is like Noe suggested. We will use our manō hae suits equipped with our best warriors and energy weapons. We will go and meet them, disable their ship and bring them here. We will find out what they want and we will decide from there. If they crave dialog and answers, we will work with them. If they crave war and revenge, we will destroy them." He glanced at Kai Malina and Mana Lani.

Kaimi followed his brother's eyes, both māhū sat stone faced. The shadows continued to cover them as if to protect them.

Perhaps the gods are shrouding them.

"Will the gods support and help us?" Koa asked them, his voice raised to ensure no others spoke and none of his siblings or the elders interrupted him.

Mana Lani nodded at Kai Malina, who stood. Mana Lani's withered face appeared to have aged a hundred years over these last several months. "The gods were clear," Kai Malina spoke. "You must ensure Mu's survival and keep our people safe."

"But do we go to war, or do we have a dialog?" Koa insisted, his tone gave away his annoyance.

Kai Malina spoke, "The task is for you, the king to decide, but know the gods will be watching and judging you." They bowed their head.

Koa nodded, his nostrils flared with each inhalation, the color in his face returning to normal. "Thank you." He glanced at those around the table. "We know what we must do. I trust you all to make the necessary plans. Kaimi and I will lead our warriors."

"What?" Several people spoke at once.

Kaimi glanced at his brother. He found his voice had joined the chorus of others questioning Koa, their king.

"I will not send our warriors someplace I am not willing to go on my own." Koa stood tall, his bare chest and stomach tight. He projected all the authority and strength he had. "Kaimi worked with Noe for years on the suits. I can think of no one better to have there by my side." He faced Kaimi, these next words for him alone. "Will this be a problem?"

Kaimi bowed his head. "If you want me there, I will be there." He raised his voice along with his head and met his brother's eyes. "We will offer friendship as one. And if need be, we will fight as one."

There were murmurs from around the table, but no one countered the king.

"We are done here for now." Koa met each of the council member's gaze before exiting the chamber.

Kaimi glanced at his sisters as the elders stood and started to file out.

"You need to talk him out of this." Ulani approached Kaimi. "We can't lose him or you."

"Are you doubting our king?" Kaimi's tone tested, but his voice was calm. He had his doubts, but he would not speak them, not in public.

Ulani shook her head. "I'm worried for my brothers." She reached out and took his hand. "Our family is again whole and I don't want to lose our oneness again. I don't want to lose any more of those we love."

Nohealani moved to them. "I'm worried as well, but I have faith with you both there. We will be safe and Mu, along with Mother and Father's memories, will be protected." She offered a weak smile.

"I worry as well," Noe whispered. They had not exited the room, which wasn't uncommon. They were almost like family, well, in Kaimi's eyes at least. Still, their voice came gently. "But I think King Koa is correct. You and he need to go. The mission is important, not only for what is to come, but to show our people your strength and you are both together in this, a united front."

Nohealani nodded, and Ulani let go of her frown and glanced down at the floor.

She would not fight any further.

"Plus," Noe started.

Kaimi tapped his fingers as he waited to hear what more his scientist friend had to say.

"I want to know someone out there understands the technology. I had planned on asking if I might go, but doubted I would be allowed, so you were my next pick. You were there from the start when we worked on these suits, so you understand them."

"And I can fix them, if there are any issues." Kaimi almost smiled.

Noe nodded.

"I guess." Kaimi ran a hand over his chin. "I need to go and get reacquainted with this new tech, so I can go with our king to greet our coming guests."

*****

Karen walked the corridor of the sub, making her way from the labs. The scent of oil and machinery filled her nose, even here. *Perhaps I shouldn't have forced the no perfume rule.* She shook the image from her mind, focusing again on the labs and all their equipment. Yes, she had the interns, and she was keeping them busy, but given everything, the final inspection was her job, and good thing too. She had to send Jayden, Dinh, and Mila to her office for a couple of laptops and tablets left behind.

She passed one of the crew members and offered them a nod.

"Hello, Dr. Linn." They greeted as they passed.

"Hi," she responded.

Crap. What was their name? I'm just getting all the names set for my team and now I have to learn all the crew names as well.

She shook her head. "Speaking of forgetting. I'm sure we've forgotten something." She huffed, going through her mental checklist again.

Today was the day. All their preparations and planning, everything relied on this working. The media event, after the questions, had gone well. Well, better than they had assumed the event would go. Yes, there were a few comments here and there, but the more the press spoke to the scientists and the crew, the more they started to come around. They began to ask pertinent questions and wanted more details on her research. She even considered offering a couple of them a spot on the trip, but she didn't want reporters underfoot, even though having them present might have been good PR. What she did agree to was to have two of her interns Amanda and Hanh record everything, well not everything, but document all the important stuff. That way, they would have a record of their research and their journey. Alister had even offered to help, since he had experience in the movie industry. This made the media even happier, as she promised they would share the final product with them. All the concessions helped. And the press even began to treat Michael better, which made her happy. Especially after he reminded them of all the potential new discoveries they would be making, even without Mu or finding the cause of the Pulse.

He's good at working the media and the crowd.

"Well," Michael came up next to her. They were right outside their cabins on the second level of the sub. He wore sneakers, jeans and a light salmon colored sweater. He looked impeccable, as always. "Do you think we have everything? Is there anything I can do, or do you need me to stay out of the way?"

Karen laughed. "I've given the captain the go ahead. I think we're as good as we'll ever be."

"Good." Michael smiled as he pushed up the sleeves of his sweater. "You'll need to tell me to get out of your way whenever I get in the way."

"You'll be fine." Karen beamed. "And if not, well, there is always the wet lab."

"Ouch." Michael put a hand over his heart. "Are you sure you're not related to Sharon?" He chuckled and his whole face lit up.

I hope I'm not too bossy for him. Nah, we've been working fine together. It'll be good.

Karen smiled as she glanced around. "Fourteen days in a big metal tube searching for answers to some of the biggest questions of our time. I hope I have enough lip balm." She laughed and felt her pocket and pulled out her balm, giving her lips a coat.

Michael smiled and shook his head.

"From what I understand from Captain Abbas," Karen put away her lip balm. "We're going to ride along the surface of the water until we leave the bay, give people a chance to see us and give the media a chance to get all their photos and pictures."

"Oh, that should be fun." Michael frowned, his lips pinching together. "Maybe I should go put on my speedo and lay on the top deck and give them an eye full."

"I wouldn't mind seeing you in your speedo." Alister popped out of his cabin, closing the door as he walked over to Karen and Michael, "You know the sub's not as tight as I figured, but my room isn't as nice as your cabin and you can definitely hear what's going on out in the hall."

"What's that wonderful scent?" Karen sniffed the air as Alister got close. Images of her family and friends sitting around the table playing *Ten Thousand* filled her head. Everybody laughing as someone pouted because they rolled four fours. She even tasted hints of her sister's orange spice cake. Their house was always warm and welcoming and the dining space never cramped with all the people. Everything all cozy, loving and wonderful.

"Oh, sorry." He waved his hands around him.

Alister's words pulled Karen from her memories.

"It's my aromatherapy. The scent is orange and ginger. I sprayed some in my room to freshen the space. I guess the scent followed me out." He bit his lips. "I know you have a no perfume rule, but I didn't..."

"Don't worry, your aromatherapy actually smells good." Karen leaned in. "I may want to borrow some for my room."

"Anytime." Alister beamed. "Like I mentioned, the cabins are roomier than I planned for, but the ventilation needs some work, as does the soundproofing." He chuckled with a smile and glance toward Michael.

"We did our best to sound deaden things on the sub, but there is still going to be noise, unfortunately, same thing with the air filtration." Karen shrugged. "On the plus side, we all have our own private bathrooms. Most of the crew and research team have to share. So that's something."

"Which I'm grateful for," Michael relaxed his stance as he spoke. "I hate sharing a bathroom or showering with others."

"I wouldn't have pinned you for being shy." Karen watched him.

"I'm not shy, obviously, but I... well, I guess I don't like to share." Michael smirked. "Anyway, private bath and soundproofing are all perks of writing the check. Oh, and Alister isn't the only one with some aromatherapy spray."

"Well don't tell anyone else." Karen grinned. "And for the love of all that's holy, don't go crazy with the spray either."

"Yes ma'am." Michael offered a salute.

"I guess I'm used to sharing," Alister revealed as both Michael and Karen faced him. He tugged at his short-sleeved blue button-down shirt. "I've never had anything all to myself my whole life. I didn't have my own bed, till I moved out, even now I share a bathroom. Ah well." He glanced down the corridor.

"Hey, you might not have to keep sharing for much longer." Michael beamed as he watched the younger guy.

"I'm waiting for Mr. Right." Alister glanced at Michael with raised eyebrows.

Karen shook her head.

If these two don't end up together, I'm going to throw them both overboard.

"Did our guests find everything okay?" Michael asked of Dr. Farmin and Dr. May-Jordon.

"The last I saw, they were checking out the labs with Dr. Chen and Dr. Dubois." Karen pointed in the direction of the labs. "I hope we have everything."

"Too late now." Michael pulled out his phone and checked the device.

As if on cue, the public address system kicked on. "Attention please, attention please." The comms officer spoke. "We have been cleared to embark. Crew ensure all stations are secured, we request all guests stay to decks one and two while we clear the Golden Gate Bridge. Once we are out to sea, the captain will make her address. All crew prepare for departure."

"So, what are we supposed to do now?" Alister asked, glancing up the corridor again.

"Stay out of the way." Michael shrugged.

"Make our way to the galley," Karen gestured her hand in the direction she wanted them to go. "I arranged a welcome lunch for all us non-sailor types, figured a reception with good food and sweet treats would be the best way to keep us out of trouble."

"Good thing I brought my workout gear." Michael patted his nonexistent belly. "I have no intention of gaining weight on this trip."

"This isn't a cruise." Karen crossed her arms over her chest.

"Maybe not, but if all we're going to do is eating and researching, I'm going to be spending time in the gym." Michael offered a firm nod.

"You won't be the only one." Alister smiled.

"You guys are ridiculous." Karen shook her head, "Come on, let's go meet and greet and be social."

~ Chapter Twelve ~

Michael held a steady pace on the treadmill as he ran. He was on his seventh mile and sweating like a horse. His pulse was not as high as he was hoping. Perhaps being on the sub affected him in ways he didn't know yet. The hum of the sub was barely noticeable any longer, neither were the sub's vibrations. The first two nights had been tough. Falling asleep wasn't easy and getting a good night's sleep was almost impossible. He pulled the towel from the top of the machine and wiped his neck and forehead.

At least I slept well last night.

He continued his run and increased the incline and speed. Trying to get his heart rate up to burn more calories.

"You beat me this morning." Alister joined him on the treadmill next to Michael.

"I didn't think this was a competition."

Alister laughed. "Life is a competition and we all want to be in the winner's circle."

Michael nodded. Alister wasn't wrong. A bit pessimistic but not wrong. "How'd you sleep last night?"

"Good." Alister commented as he started his warm up, "But growing up the way I did, I'm used to noise." He laughed as his feet hit the tread and he began to move. "I can't sleep when it's too quiet, so being here on the sub, the noise is like home..." he chuckled. "Well, kind of." He picked up his pace, now at a full jog.

"I'm the opposite. I need the quiet. At least the cabin is dark, which helps." Michael huffed out as he continued. "What has life been like for you... as a kid?" He asked.

Alister shrugged as he increased the speed to match Michael. "I don't know. I mean normal, I guess."

"Really. Normal?"

Alister sighed. "Well, how I grew up is the only thing I know, so I guess normal for me."

Michael spotted the discomfort on Alister's face as he focused straight ahead and any hint of a smile gone. "Sorry. None of this is my business."

Alister shook his head. "Don't worry, I don't mind." He faced Michael, offering a bit of a smile before focusing on the treadmill. "My family's poor, no surprise, and me being the oldest I had to help around the house and with the bills..."

"Oh." Michael pulled out his water bottle and took a swallow.

"I don't talk to my family anymore, they don't approve of what I'm doing," He laughed. "But they sure don't mind spending the money I send them." He frowned.

Michael wiped his sweaty brow with his hand, then used the towel hanging in front of him to dry off his hand. "Is that why you don't have your own place? I mean, I know we pay pretty good and you have your 'Only' account. So..."

"Most of what I make, I send to them. I have younger brothers and sisters, so the money really helps them out." Alister ramped up the speed on his machine, the whir increasing along with the speed. "I keep a little for myself. I have the investments I'm starting, but yea, I rent a room to help keep my costs down."

"What you're doing is really admirable." Michael tapped the buttons on his machine, thinking he might increase the speed to match Alister's, but he didn't want to push himself and get hurt. Still he raised the effort and speed a bit—*a final burst to end my workout*—. "Assisting your family is cool."

"I suppose, but helping them never feels like enough." He grabbed the towel he brought and patted his forehead. "You must get it, given your own history."

"Yep." Michael started to slow down his pace. He wanted to grab a shower before breakfast and he had already been going for just over an hour. "Living on the streets, I know exactly what you mean, but I only had to care for myself and I had no one judging me."

"Well, like I mentioned at dinner the other night, they are a bunch of hypocrites, and even though they're my family and I love them..." He didn't finish his statement.

Michael didn't press and finished up his workout in silence. Especially as others were coming into the gym for their workouts. Once done with his 10-mile run and stretching, Michael made his way to his cabin for a shower. He couldn't imagine having a family who didn't accept you, but still wants the money you make. Alister's situation couldn't be easy and must lead to some difficult choices.

*****

Karen sat in the galley with the others on her team enjoying breakfast. Anne, the chef, had cooked pancakes, bacon, eggs, fruit and the other typical items; cereal, yogurt, granola, and milk out for breakfast today, nothing fancy, but the woman sure knew how to cook. She even had fresh muffins yesterday, but they weren't so lucky today.

"Today I want to start checking the geological data we've received, and compare today's results to what we received before the Pulse, and before we left. There have been some changes and I can't figure out how to account for those discrepancies." Dr. Dubois remarked between bites of bacon.

"All our current data seems different from what we had before we left Moffett Field, shifting somehow." Lucas declared as he worked his way through his eggs. "I'll be damned if I can explain any of our new readings.

"And nothing from Dr. Chen and her team can explain the changes, either?" Karen asked. The first two days were uneventful, but between the readings yesterday and today, the ocean shifted, and now everything was in flux. There were no earthquakes, no volcanic activity, and there were no storms. Nothing from NOAA or Moffett Field might account for these changes. "A mystery."

"Oh mysteries, down here in the deep blue sea." Michael sat alongside Karen, placing his tray with his meal in front of him. "That isn't good, or maybe it's those mermaids we were warned about."

"Merpeople." Dr. Samuel remarked.

Michael held up a hand in surrender as he took his seat.

"Anyway, maybe a mystery isn't good, but these anomalies are why we're here." Karen took a bite of her pancakes, seeing Michael had fruit, yogurt and granola for his breakfast. "Come on Michael, live a little." She pointed to her pancakes with butter and syrup. "These pancakes are fantastic. Worth the trip alone."

Michael laughed. "I'm fine with what I have, but I wouldn't mind one of those muffins from yesterday."

"Gone." Dr. Samuel shook their head with a bit of a frown at the fork full of pineapple. "And the chef said she might not make them again, given how quickly we gobbled them up."

"So, I'm being punished because all you scientists constantly eat while you work." Michael laughed.

"Hey geology, oceanography, and climatology take a lot of brain power and require muffins and snacks." Dr. Jenner glanced toward Michael, with a wave of their fork.

"Plus, we can't send the babies out on food runs for us," Mason smirked.

"Babies?" Michael glanced around the galley.

"Our interns." Karen amended. "All these fancy intellectuals call the interns 'babies'." She shook her head. "At least they aren't calling them by numbers anymore."

"Ouch."

"The teasing is all in good fun," Mike, Dr. Sanchez, countered with a grin to the table.

The others nodded.

"Oh watch out, here come Mom and Dad." Isabel stood, she had finished her meal. "I'm heading to the lab." She took her tray and started to head out.

"Wait for me." Mason stood as well, stuffing the last of his pancake in his mouth.

As quickly as possible, Karen's team shoveled the rest of their food and scurried off, much to Michael's surprise.

"What's this all about?"

"Us, I'm afraid." Dr. Farmin had their tray filled with today's breakfast selection. "May I?"

"Please." Karen pointed to the empty space near her.

Michael nodded before taking another bite of his granola.

"I'm sorry about my team." Karen remarked as she took another bite of bacon.

"We're used to the poor treatment, having us here and hovering around. I understand." Dr. May-Jordon replied as he joined them at the table. "And I don't think our popularity was helped when I asked about the anomalies they've been finding."

"Still, we should be professional." Karen huffed and picked up her tea, taking a sip, and making a face.

"I don't know how you drink that stuff." Michael scrunched his nose.

"This is tea, not coffee. I didn't put enough sugar in." Karen laughed.

"Let me." Dr. May-Jordon stood.

"No." Karen waved him off. "Thank you, but it'll be fine. I don't need all the extra sugar, especially with the syrup I've had."

He nodded and returned to his seat, settling down to eat.

"So, I know I'm not a scientist, but what is so special about all these readings and them being off? I mean, aren't odd readings normal? Aren't these findings part of why we are here?"

"There will always be variations," Dr. Farmin offered. "But these readings..." She shook her head.

"So maybe we are on to something?" Michael picked at the fruit on his plate.

"That's what me and my team have been saying, but Rochelle and Wayne here don't agree." Karen glanced between them.

"But if you can't explain these new results by normal measures—"

"That isn't how science works." Rochelle declared, putting her fork down. "We have to ensure the data isn't corrupt and all our tests are repeatable; just because you get one odd reading doesn't mean we've found what caused the Pulse, Michael."

Rochelle and Wayne were right, and Karen appreciated what they were saying, but her team received more than one strange reading. They were getting all kinds of odd data which didn't add up and the variations were what had her worried, maybe excited. "So we go deeper, and send out the drones, have them take samples and see what they find."

"Excellent." Wayne nodded his head up and down before taking a bite of his own pancake, currently doing laps in the maple syrup on his plate. "I agree. I think using the drones now is a good idea."

"Wait, you agree?" Karen glanced at the man, surprised by his remarks, sipping at her tea again, getting used to the lack of sweetness.

"Karen, Dr. Linn, I don't know what is happening out there, but we're all here to find out." Wayne offered. "Maybe we'll find Mu. Maybe we'll find something else. Maybe we don't find anything, but since we're here, we might as well do all we can to learn what we can."

"Thank you, Wayne." Karen smiled with a glance at her plate. Should she have some more or was she finished? Always the million-calorie question. "I appreciate hearing you are on our side and not against us."

Wayne glanced at Rochelle between bites. "You didn't..."

Rochelle shook her head. "Your story is not for me to share."

"What?" Michael was curious as he bit into the last of his fruit.

"Yea, what am I missing?" Karen asked; deciding she was finished, she wiped her mouth with her napkin.

"Dr. Linn, I'm not sure what you know about me, but I've been a big fan of your research, I may not believe all your theories but I've read everything of yours and I asked Rochelle to accompany her on this expedition. You and your team may not believe me, but I'm here to help and to be part of this."

"No way." Karen laughed.

Rochelle nodded, swallowing her mouthful of bacon. "He's been working on me for years trying to get me to green light our cooperation with you. You have Dr. Wayne May-Jordon to thank for us finally coming around, well, him and your newest research."

Karen's cheeks ached from the smile on her face. "I... wow... I don't know what to say."

"Sounds like we have more allies than we believed." Michael finished the last of his own breakfast.

"And don't think we've forgotten about you, Mr. Donovan, Michael, if I may."

"Don't tell me you're a fan of my work?" Michael asked, an impish smile on his face.

"No, but we know about your foundation and all the work you do behind the scenes to help the community. Personally, I don't care what you do to make a living as long as you follow the laws and you pay your taxes, but seeing you out there helping people and doing what you can, despite what others may think, is nice."

"You didn't think we wouldn't have done our homework on the two of you." Rochelle took a bite of her pancake.

"Well, I assumed you would, but you never mentioned anything." Michael countered, placing his used utensils in a neat line on his tray.

"Down here is a whole different world; we can be more open than we were on land. As you can imagine, the President, well she has to be careful, there are a lot of people who want to see her fail. Kind of like you, Dr. Linn."

"Makes sense, but why now? Why not before?"

"Until we started getting these odd readings we, well, I, still had my doubts." Rochelle finished off her pancake. "And now." She shrugged, then added, "Perhaps there really are merpeople down here."

"There is still a chance this will all be for nothing, and don't get me wrong, we'll need to distance ourselves from you if this all blows up or turns out to be nothing, but for now, we are all working toward the same goal."

"I appreciate the heads up and our current truce." Karen glanced at her tea. She wanted to finish the drink before she had to lick it like an ice-cream. "And I think my team will as well."

"I can't wait to see those drones out there." Wayne finished off his pancake before speaking again. "This is quite exciting, and I'm hoping we all make history together."

Karen raised her cup of tea. "I'll drink to that." She took a sip as the chilled bitter liquid hit her mouth and she fought to swallow.

~ Chapter Thirteen ~

Kaimi pulled himself from the mechanical suit and the water. The salty scent was outmatched by the smells of oils and lubricants. Everything had worked as planned and the energy pulse weapon was easy to aim and use. He hoped they wouldn't need them, but they needed to be prepared. The tail stock and the fins were a bit to get used to, but they couldn't be beat for movement. The gods comprehended what they were doing with the design of these creatures, and he was pleased they had been wise enough to use the design for these suits.

"What do you think?" Koa asked as he offered a hand to his brother.

"I think in six days we've managed to train and prepare ourselves for something I had hoped would never happen." Kaimi took the offered hand and stood along the dive pool, watching the others continue their practice. He glanced into the depths of the pool and witnessed how well their warriors moved and how fast they actually were.

Impressive, they even look like manō hae, or nai'a. Or even a small koholā. Noe is brilliant.

"I know this isn't what you had hoped for, but I don't see a choice." Koa rested his hands on his hips, dripping water on his slowly drying white sarong. "The reports show they are getting close. Something is drawing them nearer to our location."

"Undoubtedly our own signals and electronics." Noe approached, glancing at his notes and checking over his shoulders at the warriors still in the pool. "I've been looking into if our energy crystals and our technology might be attracting them to us. Their ship appears to have devices much more sensitive to our equipment than what we assumed they had, plus with them focused on this part of the ocean, less is being discarded as background noise."

"We're drawing them here," Kaimi pulled in a breath with the words. He always realized this might be the case, even his parents felt this. "We're causing our own problem." He shook his head, not pleased with this new development or confirmation of his own theory.

"We can't very well shut everything off and blow out the torches." Koa ran a hand under his chin before massaging his temples. "We're well beyond that, plus the crystals would still emit their own energy signal, perhaps even more if we power everything down."

"Correct, your majesty," Noe offered as he rested his hands by his side. "I think we are beyond stopping their arrival, and from what I've learned, they should be within reach of our suits and our team within six hours."

Koa frowned, but offered a nod in recognition.

Kaimi pulled over a towel to dry himself. There was a slight chill in the air. "Six hours." He sighed, wiping away the coolness and damp. "Not long before we find out who we are dealing with and what they want."

If the gods are to be believed, we are in danger, but I still don't think they come to fight. Those we've seen tend to not look like warriors. Especially the men.

"We'll take a limited force with us, ten people tops. The rest will stay in reserve in case we need them." Koa instructed as he glanced around the group. "We will try diplomacy first."

Noe nodded. "That seems wise. After studying their machine, we found they have entry points on the underbelly we should be able to breach; we should be able to selectively disable their vessel without harming anyone or the machine."

"Good." Koa glanced at the warriors in the pool. Several were starting to come to the surface to exit. "I don't want a war and I don't want anyone harmed."

"From either party." Kaimi noted where his brother looked. "Any more news from Kai Malina or Mana Lani? Will the gods send their promised creatures to help us?"

"Nothing, and I'm not sure. They may only show if there is blood in the water and we are in a battle, but…" Koa shook his head. "I heard them bickering earlier today. Kai Malina wasn't happy and Mana Lani clearly was in the mood for a lecture. You know how they can be."

"Mother and Father always did have a difficult time reining in Mana Lani." Images filled Kaimi's head with the vocal conversations his parents would have with their māhū. He remembered asking his mother once why they allowed such impertinence from Mana Lani. Their mother only smiled and told him someday he would understand when he was king. Neither came; his understanding or him becoming king. He brushed the thoughts from his mind. "I'm glad Kai Malina is there to help provide some balance."

"Agreed." Koa used a fresh towel to dry himself. "We will need to go and speak with them to get the gods' blessing prior to going; a blessing will provide support for our warriors and a much-needed boost for myself. Plus, maybe they can make an appeal to the gods about getting the assistance of the sea creatures mentioned in the vision."

"I can't argue your reasons." Kaimi dropped his used towel in the bin with the other damp towels. "Shall we go and speak with the others and make our final preparations?"

I hope we're doing the right thing. I hope this will work out. Not only for me, but for Mother and Father's memory.

"Excited to go meet our visitors?" Koa quipped. "Or perhaps the former male body attendant from the video caught your eye."

Kaimi shook his head, ignoring the teasing comment from his brother. On another day he would have been pleased and even laughed, but today was not that day. "The sooner we go, the sooner we return and we can put all this uncertainty behind us." He grabbed a fresh towel and draped the material over his bare shoulders as they made their way out.

Ready or not this must be done.

*****

"And you're sure about these readings?" Karen tapped her tablet, making eye contact with everyone on her team, from doctor to intern. They all were gathered in the largest of the meeting rooms; this was the space they used for the reception they had on their first day at sea. Now a much different meeting, especially given all they have found, or hadn't found yet, as the case may be.

"We've doubled checked." Dr. Chen tapped her laptop and faced Karen. "Dr. Sanchez and I both agree. Something is out there and the signal is growing in strength."

Javier bit his lips but offered a nod of support.

Karen faced Michael; his eyes were larger, as were many of those gathered. But this is what they were doing here; yes, some had doubted her. Even she had her doubts. But this, this signal, these energy readings, this is why they were here. Why were any of them surprised?

We found Mu. Or something.

"And what do the rest of you think?" Karen asked her full team; now was not the time to hold their opinions. She wanted to ensure every voice spoke out; if doubt lay before them, this was the place to share concerns and solutions.

"Both Lucas and I found no geological interference that would cause the energy readings we're seeing." Dr. Dubois pinched the bridge of her nose, her glasses in her other hand.

"Same with us," Dr. Jenner followed up. "Zoey and I can't explain this from a climatology stand point. Whatever this energy source is, it's coming from down here or deeper out in the ocean. I can assure you all what we are finding is not a storm or anything natural."

"From what we've seen, and based on the latest satellite imagery we received, you couldn't ask for any better weather up there." Zoey, Dr. Samuel, offered by way of confirmation, pointing towards the ceiling.

"What about whales or some other marine life?" Michael asked.

"We shouldn't be seeing readings like this." Isabel's voice was loud enough to be heard, but barely. "There is nothing living out there able to cause these kinds of readings—"

"That we know of," Mason interrupted.

She sighed. "Mason and I have been going back and forth since we first noticed these...I don't know... abnormalities... but..." she trailed off, her gaze dropping back to the table.

Karen ran a hand over her device, making a few notes and double checking all the results against her own data. "Dr. Farmin. Dr. May-Jordon. Thoughts?"

"I can't find any other explanation." Dr. Farmin reviewed the notes and data as Dr. May-Jordon nodded his agreement. "If I had any doubts, those ended two days ago," she continued.

"I've confirmed with Captain Abbas, Chief Thomas and the comms officer the signal and energy readings are nothing from the sub or any other vessel." Dr. May-Jordon added. "We're running silent for the most part, and our equipment can weed out any other background sound or noise from passing ships or other subs."

"Dr. Linn," Hanh started. "Does this mean we found what we're looking for?"

"Fantastic." Ezekiel bobbed up and down in his seat like a little kid excited to go on his first ever roller coaster.

"Do you know what this means?" Dinh pulled out his smartphone and took several shots of the people and the room. "We have to document everything."

"But why now?" Karen asked. "Why are we getting all these readings now? What's changed?"

"Us." Michael's tone was flat as he glanced around at the group. "We're here. You've said no one's ever been this deep or in this location before, well not for long anyways."

"What I'm hearing is…" Jayden started. "We're not alone down here. Imagine what we're gonna find." He clapped his hands together.

"Holy Hell," Mila commented.

"You're not serious." Amanda's head shook. "We don't know anything yet."

"Well… I can't think of anything else. Unless another sub is planning to attack us." Dr. May-Jordon offered as he let out a nervous chuckle.

Michael glanced at him with a frown firmly placed.

The doctor's nerves continued to give him away with his poor choice of words, but the joke was not appropriate, even if an attack may be a distant possibility. "Okay." Karen glanced at Alister, who held a camera on her as he recorded the meeting. How anyone enjoyed being in front of a camera like this lay far beyond her. However, since the trip began, Alister and the interns had been recording everything. She still wasn't used to having a camera in her face. There were times she wanted to snatch the gadget from his hands and throw the mechanical beast on the ground—*why did I agree to this and why am I continuing to allow them to film*—? "As Amanda rightly commented, we don't know anything yet. I think now's the time for the drones. We send them out, have them search and scan, afterwards we send out Bob, if need be. I want to ensure we're doing all we can to not rush into anything. There are a lot of people who will use any miscalculation on our part to discount our findings."

There were nods from around the table. Being cautious now appeared to be the smartest move.

"Are there any geological worries?" Karen faced Dr. Dubois and Lucas.

"Typical undersea mountain ranges. Nothing we don't know about and can address. The area isn't flat, but there are no surprises, at least for now." Dr. Dubois glanced at Lucas, who nodded in agreement.

"Caves?" Michael asked as everyone focused on him.

"Oh yes," Lucas nodded as he glanced at the monitors and the devices in front of him. "There are lots of caves. Which is why we have the drones." He continued. "Now our focus is pinpointing where and which cave will give us the best entry point so we can go exploring."

"The signal might be coming from there?" Michael shook his head as he pointed to one of the mountain ranges on the screen. "Sorry if you have to explain this to me like I'm five; I want to make sure I understand. I mean, clearly there is nothing on the bottom of the sea, we would've seen or known about some ancient civilization here by now, so whatever we've found has to be in some giant cave or part of these undersea mountain ranges... right?" He scanned those attending the meeting.

"Nothing to be sorry for." Karen reassured him. "We'll scan the mountain range and see what we can find; we can send in a team with Bob and give this area a real good search. If we're lucky, the Pontus will be able to enter and we can decide from there, but we're stretching things and I doubt Captain Abbas or Chief Thomas are willing to risk the vessel, no matter how big a cavern we find."

Michael nodded his agreement.

"Okay." Karen stood from the table leaning forward. "I'll speak to the captain, tell her where to stop us and we'll send out the drones." She clapped her hands. "I want all our tests and investigations run by the numbers. I don't want anything left for chance or interruption. Let's get to work, everyone."

*****

Michael stood in drone command. The noise from the sub and everyone who had been rushing about had finally settled as the drones were launched. This space was tight, given everyone who was present. Karen stood at the monitors along with a couple of the interns, Hanh, Amanda and Lieutenant Morin, who was manning the drone controls along with Ensign Bianchi. Alister moved around with camera in hand, documenting everything and himself. All the others were at their various stations and following up on the signal. Captain Abbas had called all crew to stations, even those who were off shift. She wanted to be ready for anything, especially as they approached the undersea mountain range.

Michael couldn't believe the images playing out before him; there were no other words for what they saw. They were indeed staring at a mountain range; how anything this large existed in the ocean was beyond him. However, clearly undersea mountains did exist down here, but he had no idea how. When he had read only about 20% of the ocean had been explored, he didn't fathom how that was possible, especially with all the satellite imagery out there, but standing here and seeing what he observed now, he had no doubt no one really had any idea what lay beneath the waves. "Amazing." The word escaped his lips along with the oxygen in his lungs.

"And we're going to be the first people to go exploring." Karen's eyes were focused on the screen.

"Dr. Linn." Bianchi began. "The first set of drones are in position."

"Let's get this party started. Activate cameras, sensors, and lights. Let's see what we have here."

"All drones are coming online." Morin stated as live images started to fill the screens as he continued to work the controls at his console.

"These images alone are going to change what we know about this part of the ocean." Amanda commented as she worked her tablet.

"Make sure you capture all this," Hanh instructed Alister, pointing to the equipment and the monitors. "This is going to be huge and we want everything documented."

"I'm on it." Alister checked the camera and pointed the device at who spoke. "You don't have to worry about me. You keep doing your sciencey stuff and I'll make sure people see you for your brains and not your looks."

Amanda and Hanh laughed.

"Enough flirting." Karen instructed everyone. "Let's focus."

The command room fell silent as the drones continued to explore, there were caverns and caves, but nothing big enough for them to fit into and with the lights on a lot of creatures were coming out to investigate on their own and see, or sense, what was happening to their world. "I've never seen fish like these." Michael watched the monitors.

"Most are bioluminescent creatures living out their whole existence down here." Karen glanced over her shoulder at him. "They are probably as ignorant of our world as we are of theirs."

"Amazing." Michael's gaze bounced around the different monitors, unsure where to look and what to focus on.

"Well, hello there." Bianchi pointed and smiled at the main monitor.

"What?" Karen and Michael responded in unison as they focused on where Bianchi watched.

"Looks like..." He paused and leaned in.

"Ensign, what are you seeing?" Morin demanded as they adjusted to see better.

"I thought I saw a shark or something big, but now..." Bianchi tapped at the monitor before moving to the manual controller. "No, hold on." He started moving the joystick and the drone moved, the image listing and shifting before blinking out. "What the hell?"

"Did we lose a drone?" Karen asked, glancing between both officers.

"Seems so." Morin banged his hand on the desk space again.

"Play the last visual." Karen commanded as she leaned in. "Morin, keep your eyes on the other drones. I don't want to lose anymore."

"Ey." Morin acknowledged, wiggling their fingers and taking control of the stick again.

Bianchi typed away and put the image on the larger screen as Michael and the others watched the screen. "I don't see... wait, what was that flash?"

"An eel?" Amanda offered.

"No. A pulse of some kind," Karen countered, arching her neck to see better. "But from what?"

"Jesus!" Morin yelped, pushing back from their control station, quickly pulling in again, leaning closer to the screen. "Mario, did you see what we caught? The creature, or whatever, is huge."

"What?" Karen asked. "What creature? What did you see?"

Alister bumped Michael as he shifted to record Morin and Bianchi. "What did you see, another flash?"

"No, a creature, I think, like a shark or a dolphin, but not like any I've ever seen before."

"They can't be this deep." Karen countered to the room, "well not a dolphin, maybe a great white? But?" She shook her head. "We'll want to send all the images we have to Dr. Chen, Dr. Sanchez, Mason and Isabel so they can figure out what we have down here."

"You said yourself there is a lot we don't know about this part of the ocean." Michael ran a hand through his hair. "Can these animals affect the drone?"

"Drones?" Morin amended with a frown. "Both drones two and five are now down."

Several people spoke at once. Even Michael had jumped in, not sure what was going on and wondering if they might be in some kind of danger.

"Okay, everyone take a breath," Karen spoke over the group. "Mr. Morin, if you would please circle drones one, three, and four and send them to where two and five were, let's see what we have here." Karen instructed, trying to regain control of the situation unfolding around them. "We planned on losing some of the drones to the sea life. These organisms are probably as curious about us..."

"There." Morin shouted, standing up, calling all the others over to the main monitor he watched. "The creature... holy hell...a mermaid."

Did he say; mermaid?

Immediately, the warm light vanished, replaced by a wave of red light as an alarm called out to all of them. Before Michael managed to speak the decking under his feet shifted and a sudden bang along the hull filled his ears. Sparks rained down on them from the consoles as each of the drones or their respective monitors blinked out. The captain's voice rang out from the speaker. "All hands. We're being..." The lights flickered and everything went dark and quiet. The next hit to the sub was larger than the first; the sub rocked and Michael felt himself falling and reaching out to grab for something to brace himself. Alister, or someone, crashed into him as shouts and screams filled his ears.

Michael tried to get his footing but, in the darkness, finding where to stand now impossible. He held on to someone and they rocked again. This time, an explosion filled the space with light for a brief second. All he managed to see was blinding light and chaos. He felt something hit him square in the shoulder and neck, knocking him to the ground, as a thud hit next to him. A blast of air made his ears pop as a rush of heat blew by his face. Next to him, the hatch slammed shut.

What did we hit? What hit us?

*****

Kaimi moved through the water with ease. He had some initial concerns the suits would work differently in the deep blue versus in the training facility, but the suits couldn't have performed any better. After taking out the small swimming devices, they spotted the visitor's vessel; the boat was huge, much bigger than he judged given what we understood about them. Even the larger creatures stayed away, leaving only the glowing fish around to explore. Koa wasn't too far from his position as the team of ten moved toward this undersea beast.

"Look at the size of their ship." Koa spoke through his earpiece.

"Their boat is gigantic... no wonder they were able to reach us," Kaimi responded.

"We disabled two of their devices," one of the team reported.

"Were they hostile? Did they try and attack?" Kaimi asked, trying not to show his annoyance.

"No, but..."

"Now's not the time." Koa replied. "Let's make our way to the lower hatch and the upper hatch. Teams of five. Kaimi, you go to the upper and I'll take the others to the lower."

"Agreed. No more energy weapons. We don't want to kill or hurt them." Kaimi added. "Agreed, your majesty?"

"Agreed." Koa pointed to the team members. "No firing on anyone or anything unless the order is given by me or Kaimi."

A round of 'understood' came through their earpieces. Kaimi took his team to the bottom of the beast and observed the hatch doors were open, —*clearly not here for a fight.*— he moved closer to the hatch as did the others. At this point, he stopped speaking and used hand motions to direct his team. They reached the hatch, and he breached the water, seeing three people working on various machines and moving a smaller ship into a launch position, if he was correct. As he motioned, one of the men in the ship let out a shout and ran to one of the machines, pushing something on the panel as lights turned red.

The water around Kaimi and his group was upended as an explosion of water, fire, and light erupted. Kaimi and the others moved as quickly as the suits would allow. He and his team swam clear of the vessel as he witnessed a pulse hit the outside of the ship. He glanced at the location and established the shot came from Mu. "Who fired? Koa! Did you authorize?"

"Hold all fire!" Koa shouted. "Hold all fire! Noe, did you fire the pulse weapon?"

Kaimi watched as a second pulse hit the vessel. He couldn't believe what he witnessed. This ship. Those people on the ship wouldn't survive, the ship, sub, vessel, whatever wouldn't survive. "Koa, we must act."

An implosion from the vessel caused the water around them to glow bright as the shock wave hit faster than expected. Several of the team, including Kaimi, took a tumble, making getting oriented difficult; quickly he focused on his air bubbles as they showed him the direction to the surface waters, helping him find his bearings. Between him and the suit's ability to compensate, they were righted almost at once. Within moments, Kaimi had found Koa and the others making their way toward him.

"What do we do?" Kaimi asked as he continued to make a mental note of the team and their surroundings. The mountains continued to be stable and none of the outcroppings appeared in any danger of collapse, still this reminded him of why they so seldom ventured out this way. "And who in the name of the gods fired our weapon?"

"We help them." Koa instructed his guards. "I will not leave these people to die because of something we caused, or allowed to cause." Koa typed something before speaking. "Brother, I swear to you, I did not order this attack. We will do what we can for them. This is not what I wanted."

Kaimi understood they were on a private channel. "The location we headed for is, or was, open so we can enter through there; I saw another hatch on the bottom we might be able to access."

Koa nodded and typed again before speaking and laying out the rescue plan for the people on the ship. They only had moments to do what needed to be done to save those they would be able to save. Kaimi watched as his brother called for the rest of the warriors to come assist; they might not fully understand the technology of the vessel, but they comprehended enough to assist and rescue. This would not be easy and they would need help from Mu, but if the gods were on their side, they would make this right.

~ Chapter Fourteen ~

Kaimi bent down and checked the bodies in front of him. He closed the young man's eyes and offered a prayer to the gods. He stood up. The space he had emerged from when they were going to make contact now held dead bodies. The vessel appeared to have minimal energy, and only the most necessary systems seemed operational. The air had a charge, and a haze of smoke filled much of the research area, or boat launch.

"The smaller vessel seems in good order and undamaged. From what we can tell," Alanah commented, as she knelt next to Kaimi. Glancing at the face of the man, she looked at the other bodies around her. "They don't look much different, do they? They could be from Mu."

I can't believe we did this. All this blood is on our hands. They never had a chance. And we never gave them one. Why?

Kaimi shook his head. "Is there anyone alive here?"

Alanah was quiet.

Kaimi knew the answer, but wanted to hope.

"Not so far." Kelii's voice rang out from behind Kaimi. He arrived with the rest of his group. "This level had a lot of function for the vessel. Unfortunately, most of the people here are dead. Where they housed the propulsion suffered a lot of damage; however, their fire suppression system appeared to work." He commented as he joined them.

"We need to meet up with the king and the others." Kaimi glanced at their suits and frowned. "Alanah and Kelii stay here and watch for the rest of our people. When they arrive, start seeing to the dead." He cracked his neck as he studied the space. "I would love to know more of what this vessel was like and what this space was for."

Perhaps we can save the vessel and learn more about the ship and the people.

"Let's go." Kaimi motioned to the others as they made their way through the opened hatch. They managed to open several of the locked or blocked doors, revealing some small shared rooms, and more functions for the vessel. This space was tight and had a lot of machinery running through the passageways. He found Koa and Kalea working on one of the hatches. "Where are the others?" he asked as they reached them.

"I sent them to the next level up." Koa didn't face his brother as he spoke. "They are trying to find the control area. We think people might be alive in here."

"Thank the gods." Kaimi pointed to the door. "Give Kalea a hand." He gestured to Mana. "The rest go up to the next level and search. Meet up with the king's group." They nodded and were off; Kaimi took his brother's arm and pulled him away from the door.

"Who fired?" Kaimi asked in a hush tone as they moved away from the two working on the door and out of hearing range.

"I have no idea," Koa's lips were pinched together, dirt or grease smudged on his face, shoulders, and chest. His brows heavy on his head. "Maybe Noe."

Kaimi leaned against the counter and shook his head.

"They have the access." Koa countered to the unspoken argument. "Still, I doubt they did this." He ran a hand over his forehead, adding to the smudges. "Once we return to Mu, I'm going to find out." His tone met his brother's. "Not only did they kill these people, but they almost killed us."

"Do you think whoever did this is the same person who killed Mother and Father?" Kaimi leaned against the wall filled with mechanics and blinking lights. The smell of fire and battle was lessening as the vessel's rebreathers continued to run.

For now.

Koa stayed quiet, but his furrowed brows and frown said all Kaimi needed.

We have a traitor.

"Your Majesty," Kalea called as a crack of the hatch met their ears.

Kaimi and Koa returned to the door as smoke emptied into the corridor. There was a creak from the vessel. "How long do we have?" Kaimi waved his hand in front of his face to help clear the air.

"We'll know better once the others arrive; I called for our technicians and Noe to join us." Koa peeked through the door into the darkness, only seeing the lights from his people in the space.

Kalea peeked her head out of the door. "There appears to be some alive, but unconscious. They are going to need help."

Kaimi smiled at his brother.

Some hope.

Koa nodded and faced Kalea, "Let's get them to safety and keep searching."

"Some good news." Kaimi offered as he moved to help Kalea and the others with the survivors. Perhaps the gods would be kind this day.

*****

Karen shifted and coughed. There wasn't a part of her not aching. Especially her head and her now blossoming headache. Nothing seemed broken, but open wounds didn't mean she wasn't injured—*probably a concussion*—that wouldn't be good. What happened? The drones went off line. The alarm. The hatch closed and an explosion. She coughed again.

Did someone say mermaids?

A pair of dark eyes met her gaze. Their mouth moved, but she didn't hear them or, maybe, understand them. She went to sit up and met only darkness.

*****

Michael hurt. His leg screamed in pain and his back stung with millions of needles poking deep into him. He remembered the alarm. The sounds of burning electrics and a flash of blinding hot light. His ears popped as air rushed past him. He winced as something jabbed him in the arm.

"Dr. Rizzo." Michael tried to force words out of his mouth. "My leg. My back...something."

Michael heard someone speak, but the voice didn't sound like Dr. Rizzo or one of her team, but Michael didn't speak Italian or was the language Sicilian? He didn't remember.

His chest expanded with the air he brought in, breathing much easier now. A bonus for sure. The medicine must be working. The pain of his body was slowly vanishing. There was a lot of speaking around him and there were sounds of equipment and people rushing about. They must have moved him to medical.

Good, the sub is still in one piece at least.

"How are the others?" Michael tried to turn his head and open his eyes, but his vision was still blurred so he continued to blink, keeping his eyes mostly closed. Did the words come out, or were they only in his head? Had he spoken out loud? A man checked his arm and tended to his other wounds. He didn't recognize the medical personnel, he appeared Hawaiian, maybe Samoan, he didn't look familiar, but Michael didn't remember all the crew. Plus, his head continued to be fuzzy. Maybe the person had been cross trained in first aid and now helped the medical staff.

The man smiled at Michael, again speaking, but Michael wasn't processing the words. His arm felt warm and something warm moved through his veins and sleep found him one more time.

*****

Kaimi reviewed the others. They had managed to secure the vessel, but still the ship had been severely damaged and many of the spaces had to be sealed off for now; they would need to bring the vessel closer to Mu. Right now they were limited, and the broken equipment didn't help nor did the foreign words marking everything and on the monitors. The language would be problematic, even with their equipment and more people, because they would not be able to bring the beast into Mu proper. Attending to the ship and making repairs would not be straightforward, especially with all the casualties.

"We've done all we can for now." Noe reported as he reached Kaimi.

"Did you inform Koa?"

"Yes." Noe nodded. "He's speaking with the captain of the vessel. Most of the ship's crew and scientists were killed in the attack. We will have to speak English with them. They do not understand our language. Even one of the crew who speaks 'Hawaiian' doesn't understand us, even though we use many of the same words."

Kaimi's lips pulled tight, "Wonderful." He pulled over a tray of medical supplies. "Most of the words here I don't understand, none of their medical team survived, so I've been using our medical equipment, but they have equipment and devices I've never seen before, some of this medical gear appears more advanced than ours, and I don't think everything is in English. Some other language maybe." Kaimi pulled out a box, "Bandages." He pointed to the word on the box. "*Bendare*. Do you know the word, 'cause bendare is not English?"

Noe shook his head.

"Well, we knew the differences in language might cause issues." Kaimi put the box down. "I suppose we'll have to figure what other languages the crew speaks later." He checked the bandage on the man before him and checked his pulse. Before running a hand through his short hair.

"How are they?" Noe pointed to the people sprawled out in the medical facility.

"Some major wounds, but we have most stable for now." Kaimi pointed to the man with the dark short hair with hints of gray throughout and olive complexion, who lay there still. His face was defined and his lips weren't as full as he was used to seeing, but overall this man was attractive, not as much as when he spoke in the video, but still, even lying here, he looked good. "He has several cuts. He suffered a fracture in his leg and, I believe his spine has been bruised. He came to, but I medicated him enough for sleep, so we can move him. We should be able to heal him once we reach Mu, but I wish our medical people were here."

"You and the others will have to make do for now." Noe directed. "If you can go to the command center, the ship's captain refuses to leave, but she needs medical treatment."

"I'm not a healer." Kaimi huffed and grabbed a first aid kit and some of the supplies he had figured out. "Keoki, please watch over them; once we are able to move them, do so. The sooner we can get them out of here, the better. See if, perhaps, we can use the smaller vessel of theirs."

"I believe Lolani and Nana are working on additional emergency transportation to Mu," Keoki commented.

"Good." Kaimi grumbled out the response as he and Noe made their way through the vessel, this part of the ship almost looked as though nothing happened, there were hints of smoke and burn in the air, but for the most part things checked out. The lowest level and parts of the third level appeared to be in the worst shape. This space offered high-quality appointments and comforts, which surprised Kaimi given the nature of the ship.

This doesn't appear to be a warship in the least.

They reached the command center, and many of the monitors and devices did not appear working. Those who were alive and uninjured worked succinctly to make as many repairs as possible.

"I appreciate what you're saying." The female captain responded as she held her wrist. There were several gashes on her head and her uniform was ripped in places as well. "However, I need my people here on the ship. Whatever you people hit us with almost destroyed the Pontus, and I refuse to lose her like this."

"Captain." Koa's words were firm and slow as he spoke English. "We don't have the luxury of time. We are here to... help you...and... your people."

"Why did you attack us and board us?" The captain's tone filled with venom and anger.

"Why did you come here?" Koa countered. "Why did you send those...attack fish?" He wiggled his hands in front of him, trying to mimic their movements. "At us. I can ask you all the same questions. We came to find out more, not to attack and I... promise you... we'll find who did this and punish them. In the meantime, we need to get you and... everything...everyone... off this ship."

"Why? So, you can pick our sub apart and steal all our technology?" The captain stood taller.

He laughed, as did Kaimi.

Koa faced his brother and started speaking in their native language. "Can you see to her wounds? She is stubborn like Mother and loyal to her people like Father."

Kaimi rested the first aid kit on one of the open chairs and began pulling out the supplies he would need. "You like her."

"Indeed."

"My brother, Kaimi, will see to your wounds." Koa reverted to English. "And Captain, I assure you, we have no interest in your technology."

The captain's face contorted as if her wounds affected her more than she let on, but Kaimi sensed Koa may have offended her with his comment.

"Captain Abbas." Kaimi used his best English. He had enjoyed many of the movies and shows from America and had learned a great deal about their language. "We are not here to hurt you, even though this attack may seem otherwise. We are tending to your ship and your injured. Please let us help you. And yes, this ship is impressive, but we have no need for such a vessel or the wonders and secrets held within." He reached out his hand to her.

She frowned. "How many?" She asked, taking a seat at the navigation station, allowing Kaimi to work.

Kaimi glanced at Koa, who grimaced.

"I know about Kaya, Thomas, Morin, Meyer and Rizzo." She inhaled as Kaimi dressed her wounds. "What about the rest of the crew? And the research team, how are Dr. Linn and Mr. Donovan? Dr. May-Jordan and Dr. Farmin?"

"I can tell you many were injured, but I don't know their names. I believe the older woman, Dr. Linn, and man, Mr. Donovan, will be fine, as are most of the people in the small command room, but most of the others on the lowest deck and the stern of the ship did not fare well."

The captain hissed. *"Merde! comment cela pourrait-il arriver? Comment pourrions-nous laisser cela arriver? Tous ces pauvres gens."* She frowned.

Kaimi and Koa looked at her.

"What are these words she's speaking?" Koa asked his brother.

The captain frowned as Kaimi stepped away, facing his brother and subsequently her.

"You speak English, but not French... of course." She snarled. "What should I have expected, after all, clearly the world revolves around the United States and English. You know almost 300 million people speak French on this planet, and there are more places than the United States." Her annoyance filled every one of her words.

"I apologize, yes we know there are many cultures on the planet, we have seen much from you and have learned a great deal, but for us to know everything is impossible, plus we are limited to what we see and hear," Kaimi offered. "I know some of the words in French, but not like I know English." He explained as he finished dressing her wounds. "I think you'll be fine, but once we return to Mu, I want our healers to look you over."

"Look, Kaimi. You are called Kaimi, correct?" The captain began. "I'm not leaving this ship." There were nods from some of the other members of her crew. "I understand we're your prisoners, but I'm not leaving."

"Yes. You are." The older woman who had the head injury instructed everyone as she stepped into the command space.

"You should be resting." Kaimi stood and faced her. "You should not be up."

"I'm fine." The woman countered as she rubbed her head and winced, but refusing to show any other tells of soreness. "Now hush."

"Karen," the captain stood, and a smile grew on her face. "Dr. Linn, you're alive." Relief poured from her and her words.

"I believe so, for the time being." Karen took a few steps, holding onto the console next to her. "As I understand our situation, the Pontus needs to be repaired. Most of the crew are dead or need medical treatment. We can't risk staying on this ship out of some maritime act of loyalty. We need help and if the king and his brother are offering the assistance we need, we will take the offered assistance."

The captain dropped heavily onto her chair. Remaining quiet for a moment.

"Susan." Karen approached and Kaimi moved to the side, "We both lost a lot of people today, and this whole nightmare is my fault, something I'm going to have to live with. I put you all in danger and here we are, well I'm not going to risk our lives anymore."

"We can't abandon ship." The captain shook her head. "The Pontus is our only way home." She slapped her good hand on the console. "And you didn't do this, they did. We only came to find out what caused the Pulse, and why they attacked us five years ago."

"I never said we were going to abandon anything." Karen countered and took a step closer. "The Pontus can't get us home at the moment, and I don't want to see any more people we care about die. Do you?" Her gaze focused on the captain. "Plus, maybe seeing as we all know each other, we can find out what happened five years ago and why."

Kaimi noted Dr. Linn remained careful in her word choice. Not choosing to blame them for the pulse attack five years ago, which she rightly should have. He glanced at Koa, who, he hoped, had noted the same thing.

There may be hope to save this first contact.

The captain glanced around at the few faces of her surviving officers. "Commander Levy, you're now my XO, what are your thoughts?"

A heavy sigh came from the woman. "A compromise. We remove all the wounded and keep a few of us here to assist with repairs. I doubt our new *friends* will fully understand the inner workings of the Pontus. I will offer to stay here, and I'd like to have Renard and Meyer remain as well."

The captain looked at Karen and again at Koa and Kaimi. "She's not wrong. You're going to need our help to fix our ship. Especially since not everything is in *English*."

Koa glanced at Kaimi. "Having some of them here will make repairs easier. We can leave enough suits here should they need to evacuate, and we'll use their smaller ship to transport the wounded."

"Smaller ship?" Karen's eyes grew large and an expression of joy filled her face. "You mean *Bob*? He survived?"

Koa took a moment to answer. "Yes, if you mean the little six-person vessel, the ship appears in one piece. We were hoping to use...*Bob*... to move the wounded to Mu."

Karen laughed. "What about the drones?"

"Ah, the little fish swimming around the mountains and caves," he wiggled his hand in front of him. "Yes, but the control room for them was heavily damaged." Kaimi responded.

"Captain," the woman in charge of security spoke. She hadn't commented much and had put up a lot of fight when they first arrived. "I'm not comfortable with leaving the Pontus unprotected, but I don't want you all to go off without protection, either."

Abbas glanced at the woman. "I think having you stay here with the uninjured crew is our best course of action. The sooner we make repairs, the better."

Koa raised his gaze to the ceiling. His lips moved, but no words left his mouth. "Agreed. We will make...match... your numbers one for one. We will offer any and all support we can. Noe will work directly with you from Mu."

"How?" Abbas asked. "Our communications are out."

"We will use our communications for the time being." Koa stepped forward. "And we will ensure communication is kept...minimal... so no further surprises happen."

Kaimi wasn't sure how he felt about all this, but they had more problems than answers at the moment. But at least they were making some progress, and neither party seemed interested in fighting with the other, which made for a good start, but how long would the peace last? There were questions remaining; including who fired the pulse weapon? Who the traitor was? And how would the gods and their people react to these visitors?

Only time will tell.

~ Chapter Fifteen ~

Michael's eyes fluttered open again. Lemongrass and coconut filled his senses. He couldn't help himself as he inhaled much deeper this time. The scents assisted in returning him to consciousness.

Clearly the Pontus is in better shape than I imagined.

"Dr. Rizzo." Michael called as the light filled his range of vision. More of the space came into view. The tightness and throbbing in his back gone, sore, yes, but the pain no longer vexed him. Even his breathing came with ease.

"You're awake." Alister squeezed Michael's hand. "We were worried about you."

"I'm fine." Michael commented and started to take in his surroundings. "Where? What? Where are we?" The room surrounding him was a calming blue with warm light, but this space was clearly not like any medical facility he'd ever seen or been in. Crystals lay embedded in the walls and provided a warm light. The floors were a polished grey stone. The medical equipment, monitors, bed and gurneys weren't made of any kind of metals or plastics he recognized. There were no windows for him to look out of, but warm lemongrass and coconut air still managed to tickle at his nose.

"That's a complicated answer." Alister gave Michael's hand another squeeze before standing up, his head dropping as he did so.

"I see you are awake." A familiar male voice spoke out. "I'm glad I was more wrong than right about your injuries."

Michael faced the voice that spoke before him. "I know you?" Michael reached up a hand. "I've seen you before." Before him stood a bare-chested man in nothing but a white glorified diaper. His hair was long and black and his eyes were a deep brown with hints of green. He had high cheek bones and full lips. In his hands, he held something akin to a smartphone.

The man from my dream. No. He had been a fantasy. He probably looks like someone I've seen before.

"I attended to your wounds on your ship." The man responded. "On behalf of my brother, the king, welcome to Mu. I'm Prince Kaimi, but please call me Kaimi."

"What?" Michael tried to sit up but halted as the blanket dropped, sending a chill through his body. He was bare chested and hooked up to an IV, or what he assumed to be an IV, considering a tube went from the machine nearest him to the back of his left hand. "What happened to the Pontus, the crew, Karen, the rest of the research team?"

"Your ship is being tended to." Kaimi moved to the IV and the man's arm. "Dr. Linn is fine, as are several others..." He trailed off. "Dr. Latu." Kaimi called and an older man approached. He wore a smock, or scrubs, and gloves. Tattoos covered his exposed right arm, and must have continued up, as there were hints of the markings around his neck. They began speaking in a language Michael didn't understand. Once they finished their conversation, Kaimi, the Prince, or whatever, smiled at him. "This may pinch, but please remain still."

The doctor or medical professional Kaimi spoke with, greeted Michael with a kind smile and pointed to his arm with the IV and bowed with raised eyebrows.

Michael glanced at Alister, who nodded. A pinch and the IV had been removed from Michael's arm and the doctor wrapped the wound up. "Thanks." Michael moved his arm, no stiffness found him and the pain from earlier vanished. "Prince Kaimi is it? Can someone please tell me what happened?"

Kaimi glanced at Alister.

"I think for now you should speak with Karen. She can fill you in." Alister's tone came out gentle and soft. Relief dripped from his shoulders and neck as he appeared to relax. "You've been out for little over a day."

Michael frowned. "A day."

Alister shoved his hands deep into his pockets and shrugged.

Michael stroked his chin, his stubble a clear indication of how much time had passed.

I need a shave and probably a shower.

He pulled at the blanket, only warm air separating him from the soft coverings.

And clothes would be nice.

Kaimi called over to someone who appeared to be a guard. The two spoke in their native language, and the guard left with haste. The dark-haired Kaimi faced Michael. "I'm sending for Dr. Linn now. In the meantime, how do you feel? Are you hungry? Would you like something to eat? Is anything sore?"

Michael took several deep breaths, trying to keep his composure and not freak out. Seeing Alister here and in good spirits helped, but he wanted answers and he wanted someone to explain what was going on. He would have imagined he was dreaming or in some drug induced state, but the soreness he felt and the pinch from the removal of the IV proved he was awake.

By the time Karen arrived, Michael had sat upright and sipped on some broth, or soup, he wasn't sure. He enjoyed the flavors; the soup tasted like crab, but there were other bits of protein in there as well. "Oh Karen, thank god." He moved the soup away, resting the bowl next to the cup of water on the table next to him. "These two won't tell me shit," he pointed to Kaimi and Alister. "What happened?"

Karen looked at the others. "Can you give us a minute?"

Alister's mouth opened and closed before he spoke, giving himself a moment. Finally, his words came out, "I'll return in a little while."

"I should go and provide an update to the king." Kaimi offered a slight tilt of his head, then glanced at Michael from head to feet, hints of pink dancing at his neck and cheeks. "A pleasure meeting you, Mr. Donovan."

Michael watched them leave. "king. Mu. Prince Kaimi. Mermaids. What the hell happened? How hard did I hit my head? And are we sure I'm not dead... we're not dead... in some kind of shared hallucination?"

Karen sat on the edge of the bed, resting a hand on his draped calf. "What do you remember?"

Michael focused and a few blurry images filled his mind: smoke, emergency lights, the drones. "We were in drone command. Drones two and five went dark, but as we played the video, we spotted a giant fish or..." He faced her. "Them?" He pointed towards where Kaimi left.

She nodded.

"But we were hit by something." Michael pinched his lips together, trying to focus on the images in his mind. "They attacked us." He waved a hand. "I remember something hit me and I woke up in medical." He glanced around. "Now I'm here."

Karen nodded. "We were hit by a lower level pulse, similar to what hit us five years ago, but this was a more targeted attack, directed right at us, and the king and his party who were coming to greet us."

"What?"

"I know this is a lot." Karen pat his leg. "They are still investigating who used the weapon on us. The king, Koa, and Prince Kaimi claim they didn't authorize the use and Captain Abbas and I tend to believe them. They were hit in the pulse as well, but their suits protected them, but the Pontus and most everyone in her..." Karen trailed off.

Michael processed the words. And based on Karen's falling expression and draining color, his stomach dropped and the soup he had eaten threatened to vacate his stomach. "Oh lord. How bad?"

Karen scowled and shook her head to the right and left as she sighed. "Bad enough. Susan, Captain Abbas is fine. So are Commander Levy, Lieutenant Renard, Ensign Bianchi, Commander Roy and the Doctor and five of the crew, As well as Anne."

"God, and your team...our team?"

"Dr. Chen, Lucas, Mason, Jayden and Amanda." Karen's voice cracked as she spoke their names. "Dr. Farmin survived, but Dr. May-Jordon..." Her head dropped and she quickly swiped at her eyes.

Michael rubbed his temple as a dull ache clawed behind his eyes, burrowing deep into his skull. "Almost forty people dead, how? What're we gonna do? How long are they gonna keep us hostage?"

"We don't believe we're hostages." Karen took a breath. "And the attack wasn't intentional."

"Come on." Michael watched her.

How else should they interpret these... happenings.?

"Some didn't want us here." Karen mentioned with a glance around the space and lowered her voice. "And they are trying to find who. In the meantime they are helping us fix the Pontus. The officers and crew who were uninjured are on the ship conducting repairs and everyone else is here in Mu."

"This is not what was supposed to happen." Michael reached out to Karen, grabbing her arm and squeezing. "All those people, we did this. We are responsible. What are we going to tell their families? Their friends?" He started to shake as his heart beat faster, his stomach wrestled inside him like two teen boys wanting to kill each other or fuck. "What was this for? We got them all killed." He released Karen's hand.

"Michael, you listen to me." Karen focused on Michael, her gaze and brows as firm as he had ever seen. "Everyone realized what they were getting into, everyone accepted the risks. We didn't force anyone to come with us—"

"Do you think their families are going to care? Do you think I care?" He looked at his hands, rubbing them to the point of raw redness.

"I was where you are when this happened." Karen took both his hands in hers. "I said the same thing to Captain Abbas. I'm not going to let you walk off the ledge. We prepared for everything. We believed we identified every eventuality but we were wrong. Now all we can do is pick up the pieces and make sure nothing like this ever happens again."

Michael glanced at his hands. Karen released them. He swiped at his eyes. He rubbed his temples, hoping to massage away the pain, regret, and anger. "Fine, but I want to meet this king guy, and I want explanations. Someone is going to be held accountable for all those deaths."

Karen nodded.

"Get me out of here."

Karen stood and offered her hand in support.

Michael tossed his feet over the edge of the bed and went to stand, but stopped. "Son-of-a-bitch, I need some fucking clothes."

*****

Dressed in clothes apparently pulled by Alister for him when they were being evacuated from the Pontus made Michael feel more like himself. And much to his surprise, everything smelled fresh, which had him wondering if they had cleaned all their clothes once they arrived. Soreness lingered in his leg, but according to Karen, the inhabitants of Mu had some advanced medical treatments, so if his leg had been broken he wouldn't know now, and his back felt better than in a long time.

As he, Alister and Karen made their way through the passage, Michael stopped, leaned against the wall with small crystals and what appeared to be shell patterns embedded as some kind of design. "I didn't get a chance to say, I'm happy you're okay. I know we lost a lot, but I'm glad you're here."

Alister smiled, "Well lucky for me, when I toppled I landed on you. Hopefully, I didn't make your injuries worse. Sorry, by the way, I still managed to hit my head, but otherwise I'm okay, just some smoke inhalation. Unfortunately, the camera got busted up and the SIM card was smashed."

"The camera's not important. We were lucky." Karen rested a hand on Michael's arm. "The drone command center had been far enough away that we..." She sighed, not needing to finish what she had planned on saying.

"I'm assuming the others will meet us there." Michael started to walk again, the bright glow from the veins running through the floors catching his eyes.

"Yep," Karen agreed as they moved forward.

"What is this whole thing about?" Michael asked. "You've been around them a lot more than me."

"The king is going to welcome us and introduce us to his family. There will also be the council of elders. We'll probably have to be polite and thank them. They are also hosting a lū'au in our honor as a way to show us as invited guests."

"Why are they doing this?"

"To make amends, I think, but I have a feeling to show us off to their people." Alister tugged at his short-sleeved shirt and played with the buckle of his belt. "I don't mind. We can use the break."

Karen nodded. "I agree. They want to show us as welcomed, honored guests and ensure their people don't see us as a threat."

"And to honor the people we lost." Alister added.

As they made their way down the hall, Michael spared several more glances at the design of the space. This area was nothing like what he dreamed (if he allowed himself to dream of such a place); blue polished stone floors with what looked like marble stone walls. The walls had a bright glow of veins running through—*clearly, they incorporated some kind of bioluminescence into the design, or the glowing stones are natural here*—. As they walked, he peered out the large windows looking out on Mu, which appeared to be huge. Close to where they were, gardens with several tide pools lapped about, the sounds calming and easing any tension or worry he might have.

How is any of this possible?

Buildings of all shapes and sizes lay beyond the gardens and tide pools. Additional rich gardens and ponds spread out everywhere. The city, alive with activity. None of the buildings were huge, but they rose several stories. Beyond the city lay groves and fields with crops. He even noted a bay with various boats moored at several different docks. All active with life. The whole city, and surrounding areas, had been laid out in a massive cave under the sea, with brilliant crystals providing enough light to make this time of day feel like midday in San Jose. These crystals even caused more sparkle from the gold and crystal highlights throughout the space. Scents of salt water and ocean mist found their way to his nose. This building was clearly the palace or...he wasn't sure what the citizens of Mu called the structure, but whatever the native people named the site, clearly this was where the government met and ran things.

They met guards at two open doors leading into an even larger hall; the space filled with people who were wearing variations of the style he was coming to understand for Mu. The men, mostly bare chested with intricate tattoos covering their bodies, wore long skirt wraps of different colors and patterns. Some even had crystals stitched into the material, creating patterns reflecting off the light. The women wore wrapped dresses, matching the men's in colors, patterns, and crystal filigree. Many adorned themselves with flowers in their hair.

The assembly stood waiting for them. Or maybe they were interrupting something with their arrival. Michael couldn't be sure, but the guards nodded at them and they continued. At the front of the hall on a raised platform sat a man with several people on either side of him. He wore some kind of ceremonial dress of all white, and as they moved closer, he noticed a crown on top of his head.

"King Koa," Michael whispered as they walked forward.

Karen nodded.

"Welcome. Friends." Koa greeted with outstretched arms. "Please come forward."

Michael gulped as they continued to move in. He spotted off to the side, as they reached the front, Captain Abbas, Dr. Farmin and the rest of those from the Pontus who were here and not on the sub getting her repaired.

"Talk to you later." Alister moved over to the others.

"What?" Michael's eyes were large as Alister moved to the side.

"We are pleased to address Dr. Karen Linn and Mr. Michael Donovan." Koa continued, his arms still outstretched. "I'm King Koa Tupu." He pointed to the man on his right. "You know my brother Prince Kaimi."

Kaimi bowed his head.

Michael offered a nod in recognition.

"These are my sisters, Princes Nohealni and her children, Princes Allyn and Prince Palani."

The three glanced at Michael and Karen.

"My sister Princes Ulani."

She nodded at them

"And our family Māhū," He paused. "I believe you would say, Spiritual Healer or Spirit Guide, Mana Lani and my sibling, Kai Malina." Neither responded to them, but continued to watch.

Koa broke from his family and stepped forward. "We are pleased to welcome you to Mu, and we weep with you at the loss of those who now rejoice with the gods."

Karen nodded. "Thank you."

Michael's expression remained neutral. "Yes, thank you."

"As you are unfortunately aware, our pulse device was used without my authorization, which caused the loss of life, and as promised, we have launched a full investigation. We have also offered your people whatever aid we can to repair your vessel, the Pontus."

Silence filled the halls and Karen spoke once again. "We appreciate all your support."

"This assistance is but the least we can do," Koa offered, as he stretched out his arms. "We also welcome you to our home and offer all the hospitality we have to share. Additionally, I would like to request your help in the investigation..."

There were murmurs around the room and many sour expressions greeted them, including several from the royal family.

Koa waved his hand. "Please, please, we cannot expect them to sit and do nothing with so many harmed by one of our own; this openness is made in good faith and after discussing the matter with our Māhū..."

"I was not consulted." Mana Lani stepped forward, quickly adding. "Your Majesty, I do not recall such a conversation between us."

"You are correct, I spoke with Kai Malina as you were not available." Koa countered, his words almost a dare for them to say more.

Mana Lani lowered their head and stepped back.

Michael glanced at Karen. He had no doubt they wore a similar expression and probably had a similar thought.

Mana Lani was trouble.

"Now I wish there was more I had to share with you at this time," Koa gestured to the sides of the hall, "but for now, let us share a meal and enjoy some of the finest music and dancing Mu has to offer." He clapped his hands and musicians appeared and started to play. Several servants came from every corner of the room, bringing out tables and food as the guests moved, allowing the parade of servers to do their work.

*****

Kaimi watched as the commotion around them became a dance of organized chaos. The room buzzed with activity and reminded him of all the events his parents had. Such celebrations. A smile tugged at the sides of his face. Despite the tragedy, life should still be celebrated. And Koa had made the smart move, welcoming the members of the Pontus in this way. He found his eyes on Michael; the man looked so much better in person. He didn't understand his, and the others need for so many articles of clothing. Michael wore long dark blue pants, and a burgundy long sleeve button-down shirt accented with glossy black shoes and a black belt.

I wonder what he's like. I've only seen him through their media broadcasts. I wonder who he really is?

"He's quite handsome." Nohealani commented as she moved to him. Her white dress similar to one of their mother's. Sparkles from the gown danced on the floor and walls as she moved. The crystals finding all the light in the hall.

She looks so much like Mom.

"What?" Kaimi offered a slight chuckle.

As they spoke, dancers entered the hall and began their performance. A way to keep everyone entertained as the staff finished setting the space for dinner.

"Your eyes have not been far from him since you brought him from their ship." She rested a hand on his arm.

"He had severe injuries, and I wanted to ensure we cared for him." Kaimi countered, warmth starting to build up around his collarbone and neck. "His, and all their injuries and deaths, are our fault after all, and I believe me being there for him, and them, was the least I should do."

"Such care." Nohealani offered him a raised eyebrow.

"Taking care of the wounded was my charge—"

"However, as you reminded us, brother, you are not a healer." Koa joined them. "And yet, every time I needed you, we found you by his side or checking with Latu about him. Clearly, our best healer didn't need your unskilled hand, did he?"

Kaimi remained silent, but heat had found its way to his cheeks and neck.

Nohealani chuckled.

Kaimi met her laughter with a glare, subsequently facing his brother. "What was the exchange between you and Mana Lani?" He tried to deflect the conversation, but his tone filled with defensiveness, but hopefully not anger.

Koa bit at his lower lip as a server brought him a drink. He took a sip before shaking his head. "Nothing. Well, maybe something, but nothing for now." He tapped the side of his drink.

Kaimi glanced around the great hall, as the server offered him and Nohealani drinks as well, before vanishing to take care of the rest of their guests. The space came to life with music and the smells of food. The crystal lights played with the embedded stones and shells in the walls, making the patterns dance. As the first round of dancing ended, more would come later. This first performance ensured the guests had something to focus on until the meal was laid out. Kaimi peeked at his brother, seeing worry spread over his face, but vanishing as soon as he took another sip of his drink. He realized not to push his brother, and for an attempted change in conversation, this might not have been the smartest choice. "Apologies."

Koa faced him and offered a warm smile. "No apology needed, now go greet our guest." He nodded to Michael and moved off to speak with some of the elders who were eyeing him.

"Koa's right." Nohealani sipped on her drink. "Time has moved on for both of us. I at least have my children." Her mouth raised in a smile. "I will never forget Malo, but if there is another for me to find, I hope I do, and I think Makani would want the same for you."

Are they right? Should I move my life forward? This man may not even be interested. So where is the harm?

"Moving forward is not easy." Kaimi found he once again stared at Michael. His head filled with questions and thoughts he had not had in a long time.

"You both have suffered loss," Nohealani remarked, her voice growing soft as her gaze moved over his face. "At the very least, this gives you a place to start, see what is in store, but you must try."

Kaimi nodded. "Very well." He reached out and took Nohealani's hand. "Thank you."

*****

Karen watched in amazement at what happened around them; the music, the dance, the laughing. All of the activity. She had been to Hawaii once ,and went to a lū'au, but nothing compared to what they were seeing here tonight. Even the sky, well the top of the cave appeared to resemble a late afternoon sky, she had seen the large crystals glowing, and noted how the crystals dimmed as the hours moved them to what she assumed to be dusk, and soon to be night.

What an amazing experience.

The food and the fire dancers were incredible. Seeing the performance, she wondered how much more she would enjoy the display if she understood the words. However, with the music and their movements, she followed the story the dancers shared. The show made her almost forget everything happening around them and on the Pontus. Here she sat in a world that only a week ago she never dreamed she would find. Everything she had dreamed in front of her...

Well, not dreamed.

Yet none of Mu surprised her. The people of Mu being Polynesian only made sense considering they were located in the Pacific Ocean. The inhabitants would clearly be Polynesian in ancestry, especially given how far they traveled. Some scientists and people even suspect the ancient Polynesians traveled all the way to North America, much like the Vikings had on the East Coast.

There was so much to learn here, so much they had gotten wrong and so much knowledge they had to share, but what would an exchange look like? How would people at home react to these people, especially knowing they caused the Pulse, well not all the people here, but maybe some of them. And how would these people of Mu react to the rest of the world? Studying us from the above world through media versus actually being among us in a room is something completely different.

What are we going to do?

"Hey." Michael called her from her thoughts. "You okay?"

She glanced down at her plate of food, before her lay a wonderful spread of crab and lobster and other bounties from the sea. To her amazement, some of the side dishes were familiar to her. They managed to grow and farm all they needed for their society, and clearly, they had a rich and full diet. "Just thinking."

"I know, Mu is a lot." Michael glanced out one of the large windows as the light grew less and more of the white-blue light from the smaller energy crystals filled the space along with the torches. "How is any of this even possible?"

"There is a lot about their world we don't understand." Dr. Farmin commented between bites of her meal. "Their energy crystals, for one. Are the crystals natural or something they created? A form of clean energy. What about the bioluminescent stone they use in their architecture?"

"And did you see the pearls they have?" Alister put down his cup. "They are as big as my head, and must be worth a fortune. So much potential for... well, this place is incredible."

"I keep asking myself what happens next." Karen moved her plate of food to the side. "This place is unbelievable. So now what?" She shook her head.

"We fix the Pontus and go home." Captain Abbas responded. "Yes, this place is remarkable, but we need to take care of our dead." She leaned forward. "Don't get me wrong, this city and all its wonders are not lost on me, but we aren't equipped for any kind of exploration of this magnitude. We leave and return when we are better prepared."

She's not wrong. I wish I had thought to bring on an expert in Polynesian culture and history. Or perhaps a regional historian. There is so much we're going to miss.

"Easier said than done." Dr. Farmin sipped her drink. "We know about each other now, clearly they've known about us, which explains the secrecy, but now we know about them, and when we return, the rest of the world will know about them too."

Michael glanced at those around the table. "Well, everyone did have to sign NDAs. So..."

"Do you think NDAs are going to keep everyone quiet?" Captain Abbas didn't sound sure.

Michael exhaled, not willing to admit the NDAs may not be enough.

"And that will cause all kinds of issues." Karen leaned forward in her seat. She pulled out her lip balm and coated her lips before putting the gel away.

"Honestly, I wouldn't mind sticking around." Alister peeked around the room. "Think of all the things they can teach us. Not to mention their tech. I bet there is a lot of money to be made here, enough for everyone."

Karen wanted to disagree with him, but he wasn't wrong.

"And I know I'm not the only one." Alister continued. "Dr. Chen and Jayden mentioned the same thing to me earlier."

Karen glanced at the rest of her team, wondering how many of them would stay given the chance. For that matter, would she? She sat taller, taking in the group. Some were eating, others enjoyed the entertainment, all were lost in the beauty and wonder of Mu.

So much to learn and see.

"Tell me you're not serious." Michael commented. "What makes you think they would be willing to share any of their technology, or allow any of us to stay? Despite all this hospitality, I think they want us gone as much as we want to be gone." He shook his head. "Imagine what would happen if people got their hands on their pulse technology. Nowhere would be safe."

"Well, I wasn't thinking about the weapons." Alister picked up some of the crab in front of him. "There is a lot here and Mu is beautiful, plus what's wrong with thinking about what we can do for each other? Not everyone is sitting on a personal fortune."

Michael's face filled with hints of red as he glanced down at his plate.

"Alister has a point." Karen used her best diplomatic tone. She didn't need there to be any drama from any of her people. "There is a lot we can offer each other and, right or wrong, there is a lot of money to be made as well as a lot of scientific discoveries. Think of all the scientists who will want to come and study here. Some of the medical tech alone might keep researchers and doctors going for years. And then imagine working together, all the great things we'll accomplish."

Michael nodded. "Okay, fair." He glanced over at Alister. "Sorry, this is so beautiful and they all seem so gracious. I know they aren't perfect, but..."

"Hello." Kaimi greeted. "I wanted to see how you were enjoying the lū'au."

"Everything is quite good." Michael's head snapped around and beamed up at Kaimi.

"Yes. Quite." Karen noted Michael's reaction. His current response hadn't been seen before and she wasn't the only one taking notice if the contorted expression on Alister's face was any indication.

So much for no drama among our group.

"I have spoken with the king and I wanted to confirm your tour of Mu with Noe tomorrow." Kaimi smiled, the white of his teeth played well with the white of his *lava lava*. His bare chest showed off a necklace of gold with large pearls and bones from some creature. He created quite the form as he stood there.

"Can't wait." Dr. Farmin responded.

"Unfortunately, me and most of my crew will be working on the Pontus." Captain Abbas explained and offered a slight bow of her head. "But thank you for the offer."

"How unfortunate." Kaimi's lips pulled down in a slight frown.

"We don't want to overstay our welcome," Captain Abbas added with something akin to a politician's smile, all teeth and very little sincerity.

"Well, I'm looking forward to the tour." Alister picked up his drink. "I have so many questions and I'm hoping to learn more about your home." He sipped his drink.

"Noe will be the right person." Kaimi faced the young man before glancing at Karen. "And what about you, Dr. Linn?"

"Oh, I wouldn't miss seeing Mu for the world." Karen laughed. "We were just talking. I wish I had the foresight to bring someone familiar with Polynesian culture on this trip, but..." she shook her head.

"You have one man, I believe, Tony Kawai." Kaimi spoke to Karen, "Isn't he a member of your team?"

"He's a member of my crew." Captain Abbas. "He's been on the Pontus."

"Would he be able to join the tour?" Kaimi adjusted his stance now facing the captain. "The tour might be nice for him, and some of our people may enjoy seeing ourselves represented in your group."

"Not a bad idea." Michael agreed as he turned to Abbas. "What do you think, Captain? Karen?"

Karen nodded. She liked the idea. "Fine by me, as long as Susan approves his time off the sub. I agree his presence in our group might be helpful for everyone."

"I don't see why not." Captain Abbas agreed. "Perhaps, if you and the king don't mind, I'll offer shore leave to those wanting a break. So me and my officers can run tests without people underfoot."

"We are open to all." Kaimi beamed over at her. "And what about you, Mr. Donovan? Are you looking forward to the tour?"

"Me?" Michael shook his head. "I'm not going, I'm going to rest my leg." He absently massaged where the wound had once been. "I'm still sore and I don't want to overdo or, worse, slow everyone down."

Kaimi's shoulders sank. "How unfortunate. The Crystal Caves and Torokina River are beautiful, as is all of Mu." He smiled.

"Well, I might get out for a walk in the gardens and explore the tide pools, something easy." Michael shrugged.

"You should come." Alister beamed. "It'll be fun, and I don't mind if you need to lean on me."

"If you need to see our healer again," Kaimi offered with a glance in the direction of where the healers were found. "I would be happy to take you. You should be feeling better, but if not..." he reached out a hand to Michael.

Karen shook her head as a slight smile tugged at her lips. She had to bite back a laugh as she witnessed the awkward expressions on both their faces.

And what do we have here? A potential love triangle.

She picked up her napkin to wipe her mouth, covering her chuckle.

Ah to be young…well younger.

~ Chapter Sixteen ~

Kaimi made his way through the halls to the guest quarters. He hadn't planned on doing this, but after hearing Michael would be alone today, coming by to check on him was worth the effort, and he wanted to see if Michael would like to get out and see Mu. Plus, spending time together, getting to know each other might help in their understanding of each other's culture.

Is this what I'm doing? Or am I after something more?

He stopped and glanced out at Mu; the city was alive with activity. Many of the people were excited to meet the people from above, some were leery, but uncertainty would happen no matter what, just like some of the people from the Pontus were leery about being here in Mu. Still, a buzz of excitement hovered in the air. The Pontus's mini sub was now docked in Faga Bay with several of Mu's catamarans and outriggers. Bob, as Dr. Linn called the craft, appeared so out of place, so odd with the bright orange color, but there the vessel sat, and on his way to his guest is where he found himself.

This is insane, the gods must be crazy.

He walked the rest of the way to Michael's room and glanced down at his dark blue sarong and white shirt. He chose a casual outfit, but considering they would, hopefully, be walking around and enjoying the day, the occasion didn't call for anything formal. Pleased with his appearance Kaimi knocked on the door.

"One sec." Michael called out from behind the door.

There were footsteps preceding the door opening as Michael stood there in a short-sleeved purple shirt and a pair of pants with bare feet. "Your Highness. Kaimi, Hi." He stepped to the side. "Come in."

"Actually, Mr. Donovan. Michael, I wanted to see if you'd like to go on a tour with me," Kaimi offered. "We don't have to go far and we can walk as slow as you need."

Michael peered around the room and glanced out the window. "You know what? Sure, why not. Alister almost had me out the door when the others left, but..." Anyway, he shook his head.

They must be a couple, a relationship between them would explain much.

There was a tinge of regret and sorrow in Kaimi's heart. "If you'd like to meet up with your husband, I can take you to him."

"What?" Michael laughed. "No. Alister is...well Alister is a friend, nothing more. He works for me."

"But the way he..." Kaimi stopped, unsure how to finish his statement.

"I... maybe at one point." Michael's shoulders dropped and hints of red filled his neck and cheeks. "But no. I think we're too different. He's a good guy and I like him, but he's a bit young for me. And I think we want different things."

Kaimi felt his lips pull into a smile. "I understand. Relationships can be complicated."

Michael nodded his agreement. "Let me put some shoes on, then we can go."

Kaimi moved them through the palace and out into the gardens and tide pools. The scents of lemon grass and salt water filled his lungs and tingled his nose. The smells, no matter how wonderful, always made his nose run a bit.

"How long has Mu been Mu?" Michael pointed. "I mean, you're in a bioluminescent cave in the middle of the largest ocean on the planet. Clearly, this didn't just happen."

Kaimi laughed. "No." He walked to one of the orchid plants. Picking a flower, he rested the bloom on his hand. "Our history says 12,000 years ago the goddess Hikule'o, she's the goddess of the Earth and Kanaloa, the god of the Ocean, went to war." Kaimi moved his hands to assist in narrating the story. "Kanaloa began to flood the world. This angered many of the other gods." Kaimi continued his movements. He was no story teller or dancer, but he appreciated the stories and had the movements engrained in his memory. "The god of Fertility, Lono, along with his husband Tāne Mahuta, the God of the Forest and Harvest, brought our people to this great mountain to keep us safe, but as the waters continued to rise Lono and Tāne Mahuta needed help." Kaimi pointed to the ground. "They asked Rūauoko, the god of Earthquakes, to shake the mountain and open a cavern, which he did. But the cave was dark, so they asked Kāne, the Goddess of the sky, for help." He pointed up toward the ceiling of the cave. "She captured parts of the sun and embedded them in the top of the cave giving us light. Since this gift came from the sun, the light stayed in sync with its mother, providing us seasons to grow crops and survive." He moved his arms and hands. "The gods continue to protect us and teach us, so we can thrive in this place." He finished and handed Michael the blossom from the orchid. "Your people call this plant Anoetochilus sandvicensis. We call the bloom The Jewel of Lono."

"Wow." Michael stood with the flower in his hand and his gaze focused on Kaimi. "Incredible. Thank you."

Kaimi smiled, "One of our traditional stories we are taught from birth." He stepped closer to Michael and added. "However, we now know the Earth was in an ice age, and as the climate changed and the water levels rose, our people fled the coast where they lived, moving into this cave. From what we understand, the crystals may have been from a meteorite that impacted this mountain range, but we are unsure." Kaimi sighed. "I can't imagine the suffering they must have endured being cut off from the rest of the world. But they survived and thanks to them and their hard work, we have this wonderful place to call home."

Michael laughed. "I like the first version of your story better."

"Many of us do." Kaimi acknowledged.

Which is why we have the issues we have.

"My dance and storytelling are nothing like my husband's. He was so gifted." Kaimi glanced out at the water.

"What happened?" Michael asked before adding. "If you don't mind me asking."

Kaimi faced him, "When the pulse first went out." He began. "The queen and king, my parents, were murdered. Nohealani and I wrongly assumed our brother Koa had killed them."

"The king?" Michael glanced towards the palace.

This must be so strange for him.

Michael faced Kaimi again.

"Things were in chaos and a lot of mistakes were made." Kaimi acknowledged. "I will spare you all those details, but as things went, Nohealani and I were on the wrong side of history. My husband, Makani, died, as did my brother-in-law Malo, for our folly, but time has passed. And our family has, or is, healing. As is my heart."

"Oh, I'm so sorry," Michael offered.

Kaimi nodded, speaking of Makani and his death had not been easy, but with Michael he found the pain less, and the memories of his time with Makani brought him joy. "From where you sit, we must appear so idealistic, so different from your world, but...we're still human."

"An unfortunate truth for us all." Michael glanced out at the water. Kaimi followed his gaze. "Shall we continue our tour?"

*****

Michael couldn't get over the beauty of Mu. Based on everything Kaimi had shared with him, this place felt magical. He knew better, but hearing the story and history of Mu made him wonder if, perhaps, the gods, or god, did have a hand in its creation. Michael picked up a stone and tossed the small rock into the water. "With this bay being so large, how does the water pressure and air pressure stay level?"

"Much as with how your open compartments must work on the Pontus, this insight is how we knew we would be able to enter from the bottom of your ship, in the sub launch and dive hatch." Kaimi responded.

"But at depths such as here..." Michael shook his head.

Kaimi laughed. "If you are truly interested, I can explain the science to you, or we can ask Noe? They love chatting about such matters."

Michael's lips pinched together. "No, I mean I'm interested, but..." He shrugged. "This place is so astonishing. I wish I understood better." He paused. "Don't get me wrong, I'm not stupid, but science wasn't my thing. And still, I'm not sure even science can explain all this." He motioned his hands about.

"I never assumed otherwise." Kaimi's lips spread in a coy smile. "Any man who can take being a body attendant and become as wealthy and as successful as you must be intelligent."

"Body attendant?" Michael asked.

What the hell. Does he know what I do?

"Yes, your business." Kaimi frowned, he paused glancing around, his eyes darting back and forth. "The work you and Alister do. Isn't body attendant the right term..."

"Oh." Michael's voice cracked. "Oh!" He took a step away, his voice grew louder. "How do you? I mean, when did you?" His face burned.

"When we viewed the broadcast announcing you were coming." Kaimi took a step closer. "I found the information on your company and learned what you did, and what you turned those talents into." He smiled. "You've accomplished a great deal and impressively so, our body attendants don't have those kinds of opportunity, since our community is so small and we don't use them to the extent you have been used. Their service is much more private." He continued. "My body attendant, Timu and I never engaged in sexual relations, nor your kind of role play, you and the others like you, have engaged in. Not that when I was younger I wouldn't have minded, but we are friends and have a close relationship."

Michael nodded, finding the saliva much easier to swallow. "What I do doesn't bother you? Knowing what I do, or did in my past isn't an issue?"

Kaimi's eyes narrowed. "Should I care? Does your job bother you? Your work as a body attendant doesn't appear to bother those you are with," he shrugged. "Why should I care what you do? You live your life the way you want and are successful. Not to mention all the good work you've done."

Michael laughed.

Am I actually hearing this correctly? Kaimi doesn't care how I make a living. Clearly, he's seen what I do and he doesn't seem the least bit fazed.

"Thank you." Michael found those the only words he could speak at the moment.

"For what?"

Michael couldn't help but relax as his words returned to him, "You've known this whole time and have not made me feel small or ashamed of what I do. The only other person to act this way toward me, well and the people in my business circle, is Karen." Michael's shoulders released and the pain in his neck he had been unknowingly carrying vanished. "I wish more people were like you."

"Well, I can assure you, no one here in Mu will care. Being a body attendant is an honorable profession. Especially if you work for the royal family or one of the Elders." Kaimi offered. "May I ask you another question?"

Michael tried to hide a frown threatening to form on his lips. He gulped in some air to hide his disappointment.

Here comes the question, this is when all the pretty words of under-standing fly right out of the window. Five-to-one, he's going to ask if I can show him my dick.

"Sure." Michael responded, preparing himself for the question and glancing around to ensure they were alone.

"Why did you decide to fund this project, when so many people in your government and scientists judged the task to be foolishness?"

Michael laughed again, this time from his whole body. Maybe Kaimi was for real.

"Well." Michael inhaled. "And sorry for laughing... you've surprised me... anyway, Karen, Dr. Linn, is sincere and wanted to find out what happened, or that's what she told me at first. The Pacific Pulse, you have no idea what a disaster the event was for us."

"I'm sorry again," Kaimi offered. "We will find out who caused this, and hopefully who also killed our parents."

Michael focused on Kaimi. "You don't know who murdered them? Still?"

Kaimi sucked in a lung full of air. "No. As I mentioned, we credited Koa with the blame, but the attacker wasn't him. Once the second pulse occurred when you arrived, we were certain. However, we believe the three events are related, which is why Koa wants to investigate, especially with your people here. We're hoping doing so will flush out the traitor."

Michael walked to the edge of the water. "They may strike again."

"No." Kaimi joined him at the water's edge. "The system has been completely recoded, so no one can use the pulse again."

"Good." Michael turned and faced him. "Hundreds of thousands of people died. And large sections of North America were destroyed. I would hate to see your weapon fall into the wrong hands and be used again."

"We had no way to stop the pulse. We tried, but when we got to the lab, we were too late."

"Why did you even develop such a weapon?"

"When your scientists developed the atom bomb in the 1940s, we didn't have anything to protect ourselves. We didn't have the resources to create such a weapon. With the world in the middle of a war we were unsure how things would turn out." Kaimi motioned around the space finally returning to Michael's gaze. His gaze almost pleading. "You have to understand the weapon was never meant to be used."

Michael huffed and nodded. "I can't blame you. World War II was hell and things haven't gotten much better since."

"The device was only meant as a deterrent." Kaimi added.

Humans. We are nothing but lust and fear, even in a place like Mu we are no better.

~ Chapter Seventeen
~

Karen tried to focus on the king as he spoke, but she couldn't believe what they were hearing. She studied her surroundings. The meeting room was smaller than the great hall, and was designed for function. Still the illuminating veining ran through the stone walls sparkling. Around the windows, crystals and shells were added to give the space character. Even the monitors, which were off, blended into the room's design. The tour with Noe, had been enjoyable and, as she already realized, there was a lot to be learned here in Mu. She could spend the rest of her life studying and exploring this place and its culture. However, the news about how the pulse happened and about the former queen and king was disturbing. She glanced over at Michael; based on his lack of reaction, he must have already been told about this.

Although he does have one hell of a poker face when he wants.

When they first returned from their tour, Michael was nowhere to be found. She inquired about his location to one of the guards, who spoke English, and he let her know (or tried to explain) Michael had gone out with Prince Kaimi. Only returning shortly before this meeting with the king.

He must have been feeling better, or Kaimi used his powers of persuasion. Either way.

Good for him.

"As you can understand, we were horrified when the second pulse fired." Koa stated, the words pulling Karen from her thoughts. "We should have taken the weapon off line, but considering everything we had been through and not knowing what you might do, the Council of Elders and myself believed our actions were in the best interest of all, but now..." his gaze dropped to the table.

"How is the murder of your parents still not solved?" Dr. Farmin leaned forward. "You said the assassination happened five years ago."

Karen nodded. She had been mulling over the same question. Mu wasn't huge, sure there were about 75,000 people, but not all of them had access to the queen and king, or the Palace, for that matter. Even if Koa was wrongly accused by Kaimi and Nohealani there were still others who might have committed the crime. Who had something to gain or who didn't agree with the policies set by the monarchs? Maybe the people wanted more freedom. For each person who knew the queen and king a reason for their removal existed, no matter how good or bad they were. Everyone had their own agenda, figuring out each of those agendas and who would kill to accomplish their goal would lead to who killed the queen and king.

"We fought." Nohealani rested her hands on the table. "The death of our parents caused a civil war, plainly put events got more and more out of control. For years Mu was in a state of unrest."

Kaimi frowned at the comments and inhaled. The way his forehead set and his shoulders dropped, regret held him tight.

"Which is how your husband and Kaimi's husband died." Michael added. His brows slightly raised and his lips a single line, his face poured with sympathy. His hand started to move in the direction of Kaimi, but he stopped, going no further.

Koa nodded. "Those were dark times for our family and for me. Not to mention all of Mu." He intertwined his hands in front of his face and rested his chin there. "We made." He glanced at his brother and sister sitting around the table. "I made. A great many mistakes."

"We all did." Kaimi reached out his hand to his brother.

Koa took the hand and offered a weak smile. "I hoped we were all past such matters, but clearly there are some who aren't." he inhaled deeper and released the air slowly.

"The problem we all face," Karen began trying to focus them on the here and now, and not the past, "is what do we do now? How do we proceed? Who would have done this? Your Majesty, who here has the most to lose with our arrival? And who would see a war with us as a benefit to this place?"

Koa pulled himself closer to the table. "There are many who do not, and did not, want us to contact you. They feared you." He huffed, "I suppose we all did, to some extent."

"Fear; the poison behind the time of unrest." Nohealani commented, her tone reflecting the difficulty in what she shared. "Our parents considered now to be the time to reach out to you and your world, but..."

"Fear." Michael frowned and shook his head.

Nods of agreement waved around the table.

Karen glanced around the space, disappointment crawling over her. *So many mistakes.* And now here they were. Mu had a weapon still able to be used against any country in the world, and had already been used at least twice. The effects of the second blast were still unknown, except for the sub. Now, with their discovery of Mu, the rest of the world would learn about this place soon enough. The news would bring a whole new set of trouble for these people, because a lot of people aren't going to care that the attack was an accident. Even among the surviving crew, many were not pleased and wanted some form of justice for the fallen. Even in her private moments, she was angry over the death of a majority of her team.

Accident or not.

"Dr. Farmin, what will your government do?" Koa glanced at her. She was a representative from the United States, so asking her made sense. He would seek her guidance in gauging a potential response.

Maybe he should ask the others as well. Get more feedback and get a feel for the mood.

The group was small. Karen, Michael, and Rochelle. Captain Abbas wanted to return to the Pontus, and test the systems, and inspect the repairs with her officers. Karen had told her team they can, with the approval of their hosts, explore Mu and Alister joined them as did a few crew, who the captain had granted leave. This discussion and conversation weren't meant for everyone, and Karen intellectually understood, but emotions played into everything, including big decisions affecting everyone.

"I can't really say." Dr. Farmin offered after several quiet moments, "This is new territory for us, for me." She rested her hands flat on the table. "We have first contact procedures for an alien race, but not for members of a human lost continent, or city that shouldn't exist, but..." she glanced around.

"Do you believe they will be reasonable?" Kaimi asked as he leaned closer to her. "Understand as you all have?"

Michael shook his head as his expression dropped along with his gaze.

"Now hold on," Dr. Farmin caught sight of this. "Mr. Donovan, our government is reasonable." Her tone raised as did her eyebrows. "We treat everyone as equals."

"Oh please," Michael scoffed. "Look at what's happened within our country the last few years. How can you even say that with a straight face?" There were hints of red around his neck and in his cheeks. "Not to mention we have a history of crushing people we don't agree with or understand. Would you like a list, alphabetical or by atrocity?"

"Says the man with the morals of a gutter rat," Dr. Farmin snapped.

"Rochelle," Karen's voice was barely over a whisper. This forced everyone to stop and listen to her. The softer you speak the more people have to listen to hear you and this, typically, helps to bring a sense of calm. "He's not wrong."

Rochelle massaged her temples, her sudden burst of outrage vanishing away like a sandcastle on the beach during high tide. "I... I don't know... I would need to talk to the President and even..."

Koa sat deeply in his chair, his hand resting over his mouth.

Karen rested her elbows on the table. This wasn't helping. There were too many unknowns. They needed to find who sent out the first and second pulse. The discovery would give Rochelle and her a chip to play with the governments. They would have the guilty party, which would open up a dialog. And if finding this individual helped Koa and the rest of the royal family find out who killed their parents all the better.

The blare from the alarms bounced off the walls and floors as two guards rushed over to the king and the royal family. Michael stood, as did Karen. The chairs they sat in scraped on the floor.

"Come with us," Koa commanded of those gathered at the table.

"What happened?" Dr. Farmin rushed to her feet, quickly joining the others.

"What's going on?" Karen demanded as she glanced out the window. Everything outside checked out and appeared to be in order, but a calm view didn't mean anything.

No one spoke as they moved to the doors and with the guards next to them, Karen, Rochelle, and Michael had little choice but to do what was asked. The group quickly made their way through several corridors and halls to a large room. Monitors filled one wall, workbenches, and machinery ran the length of the far wall, and over to the side, a dive pool next to a much larger, and from what Karen distinguished, deeper pool. Throughout the rest of the space were tables and counters holding additional equipment and workspace.

A lab.

"Something is attacking your sub," Noe announced to the group and pointed to the monitors. They were all showing different angles of the sub and some kind of attacker.

"What? Who?" Karen moved closer to the screens to see better. She didn't see energy blasts or weapons fire.

"The gods have sent their beasts." Nohealani covered her mouth with her hand, her eyes the size of saucers.

"What?" Rochelle glanced around the space, clearly unsure where to look. "Beasts? What beasts? What kind of creature is strong enough to harm the Pontus?"

"Mana Lani and Kai Malina," Koa stepped closer to the displays "They foretold Kanaloa would send his children to fight for us and for our home, but I never..." He faced Noe and started speaking in their native language, the words flying fast and sharp.

"Ku is our God of War and Kanaloa is our God of the Ocean." Kaimi explained to the group as his brother barked orders.

"How do we stop them?" Michael questioned as he stepped closer to Kaimi and the screens.

Koa faced him. "How do you stop the work of the gods?" He shook his head.

"We need to evacuate our people from the sub." Karen pushed closer, seeing what looked like three blue whales ramming into the side of the sub, but there was something more, something larger. "What the hell is that?" she pointed. "Whales? Something we haven't seen before?"

"It..." Koa stepped closer, subsequently taking several steps away, the color in his cheeks and face drained. "May the gods have mercy... a giant *he'e*."

"We have to warn them!" Michael's voice raised as he spoke. "There has to be something we can do. Maybe they'll stop. Karen, the Pontus can withstand this, right? The hull has been hardened for the journey, the Pontus is built for this... right?"

Karen shook her head, her face and neck cooling as sweat broke out on her forehead. Bile climbed from her stomach to her throat. Her hand moved to her mouth, covering her lips. She had no words. They never considered in a million years the sub would come under attack by whales and a... a... a what... giant squid.

"I've tried to reach them." Noe moved over to the wall and began typing. They reached for a headset. "But I can't make contact." They pulled at every lever, turned every dial, typed out every command. Nothing.

"Try again," Nohealani demanded, moving to the touchscreen. "There are people there, and this can't be what the gods meant, or had in store for them, or us."

"Assemble our warriors." Koa shouted to his guards. "Get every suit ready..." He froze again, glancing back on the screen seeing the beasts.

There isn't enough time.

Karen noted they were all speaking English to ensure everyone might be able to comprehend what was going on. Using English as the common language was better than having to guess at what they were saying, like when Koa and Noe were first speaking.

"Something's happening." Michael pointed at the monitors. "That octopus-squid thing is going to crush the Pontus like a tin can. My god, the beast is almost the size of the sub!" His gaze now frozen on the monitor as he spoke, transfixed by the disaster playing out in front of them.

Everything moved in slow motion. Karen watched the images on the screen as the Pontus continued to be pummeled and squeezed by those creatures while Koa and Kaimi shouted at the guards. They were powerless to do anything. She and the others stood in horror, watching the Pontus fall under siege again. And they had no way of helping this time.

"We have to help!" Karen narrowed on the king and his siblings, taking several steps closer to them. "There must be something you can do."

"We're sending our warriors, but this will take time." Koa inhaled. His shoulders were stiff, as was the rest of his posture. "They have to suit up and launch. Once they are ready, they have to get there." He shook his head.

"Use your pulse gun... thing." Rochelle demanded and moved to the wall of monitors, tapping one of the screens. "Fire at them. Shoot the beast before everyone on the sub dies."

"No." Koa shook his head. "If we fire, the sub will be hit. The animals are too close. If we fire, everyone will die for sure. At least with us trying to get there, they have a chance."

"Don't you have anything else? Electrical shocks? Your pulse guns? Something?" Michael countered, assessing the space around them.

Karen wasn't sure what he was looking for, but hopefully, they would find or think of something. "The Pontus was weakened by the pulse. We're lucky any of us survived the first attack. I don't know how much has been repaired, but I know the structural integrity..." she shook her head.

"Michael, everything we can do is being done." Kaimi offered as he reached out for his arm. "Please."

"What's happening now?" Nohealani pointed to the screen. "Is your ship meant to move in such a way?"

Karen leaned in and saw a ripple on the sub's hull. "The hull's not going to survive. Come on, launch the mini sub, get out of there," she demanded of the screen. If shouting would help, she would have screamed.

"Bob." Noe glanced over to another one of the displays. "Is not there. The mini sub is on their way to us. I got a message before we lost the signal."

"They don't know?" Michael made eye contact with all the faces in the room. "The mini sub is out there and might be attacked as well."

Noe shook their head.

"Who was on the ship?" Koa demanded. "How many people are on the Pontus?"

"I'm not sure. I didn't ask. Trips back and forth are routine." Noe's gaze and brows dropped. "The smaller vessel can hold six, but more in an emergency, but they were not..."

Another alarm blared in the room as Ulani rushed in, accompanied by two guards holding pulse guns at the ready. "Koa, Kaimi, Nohealani you must come! Kai Malina is..."

The siblings all shared a worried expression before Koa turned to Karen. "Dr. Linn, please, all of you stay here. Noe, keep me informed. I want our people out there NOW." He shouted as they left.

*****

Kaimi and the others rushed from the lab, leaving Michael, Karen and Rochelle to watch the demise of their ship. Nothing to be done. The attack team wouldn't reach the Pontus in time. The only hope was, if their mini sub would be okay, with luck, their people may be able to get to them. Ensuring their safety. Still, how were the people from the above world going to leave? Would their departure even be possible now? Noe had mentioned the mini sub may hold six or so occupants, but how many was the 'or so'? And why did those creatures attack the sub?

Something more is at play here and I don't think any of this has to do with the gods.

The siblings and guards reached the Great Hall, and all four of the siblings stopped. The crimson liquid pooled around the figure on the floor. The scream from Nohealani echoed from wall to wall as she rushed to Kai Malina. Iron permeated everything around Kaimi, the scent so much like before, he wanted to vomit. He wanted to look away, but he couldn't. Images of his mother and father rushed to him. Light from the crystals reflected off the walls and floor, filling the space with a bright sunny glow a contrast to Kai Malina.

Gods! Not again.

"What happened?" Koa gulped at his words, moving to Kai Malina.

"When the alarm sounded," Ulani's words caught in her mouth as she spoke. "I ensured Allyn and Palani were safe. They are with their tutors." She nodded at Nohealani. "I came to see what was happening. When I didn't find you in the meeting room, I came here and found..." she turned away, tears streaming down her cheeks.

Kaimi glanced at Kia Malina, the pristine white sarong covered with a few embedded clear crystals now almost fully scarlet. There was no need to call for a healer. Their sibling now joined their mother and father in the heavens. He had seen this too many times during the rebellion. Kai Malina's chest bore a deep gash, and there was no movement from breathing. "Who?"

"Your Majesty." One of the guards approached, his crystal pike raised. "We found these three fleeing."

Kaimi turned and noticed three of the people from the Pontus. One of the scientists, Jayden, he believed. One of the crew. He did not know her name. "Alister, what have you done? WHY?" Kaimi shouted, moving close to the young man. He wanted to reach out and grab him. Shake him. Scream at him. "Why!" the word escaped his lips.

"We didn't do this." Alister glanced at the body on the ground and turned away as the color drained from his face. His face and stomach convulsed once, then again.

Can't look at the death you caused.

The splashing from the tide pools banged in Kaimi's head. They had been here before with his parents, and now they were here again with Kai Malina. He glared at his hands and rubbed them, trying to get the blood off them, but there was nothing to remove. His hands were clean.

"We found these." The guard opened a cloth bag.

Koa and Kaimi glanced in. "An energy crystal and pearls?" Koa questioned. There were some polished bone necklaces and trinkets, they all sparkled of whites and blues, a contrast to the growing burgundy on the floor.

"You stole from us!" Koa snatched the bag from the guard, tossing the loot to the floor at the three's feet. "Killing Kai Malina. Why? For this?" Koa shook his head, grabbing Alister by the shirt, then tossing him to the polished floor with the blue veining running throughout. "We would have given these things to you. You didn't need to kill Kai Malina."

"We didn't kill your brother." Jayden tried to pull free from the guard to help Alister up. "We ran when we heard the second alarm. We thought we triggered something."

"Kai was not our brother or our sister." Nohealani exclaimed, pushing past Koa and Ulani. "Kai Malina was our next Māhū! What have you done with Mana Lani?" She stepped forward and struck Jayden. "Why have you done this to us and our family? Have we not suffered enough? Is this revenge for what happened to your people?" She moved to Alister, who had found his footing again. "We welcomed you here, and this is how you repay us?"

"I swear we didn't do this," Alister pleaded. He couldn't even look at the body of Kai Malina on the ground, Kaimi noted. "Please. Yes, we took the pearls and an energy crystal and jewelry, but we didn't kill anyone. We weren't even in this room."

"Enough!" Koa shouted, bringing the conversation to an end. "Take them to Alister's quarters and keep them secured there. I want a guard outside their window as well. Take the doctor and the others we left in the lab there as well."

"Koa, Your Majesty." Kaimi tried to pull the scents of the sea water to him, to clear the traces of iron. "What about the attack on the Pontus?"

"What?" Jayden yelped as he continued to struggle against the guard.

"What about the Pontus?" The woman with short blond hair spoke.

"The gods have sent their beasts to destroy your ship, and now we know why." Koa glared at the three. Venom filling each of his words. "You will stay here and pay for your crimes."

"Brother, we must..." Kaimi started but stopped under the icy glare of Koa.

"We must do nothing but tend to Kai Malina, leave the fate of the above worlders to the gods."

Kaimi glanced at Kai Malina and the pool of scarlet around them. His hand reached up to his mouth as more images of his parents, killed in the same manner, filled his vision. All the blood and the deep chest wounds from a crystal pike. "Where is the crystal pike they used?"

"We didn't find one." The guard reported. Their words hard coming through their pinched lips.

"Probably tossed in the tide pools outside in the gardens." Koa spat with a hand raised in the direction of the tide pool. "Conduct a full search, and I want a count of all weapons. Anything missing I want to know. Talk to Noe and see what they can find out. Search all their rooms, leave nothing unturned."

The guards nodded.

"Kaimi," Koa began. "I know you have an interest in Michael, but..." He shook his head and watched the Pontus crew leave.

A pit in Kaimi's stomach grew.

Why would they do this? How could the gods punish them like this again?

~ Chapter Eighteen ~

Michael kept his footing as the door slammed behind him and the others. They were in the lab, and without so much as a word, guards appeared and all but dragged them to this room. "Alister. Jayden. Karianne." He distinguished the three, for as angry and as bad as he felt, they looked worse. "What's going on? What's happening?"

"What happened to the Pontus?" Karianne asked. "Where is the captain?"

"Is everything okay?" Jayden demanded.

"They wouldn't tell us anything." Alister responded through his frown.

"Why are we here?" Karen glanced around the room.

"Okay." Michael raised his hands to try to gain some kind of control and order. "One at a time." He kept his hands up to quiet everyone and stop all the rapid-fire questions. "The Pontus has been attacked by a group of whales and a..." he shook his head, the words coming from his mouth were insane. "And what we think is a giant squid." Alister, Jayden, and Karianne all glowered at him. "The king is sending out his warriors, but before we were brought here, the situation on the Pontus didn't..."

"The Pontus is gone." Rochelle gulped as the words hung in the air. "There is no way the sub survived... not that kind of attack." She dropped to the chair next to her.

"But the crew." Karianne stood. "The captain."

"We don't know anything." Karen's voice raised as she spoke. "The king and his people are going to go out there—"

"Doubtful." Jayden snapped, his words filled with bile. "They are going to let them all die."

"What?" Michael shook his head. "They are sending out their people and they are going to help Bob and..." he turned to Rochelle, "We don't know about the Pontus yet. We have to have faith."

"God, this is all our fault." Jayden glanced at Alister and Karianne.

"We didn't know this would happen." Karianne countered. "I should have never let the two of you talk me into this."

"Hey. Don't act all innocent." Alister glared at her. "You were part of this whole thing since the tour."

"And look how that turned out." Jayden shook his head. "We're gonna die, and for what?" He rested his head on his hand as he massaged his temples. "So much for grad school."

"Will someone please explain why we are all here now under lock and key... Jayden?" Karen focused on her intern. "Please. What the heck happened?"

He shook his head.

"Alister." Michael continued to watch the young man. "What happened?"

Alister glanced at the floor. "We had nothing to do with Kai Malina's death. No matter what the king and your boyfriend tell you."

"What?"

"Death?"

"Kai Malina's dead?" Michael questioned, taking a step closer to Alister.

"We took one of their energy crystals and some other stuff; pearls and jewelry, nothing we suspected they would miss, especially with all the stuff we saw on the tour with Noe." Alister paced back and forth.

"What are you doing?" Karianne demanded as she stood up. "Are you trying to get us into even more trouble?"

"None of this matters now." Alister faced her. "They're going to find out, and I would rather tell them the truth now before they hear whatever story Koa and the others fabricate about us."

"He's right." Jayden's words softened, as did his stance.

Karianne's lips pinched together. "Fools."

"You stole from them?" Michael demanded an answer as everything slowly came together in his mind. "Why?"

"When we return," Alister scowled at him, his voice raising as he spoke. He found his seat again. "you're gonna dump me! All those things you said you were going to do for me will be forgotten. Assuming you even go home." He glanced around, making eye contact with everyone but Michael. "I've seen you and Kaimi." Alister got up and moved to the window. "I know how this plays out, and I didn't want to be empty-handed. I'm not like you. I have people who depend on me, even if they don't give a shit about me…"

"Jayden, how could you?" Karen shook her head.

"Their crystals are a massive energy source," Jayden began. "If we can study them and figure out how, think of all the good we can do. A world no longer needing oil, or coal, or any of that." He licked his lips and implored with his hands outstretched.

"But they caught us." Karianne's words came out harsh. "And they think we killed their… their… whatever they are. Kai Malina."

Michael rubbed his head. There were so many things happening and he wasn't sure he heard any of the conversation, or words, correctly.

"My god." Rochelle rubbed her forehead. "You're gonna get us all killed, if you haven't already sealed our fate." She quickly scanned the room. "This isn't like at home. We don't know how their laws work and what their punishments are going to be. You three may have ended us."

Michael sniffed. He didn't believe their situations would be as bad as all that. But Dr. Farmin may be correct, they didn't know their laws or know their justice system.

This is insane.

Michael rubbed his head as the room dissolved into voices speaking over each other, as everyone tried to be heard and explain their situation and their point of view. All he knew for sure was the mini sub was still out there, the Pontus was, at least as far as they were aware, still under attack, Kai Malina was now dead, and Alister and his group stole from Mu and were suspected of killing Kai Malina. He couldn't listen to everyone any more, he needed a minute. Michael spotted Alister over by the window, no longer talking, and moved to him and took his arm to get his attention.

"I need to know why." Michael's voice was low.

"I've only ever had myself. You come along and make all those promises, take me to a fancy party, offer me a new job, and bring me here." He licked his lips. "You... and him... and..." He waved his hands around. "I can't compete. I did what I deemed I needed to do. To make sure I would be okay and so I would still be able to take care of my shitty family."

Michael closed his eyes and shook his head. "Listen to me, and I need you to really hear me. I've been where you are. Hell, I was way worse than you." He forced what he hoped to be a reassuring smile. "I wouldn't have dumped you to the side like some piece of trash. I made you a promise like Tom made to me. I... Alister. I should have never shown any interest in you and I'm sorry. Tom. He made helping me seem so easy. He never once did anything to make me think there would be more between us, and I didn't do that for you." Michael raked a hand through his hair. "God, I fucked this up. When we get home...and we will get home. I know you didn't hurt anyone. Murder isn't you. I'm completely sure. So, my offer to you stands." He met Alister's gaze. "Sharon already had the paperwork ready, along with the offer letter. As for Kaimi..." Michael huffed out a laugh and shook his head.

"Why?" Alister asked.

"You're my family. Sharon's my family. Tom was my family. I don't have any other relations, so I make my own and I like to think I pick well. Why did you take the items from Mu? That..." He shook his head. "Your escapades don't matter right now. We'll sort this out."

Alister nodded.

"But I need to know." Michael glanced at the others, everyone lost in their own conversation. "I don't care what the answer is, cause we'll sort all this out. But did you have anything to do with Kai Malina?"

"God! No!" Alister yelped out each word. "We weren't anywhere near them. The guard caught us on our way here." He gulped. "I couldn't even look at them." Dampness circled Alister's eyes. "You should have seen them. The gash in their chest, all the blood." He inhaled and his face paled again. He took several more breaths.

This is not the face of a murderer.

"I've got you." Michael rubbed Alister's shoulders. "We'll sort this out."

*****

Kaimi paced the king's quarters as the rest of his family assembled in silence, except for the sounds of the bay outside and his own pacing, there was nothing. The noise was a reminder of all they had lost and all their failings. Seeing the lifeless body of Kai Malina was enough to have them all dancing on the rim of the abyss. And their death did not help his mood, seeing Michael and the others locked up, even though there was no way for any of them to have done this. He didn't believe Alister or his group were capable of such a thing.

Whoever did this knew more than any of their guests ever would.

"We can't keep them locked up forever." Ulani's voice broke the sounds of pacing and the sea. "None of this is what Mother and Father would have wanted, and I doubt these people had anything to do with what happened back then. If you haven't noticed, none of them can pass for a citizen of M—"

Koa cut her off with narrowed eyes and a furrowed brow.

"The four of us is all we have left." Ulani crossed her arms over her chest. "Don't fall back into your old habits. We all suffered today and we're here trying to help."

"Don't you think I know?" Koa's voice was loud enough to drown out the lapping water outside his rooms. "I'm sorry." He waved his hand in their direction.

"The Pontus has been destroyed and the only people who survived the attack from Kanaloa's beasts have been locked up with the others." Kaimi sighed. "And as requested, Bob, the mini sub, has been secured. But to what end?"

Koa ignored him.

"At least let me go and speak to them." Kaimi suggested.

"Speak to him, you mean?" Koa didn't bother looking at Kaimi. "Has he hypnotized you with his large pike?" He sneered at Kaimi.

Ulani raised a hand to Kaimi, ignoring Koa. She got up from the lounge she rested on and crossed to Koa, sitting next to him. "These new people are now our people. You must treat them as such." She rested a hand on his. "We cannot lock them up indefinitely."

"Can't I?" Koa snapped at her. He focused on his hands. "They killed our sibling."

"Not all of them." Kaimi reminded. "Not Michael or Karen. Not the captain." He pointed at them respectively, adding, "And I'm not so sure Alister or anyone in their group killed Kai Malina."

Koa raised his head. Kaimi felt the weight of his stare.

"Brother, you saw them." Kaimi reminded Koa. "no blood on their clothing, no weapon, a weapon the guards still have not found. Plus, the wound was equal to the one we found on Mother and Father." Kaimi moved to his brother and sister, kneeling before him. "What are the odds? Plus, we've seen death and battle. Do those three look as though they have seen death, let alone taken a life?" He shook his head.

"You think they are innocent?" Koa faced Kaimi.

"Far from innocent." Kaimi nodded, a deep frown twisting his lips and expression. "They are thieves and must be dealt with, well, Alister, Jayden, and Karianne. But the others..." again he shook his head.

Koa nodded at Kaimi before facing Nohealani. "You've been quiet. Have you nothing to say?"

The frown on her lips completed the mood her red puffy eyes had started when they found Kai Malina. She inhaled. "If they did not kill Kai Malina, who? Why?" She shook her head. "Those people would have no reason to kill. They know they would have been caught. There is nowhere for them to go. No place to hide."

"But they didn't know." Koa countered. "Not about the Pontus until we told them."

Nohealani nodded. "Still, they were after our riches, nothing more."

"Nohealani's right." Kaimi glanced at the ceiling, the sparkle catching his eye. "Something has bothered me about the murder. Killing

Kai Malina doesn't serve them, or get them any additional technology or crystals."

"What if Kai Malina caught them?" Ulani asked with an uncertain glance between them.

"They were in a different part of the palace. The guard reported as much. They might have come from the Great Hall, but that is a long way to get to their quarters." Nohealani added. "We've all taken the paths, and there are much faster ways, even for newcomers, who are not familiar.

"But what if...what if Kai Malina knew something?" Kaimi offered. "Found out who killed Mother and Father. Found out who used the pulse weapon. What if they were caught, not by Kai Malina but another, who used them to cover their own wake?"

"And you think Kai Malina might have been coming to tell us? To tell you?" Ulani asked with a firm nod of her head toward Koa.

Koa rubbed his mouth with his hand.

"The Great Hall is on the way to the meeting rooms and there are ample places to slip out, as we all know too well." Nohealani added, strength filling each of her words. "However, that is a lot of 'what ifs', and would have taken forethought with an understanding of the palace and all the inner workings."

"Someone from within." Kaimi sucked in a mouthful of air. "Not one of us, we can all be accounted for at the time, but who? Noe?" He shook his head.

"Mana Lani." Koa's voice and tone were almost a laugh. "Perhaps Timu, your body attendant, or Dr. Latu, or Alanah, maybe Kelii, perhaps Nana. Or any of our guards."

"Brother." Kaimi chided. "Do not mock."

"There is no reason for any of our people to do such a thing." Koa stood and walked to the window, glancing out. "But the more we talk, the more I don't see the logic in the above worlders doing this. Maybe there is someone else here, but for what reason?"

"We all have reasons." Kaimi stood and walked next to his brother. The afternoon light was waning, the waters in Faga Bay grew more active as the Torokina River slowed. "Look what we did. We fought for years, and we had reasons; good reasons or so we believed. Our *good* reasons cost many lives." He rested a hand on his brother's shoulder. "Do not underestimate the power of faith and our own prejudices."

Koa glanced at Kaimi. He glanced around the hall before sparing a glance over his shoulder at Nohealani and Ulani. His lips pulling together in a tight line. "I have much to think on."

Kaimi nodded.

We all do.

"However," Koa added. "I believe you should go to our guests and speak with them."

"What?" Kaimi asked.

"Are you questioning your king?" Koa offered a weak smile. "Go to him. Of two things, I am now certain. One being the above worlders did not kill Kai Malina, and the other is trying to keep you from Michael and the others." He pointed in the direction of the doors and the others. "Please be mindful of what you say. I may not believe they had anything to do with Kai Malina, but that doesn't mean they are blameless."

Kaimi nodded. "Thank you."

*****

Karen walked to the doors of the rooms they had all been shut in for hours, giving the handles another pull.

"No matter how many times you try the doors, they aren't going to open." Dr. Chen followed Karen as she stalked through the double doors. "I can't believe you three." She faced Alister, Jayden and Kari-anne."

"How many times do we have to apologize?" Jayden huffed.

"And before any of you ask. We didn't kill Kai Malina." Alister's voice bounced around the space.

"What? You want a medal for not being a murderer?" Tony glared at him. "They are my people and to disrespect them like this, after all they have done for us." He shook his head.

"Oh, good lord," Karianne countered. "Your people. You've only known them for what, a week? You have no more in common with them than any of us do."

"Bitch." Tony spat at her.

"Enough!" Karen shouted at the doors; she couldn't take this.

"Sorry." Tony and Karianne responded in unison.

"We're all sorry." Alister added.

"Well sorry isn't good enough." Captain Abbas turned and faced the three, who sat together and at a distance from the rest. "While our sub got attacked, you three decided to go looting." She clapped her hands on the side of her legs.

"Captain." Commander Levy's voice came out calm. "What they did or didn't do isn't going to change anything. What happened..." She shook her head.

"We don't know what happened," Ensign Bianchi responded. So much was in question now. "Because of them, who knows if the king pulled his people or if they did the attack in retribution. They haven't told us anything since they marched us here."

"That isn't how events played out." Michael pulled himself from the window. "Everything happened at once. We heard the first set of alarms and rushed to the lab. We watched the attack on the Pontus. The alarms blared again and now we are here." He raked a hand through his hair. "I doubt, once they have time to think about all the events and the timeline, they will continue to believe Alister, Jayden, and Karianne had anything to do with Kai Malina."

"Michael's right." Dr. Farmin nodded in Michael's direction. "We were all in a meeting, so there is nothing to worry about. The truth and the details will sort themselves out."

"I wish I had your faith." Captain Abbas moved to the bed, sitting on the edge, the French undertones of her words thicker since she returned from the Pontus, and learning of its destruction. "If we would have known about the attack, we could have taken Bob and rescued the others."

"We would have all died trying." Mason countered. "Bob going against three whales and a giant squid... there is no way."

"I blame myself." Karen glanced around the room. This group. Everyone left from the Pontus. All the risks they took. All because of her. Out of almost 50 people, this small group remained; Dr. Chen, Jayden, Mason, Tony, Karianne, Bianchi, Levy, Abbas, Michael, Dr. Farmin, Alister and her.

Twelve people.

She shook her head. "I should have thought more. We should have been better prepared. I was so sure of myself, of everything, and look where we are." She tried the doors again. "I didn't even think to bring an expert on Polynesian culture with us... how stupid is that?" She banged a hand on the doors.

"Karen, none of us anticipated any of this." Michael's words came out gently as he tried to offer her some comfort, which she appreciated.

"In all my years." Captain Abbas added, "I've never heard of an attack on a sub, not by any sea creatures."

"What about the Greenpeace sub that got attacked by a giant squid in 2014?" Mason glanced around the room.

"What?" Michael asked.

"A two-person sub and everyone survived," Karen retorted, possibly harder than she needed.

"Still, they don't know why," Mason added with a glance around the group.

"Probably the lights or something similar." Commander Levy offered. "Still, nothing has ever attacked anything as large as the Pontus, and even if there is a rogue monster squid out there, how do we explain the whales?"

"Maybe the ship's sonar." Dr. Chen offered, tapping her fingers on her crossed arms. "We know sonar can affect various sea life and has even killed some."

"But could our sonar really do such a thing?" Michael asked for clarification. "I mean, is what we're suggesting even possible? Could our sonar cause the attack, and if so, why hasn't this kind of attack happened to other subs out there? Or ships? This doesn't make any sense to me."

The doors to the rooms opened causing Karen to fright and step away.

"Michael, sonar wouldn't cause whales and a giant squid to attack the Pontus," Captain Abbas huffed again, her French accent harsh to Karen's ears. "The idea... no, we would have seen this kind of attack happen before now."

Kaimi stepped into the space and glanced around at the group. "What's this about sonar and the whales and squid?"

"Nothing." Michael shook his head.

"A theory." Captain Abbas offered.

"We're trying to figure out why the Pontus got attacked." Karen offered, since the others weren't presenting an explanation. "Not to discount this new attack wasn't done by your gods." She added quickly.

"Years ago, Noe and I were studying different sound waves, and how they affected the... our..." He stopped. "we call them Manō hae or Fire Sharks. To keep them from attacking us when we go out to sea. We included the technology in our suits. These devices are especially helpful when the creatures are spawning near the mouth of the gods."

"And this technology possibly may be used on other animals, to attract them?" Karen asked. "to cause them to attack?"

Kaimi shook his head, "Why would someone what to do such a thing?"

"Why indeed?" Michael asked, with a frown on his face.

"Why are you here?" Captain Abbas called the room to focus. "*Merde.* Are you here to accuse us of something else?"

"Susan." Karen admonished, both with her tone and a strong glare. "Despite everything happening, your remark is uncalled for."

"No. She's fine." Kaimi's voice remained neutral and offered what he hoped to be a reassuring glance at the group. "I'm here on behalf of the king—"

"They're going to kill us," Jayden called out. His voice was almost a scream.

"Is that true?" Karianne asked, strain pulling at each of her words.

"You can't." Dr. Farmin announced. "Not without due process, we are protected under international law."

"Everyone, please." Karen raised her hands. "Let's hear what the prince has to say, before we freak out."

Please be good news. Please be good news.

"Thank you, Dr. Linn." Kaimi nodded toward her. "Based on what we know to be true, we do not believe any of you were responsible for Kai Malina's death..."

"I knew they would see reason."

"Dieu merci!"

"Does this mean we can get out of here?"

"However," Kaimi continued, "Alister, Jayden and Karianne were still caught stealing and theft, even though a lesser crime, is still a crime. We cannot allow you the free access you had before. I'm sorry."

"We're still stuck here?" Alister peered around the room they occupied.

"What about the rest of us?" Dr. Farmin inquired.

"We are asking you to remain here for now." Kaimi raised a hand to hold off an objection. "But if you need to leave or wish to go out, you will need to be escorted by one of our guards."

"Well, that's better than nothing." Michael inhaled.

Karen noted his polished public speaking smile, hoping for the best, but the room erupted into chatter as everyone began speaking to each other.

"May I speak with you, Dr. Linn and Captain Abbas, please?" Kaimi requested as everyone stopped talking almost as quickly as they started.

"Just you four?" Dr. Farmin asked, focusing on the prince.

"For the moment, yes." Kaimi pointed to the doors. "If you will."

Karen studied the group and offered nods of assurance. The group moved to the doors and out into the hall. The guards stayed at the entrance as they moved out of earshot.

"What's going on?" Karen asked.

"Your theory about the sonar is interesting. I'm going to speak to my brother, but that isn't what I want to speak of right now."

"Okay." Michael examined everyone as Kaimi spoke.

"Karianne is under your command Captain Abbas, as is Jayden under yours, Dr. Linn and Alister falls to you, Michael." Kaimi began.

"I cannot say what the king will decide to do as punishment; however, we do not lock up criminals like you do; in the old days we would remove a hand of a thief, or exile them to the Mouth of The Gods, but those punishments don't happen anymore; most of the time, the criminal will pay fines or provide a service for a certain amount of time."

"They won't be able to leave?" Karen asked. "You can't keep them here... can you?"

Kaimi didn't answer.

"There must be something we can say or do?" Michael asked.

"They're young. They made a mistake; everything has been returned." Karen added. "Don't those actions count for something?" She looked at the captain. "What do you think?"

"If we were on the Pontus, I would throw them in the brig and deal with them once we got home, but here." She sighed, her accent more or less back to normal. "Mu is their home and their laws hold. I don't see us as having a choice, since we are probably going to be stuck here as well."

"For now, I thought I should tell you what is happening and let you know the king still hasn't decided how to handle the punishment." Kaimi offered, giving them all a slight head tilt. "I will do what I can to steady his response, as will my sisters, but understand we have more important concerns before us."

"Understandable." Karen agreed, but still so much happened out of their control, the least of which was the murder. What more was going to happen to them? Were they ever going to get home? Was going home what she wanted? "Thank you."

"I'll come and speak to you again soon." Kaimi reached for Michael, before pointing to the double doors. "For now, this will be the safest place for all of you."

Karen sighed as their host left.

Well, at least no one is on the hook for murder.

The doors closed and locked behind her once they had all stepped in.

~ Chapter Nineteen ~

The ghastly images from all those years ago flowed in front of Kaimi's eyes as he watched the screen. He had assumed, wrongly so, most of the information from his parents' death had been lost. But Noe over the years had been able to rebuild the files. Not all, but some.

"There." Noe pointed.

"What?" Koa leaned in, focusing on where Noe indicated.

"I don't see anything." Kaimi squinted his eyes.

"The figure off to the side." Noe zoomed in on the dark figure. Pointing to the rest of the screen. "There you are." They pointed to the figure of Koa. "There are Nohealani and Kaimi over the bodies of your parents." Their voice softened. "And this other figure..." They tapped the display.

"They are hidden in the darkness." Koa huffed. "They are in shadow, and unless you have some technology to clear up the image, we can't see them."

"I've done all I can with the image; what we see now is the best I have." Noe typed a few buttons. "However, look here." A new image filled the screen.

"The same image?" Kaimi commented as the same shrouded figured hid in the darkness.

"This is from two days ago." Noe glanced between Kaimi and Koa, their eyes narrowing and their features hardening with what appeared to be frustration or anger. "See, the same person? They are in the same hiding place." They zoomed the image out. "See, Alister, Jayden, Karianne, and all of you, including the guards."

"They discerned where to hide because they had done this before." Koa nodded.

"And like before, they did not think they would be seen on the surveillance."

"Why don't we have their image as they killed Kai Malina?" Koa faced both Noe and Kaimi.

"They understood enough to corrupt those files. Hoping the newcomers would be framed." Noe nodded.

"And since they got away with the attack before, why not use the same tactics?" Kaimi shook his head, his blood beginning to boil, as heat filled his chest and neck. They had gone over every detail the last two days when they weren't saying goodbye to Kai Malina. He had presented the sonar idea to Koa and Noe, and both seemed as surprised at the concept as he was. Several of their technicians had been on the Pontus, so if something was placed there they would never know, with the vessel now destroyed. Regardless of the mounting evidence, Koa still wouldn't allow Michael and the others out of the guest quarters on their own, but now the decree was more for their own safety, and given his conversation with Karen and the rest, everyone understood, or at least did not resent the idea.

"We are looking for someone who has unhindered access, now and back when the king and queen were murdered." Koa mentioned. "And who understands the soundwave technology, at least enough to have affected the vessel and the animals?"

"Unless you still believe the gods were involved?" Kaimi offered.

Koa's lips pinched tight.

"I'm not saying the gods weren't involved, but perhaps they had some help." Kaimi amended. "Still, the list is short." Kaimi glanced at Noe. "Including Mana Lani."

This time, instead of Koa mocking him for such a suggestion, he nodded.

"We need proof. We can't accuse anyone of such a thing. We learned our lesson." Koa huffed as he glowered between Kaimi and Noe.

Kaimi's gaze dropped from his brothers. *Yes, too many mistakes have already been made.*

"Is it possible?" Kaimi questioned. "Kai Malina used the pulse the first time and again on the Pontus, perhaps, they did this and this person tried to stop them?"

Noe shrugged. "Any of the royal family may have done such a thing, but who is the person who stopped them? Why do so in the shadows? And how would this explain how one of our sound devices got on the ship?"

"Maybe they modified the suit, not needing a device?" Kaimi asked.

"No." Noe shook off the suggestion. "None of our people were on the vessel; we secured the ship enough to not need to leave any of our suits behind. They would need one of our devices."

"Why would Kai Malina do this?" Koa asked. "They have nothing to gain."

"They were against getting involved with the above worlders from the start. Kai Malina never wanted them here, fearing we would turn from the gods."

"Some don't need help to turn from the gods." Noe stated as they glanced at Kaimi.

"I've not turned from the gods. I don't believe they control our lives to the extent we give them credit for."

"Kai Malina would never harm anyone." Koa added, ignoring the side conversation. "You should have seen them during the conflict."

"Not unless they believed they were working for the gods," Kaimi added. "Kai's faith is one thing we can all agree on; since Kai Malina was selected to be our next Māhū their whole life changed."

Kai Malina would fight for our gods, and if they judged they were doing what the gods wanted, there is no telling what they might be capable of.

Koa and Noe nodded their agreement.

"Who knows about all this?" Koa asked, peeking around the room, seeing only the three of them.

Noe shook their head. "The three of us. No one else. Not even the other members of my team."

"Good." Koa nodded, a whisper of a smile finding his lips.

"What are you planning, brother?" Kaimi asked, unsure how worried he should be. A tremble started in his shoulders and rushed down his back.

"You'll see." Koa offered no more and walked out of the lab.

"The king clearly has a plan." Noe commented as they glanced at the controls and the displays.

"Agreed." Kaimi nodded, a pit forming in the bottom of his stomach.

I hope we have a well-conceived plan.
*****

"What's going to happen?" Michael peered out the window at Mu. Kaimi had come with an offer to take him for a walk. Other than a few looks from Karen and Alister, no one cared, which was fine. Plus, since Kaimi's first visit, the guards had given the group a lot more freedom, like when they first arrived. Mu hadn't changed. The city with gold roofs and white stone walls stretched out like something from a dream. Especially as the lights sparkled, even the top of the sky, or cave ceiling sparkled. The sounds of water washed over him as the sweet scent of lemongrass and saltwater found his nose.

"I'm not sure," Kaimi admitted as they continued their walk. "The king has a plan, but is keeping the details to himself."

"Never let them see your next move." Michael nodded.

"I suppose." Kaimi stopped and leaned against the banister. "At times like this everything seems normal. The noises from the market and the bay. Children running about. Everyone preparing for the end of their day, getting ready to see their families and return home." He faced Michael. "These moments are few, but nice."

"I can see why you are all so protective of this place."

"What is your life like? What about your home? Family? Friends?" Kaimi asked as he relaxed more into the railing.

Michael glanced out, an ache tugged at his heart. "Nothing like this." He pointed around the space, ending on the window and the view outside. "I mean, don't get me wrong. San Jose is nice, but not like this, and my work... well, you know what I do, or what I used to do, but running things and being the boss isn't as exciting as people might think. There are a lot of meetings. Especially with my legal folks." He shook his head.

If we get home how much time will be spent with my legal people? This trip will continue to cost me long after we get home.

"Do you enjoy the work?"

Michael faced the ceiling, then chuckled before answering, "Some days."

"What about your family and friends, are you close?" Kaimi leaned in enough so Michael felt the heat from his bare chest.

Michael turned away, the ache in his heart grew larger. "I don't have a family, not like you. My mom died when I was young, and I never knew my dad. Anyway, I lived on the streets, doing what I needed to do to survive." He turned to face Kaimi, wanting to bask in his warmth forever. "I became a *body attendant*, as you say. None of the choices I had to make were easy, but I grew up and I met Tom." His heart lifted at the memory. "I think Tom was the first person who honestly cared about me. He made me finish school, get a degree, and he taught me everything about the business. When he died, I carried on." He shook his head, forcing the tears threatening his eyes away, "I hoped to pay his kindness forward with Alister, but..."

"We all make mistakes. That's how we grow and learn."

Michael's heart and mood lightened. Speaking with Kaimi didn't feel forced. Conversation had been easy and comforting.

"I wouldn't worry about Alister or the others." Kaimi reassured. "Koa is many things, but he is not heartless. He will take all things into account."

"I wish we..."

"What?" Kaimi leaned closer.

"Honestly, I wish we never found this place," Michael admitted. "Don't get me wrong, this place and you are amazing, but now..." He shook his head. "If we're stuck here, at some point people will come looking for us, and if we return with news of this place..."

"The world will change for both of us and our people," Kaimi offered.

"And the changes won't be for the good." A frown pulled at Michael's lips.

"No. I suppose not." Kaimi glanced out at the city before him. "My parents wanted us to join the world above. I did too, but now..."

"Careful what you wish for..." Michael sighed. "No matter what we do now, we won't be able to put this genie back in the bottle."

"Perhaps." Kaimi agreed. "Maybe this brave new world won't be too bad. I wouldn't mind seeing your city and where you live. Some of the images we've seen are glorious, and to be out in the sun again is something I would love to experience."

Michael shifted his head and faced the cave's ceiling, "The sky is something to be seen, as are the stars and the moon."

~ Chapter Twenty ~

The great hall filled with not only various servers and performers from Mu, but with the council of Elders, several guards, and Karen, Michael, Dr. Farmin and Captain Abbas, who were to represent the survivors of the Pontus. The idea that the whole team had not received an invitation annoyed Karen. What were they hiding? Or afraid of? But they didn't have a choice in the matter and given that Jayden, Alister, and Karianne still hadn't been punished, or tried for stealing, left them no grounds for an argument. Still, the chamber was a sight to behold, as the walls continued to sparkle with crystals, as the bioluminescent veining throughout made the space glow. The air was heavy with the low hum of conversation and, for Karen and the rest of their people, worry. Three days had passed since the murder and with little to no news as to what their future held. In the morning they were escorted to the hall for an audience with the king and the council.

And here we are.

"What do you think is going to happen?" Karen leaned over to speak to Michael, the pounding in her head only matched by the low beating of the drums.

"I'm not sure."

"Kaimi didn't say anything to you last night?" She bit at her lower lip, wishing she had her lip balm with her.

"Well, that's not helpful."

"No, sorry." Michael peeked around the chamber. "Do there seem to be more guards here?" He continued with a huff, raking his hand over his face. "They have all the exits covered. Why the show of force?"

Karen's gaze followed Michael's. There were definitely way more guards present than at any other time before. "Interesting. And Kaimi mentioned nothing to you?" She exhaled as they waited. Her hand tapping her leg lightly in time with the thumping of the performer's drum beat.

"I don't think he knew either, but..." Michael shook his head, his focus now on the throne and the raised polished floor underneath.

Near the throne, the drummers started beating louder, filling the space with a steady rhythm as the royal family entered. The last member to appear was Koa, and he took a seat on the hand carved throne that had been embedded with crystals, polished shells and fish bones. The throne appeared to be an interpretation of a whale or large undersea mammal. He was dressed much like he was the night of the welcome ceremony; he was in all white with embedded crystal on his lava lava. His chest was bare, similar to Kaimi's; however, unlike Kaimi, Koa had several tattoos speaking of his accomplishments, highlighted by the polished crystal and bone necklace. On his head rested his crown, and in his hand he held the ruling staff. He looked every bit the king and leader of these people.

Even more guards entered with the family, taking up additional stations throughout the great hall.

"I address you all in the language of our guests." Koa nodded at the group from the Pontus. "The murder of Kai Malina has taken a great toll on all of us." He began addressing the various people in attendance. "Not since the battles after the death of the queen and king have we seen this kind of brutality, and I must ask myself, are the gods punishing me and my family?"

There were murmurs from the council of elders.

"I'm calling forward Mana Lani who can, hopefully, provide us with the wisdom of the Gods." Koa stood and pointed his staff toward the shadows where the old woman stood. She moved forward approaching the group, the shadows around her managing to hang onto her every move before giving up to the light. She too stood adorned in whites with patterned stitching catching the glow of the light.

Karen figured Mana Lani had a few years on her, but still moved with grace and purpose. She held herself with the presence of any priest or priestess Karen had ever seen. There was always an aura of assuredness around such people, similarly, she supposed as a teacher or a professor. Even so, seeing the woman and how she walked, Karen never considered herself old, until she observed people her age, or a bit older, and realized how others must view her. This insight was always a shock to the system. Still Karen understood, you never underestimated people, especially older people, and chiefly people who had spent their whole lives teaching, or in this case providing insight or wisdom.

"How can I serve the king on this most terrible of days?" Mana Lani spoke with a reverence that didn't make its way to her eyes. The woman's gray hair appeared to be the softest thing about her. The strands pulled up in a loose bun with several orchid flowers placed around, but even the flowers didn't offer her any tenderness.

"Tell me, have the gods spoken to you in recent days?" Koa asked. He watched her carefully, almost as if watching a snake waiting for the creature to strike. "Have Ku or Kanaloa said anything more? Since the events leading to the destruction of the Pontus, and the murder of Kai Malina?"

"I'm sorry." Mana Lani bowed her head. "Not since the night, so long ago, have the gods spoken to me. I've spent many hours in worship trying to reach them..."

"A shame." Koa glanced toward his brother and sisters before meeting each of the council of elder's gaze. Finally, he faced Karen and the others before looking at Mana Lani. "Would anyone be surprised if the gods spoke to me? I am the king of Mu, after all." He asked the older woman, but faced those assembled. "The Gods came to me in a vision."

There were gasps from those gathered. Even members of the royal family reacted in surprise by this news.

"What?" Mana Lani asked, clearing her throat. "Such glorious news." She added quickly to hide the clear surprise on her face.

"Indeed." Koa announced, his shoulders straight and his chest puffed out. "But imagine my surprise to learn the god who spoke to me wasn't Ku or Kanaloa." He addressed the council now. "Not even Hikule'o." He shook his head.

Karen's gazed narrowed on him.

A bit dramatic.

"The god to visit me was Milu." Several of the elders gasped, and Mana Lani took a few steps away and peeked to either side.

"The God of the Dead." Karen heard a younger man from the council say around in hushed tones.

She noted even the guards with the bulging muscles, pulsing veins in their necks, and their tighter stance, appeared caught off guard by this news.

"The God of the Dead?" Michael leaned in and asked Karen. His eyes were large and his lips a thin line.

"I thought they were supposed to be Kanaloa, but I'm not sure now." Karen kept her eyes on the king. "My Polynesian folklore isn't what one would hope," she added.

Plus, Mu is unique, so who knows? Still, I should have brought an expert with us. Stupid.

"We're cursed." Another council member squeaked near the Pontus group.

"Why is this so important?" Dr. Farmin leaned in, whispering to Karen.

"Whenever gods are involved, matters are always important." Captain Abbas responded to Dr. Farmin with a shaky voice.

Karen nodded. They weren't wrong. All the divisiveness religion has caused for the world above. Yes, there were good sides to faith, but how many wars have been fought for God? How many people have died in their name?

"And what did the Ruler of Lua-o-Milu say to you?" Mana Lani asked, finding her voice. She tried to project confidence, but the slight tremble was not lost on Karen or Koa from the looks of things.

"He showed me a great many things." Koa raised his hands. "I can assure you I wasn't ready to see or learn what they had to say, but I listened to their words." He started to pace back and forth along the raised platform. "He showed me who killed the queen and king... and who killed Kai Malina. I noted they were one and the same, and they may not be our guests from the above world."

"But the guards found them." Mana Lani countered, glancing around the chamber hall. "Found them fleeing this space."

"Are you questioning the gods?" Koa's voice raised. "And the vision they showed me?" He zoomed in on her.

"How did she know?" Captain Abbas asked in a hushed tone.

"I assumed..." Michael's words were more for himself than anyone else.

Mana Lani remained silent.

"Milu pointed out the wounds on the queen and king matched the wound on Kai Malina." Koa shook his head. "I asked how this can be possible? But the god was angry. Furious even, that I... that we...

had accused innocent people for such crimes." He pointed his staff at Karen and the others. "The God of the Dead does not like to be lied to or taken for a fool."

"Who killed them?" Kaimi asked as he stepped forward.

Karen's gaze turned toward Kaimi.

Why is he so stiff, his voice seems off, like he's reciting lines?

"I'm glad you asked, my brother." Koa faced his brother, then turned to the council and Mana Lani. "For this is the same question I humbly asked Milu," he acknowledged, his head bobbing up and down, "but they did not say. Only told me all would be made clear today. That He, Milu, would come before this council and point the finger at the one who did this to our family."

Cries and gasped filled the room as everyone, including Karen, glanced around the space looking for someone to appear.

"No!" Mana Lani called out. "The God of the Dead cannot come here. Such an event would curse us all."

"But they must, if we are to learn the truth." Koa countered and stepped toward Mana Lani. "We risk all of Mu. I understand this, but I don't know what more to do. Maybe the god will be placated if the criminal comes forward now." He waved his staff about the room waiting for someone to step forward, but he was met with more fear-filled mumbles and people grasping for their nearest loved one or neighbor. "No. Well, I begged Milu not to come, to show me who did this, but his anger was great and even my words and promises fell flat. I offered myself to him and the gods in exchange for the truth. To spare all of you, and our people."

The crystals cracked from every corner of the great hall as the lights flickered in and out. Even the bioluminescent features blinked on and off, appearing affected by what was happening around them all. Several bellows bounced around the chamber, two of the council members stood and appeared ready to run, but the guards stood their ground, keeping the panic and people in place.

"E noho ma kou wahi!" a male voice filled every corner of the hall.

"What the hell." Michael peeked around the chamber.

"Listen." Koa called out. "The voice of Milu. We must listen and stay where we are. I know fear is easy now, but we must hear him out. Or who knows what curse he will bestow on us."

The royal family stood their places, as did several members of the council. The guards moved in, closing a circle to protect the royal family.

"Hāʻawi wau iā ʻoe i ka mea kaua a ka mea pepehi kanaka!" A loud thud hit the ground as something skid across the floor, stopping at Koa's feet. Karen followed where the sound came from and spotted a figure shrouded in darkness.

"Milu?" Her voice gasped as several other people turned in the direction of where her gaze landed.

"I know that voice," Captain Abbas whispered.

"No!" Mana Lani called out. "How did you find the weapon?" She wasn't looking at the god, but at the crystal pike on the floor.

"You cannot hide from the gods, none of us can." Koa pointed to Milu standing in the darkness.

"I had no choice." Mana Lani begged, dropping to her knees. "I did what the gods needed me to do."

"The gods." Koa shouted and pointed between the shadow figure and Mana Lani. "Milu is one of our Gods. You're saying you did this for him?"

"The queen and king would have destroyed us," Tears began to flow from Mana Lani. "They would have brought the outsiders, the colonizers here and they would have destroyed us. Abolished our gods like their missionaries did to our sisters and brothers on the outside.

Replacing our Gods with theirs, killing us if we did not comply... but they would have destroyed us and Mu." She called out and tried to move to the shadow figure, but the guards stood their ground, not letting anyone leave. "I did this for our gods." Her head dropped.

"And what about Kai Malina and the pulse?" Kaimi demanded, his voice stronger again. He no longer sounded like a bad actor reciting barely memorized lines.

"They wanted to speak. They wanted to tell you," Mana Lani wept. "But I needed to keep them silent. We had done too much, risked too much to give up." She continued through her sobs. "We had to attack the outside world before they attacked us." She pleaded. "Milu forgive me. Hikule'o I did this for you, for all our people, and to keep you with us." Tears streamed down her face.

The room fell deathly silent as everyone listened to Mana Lani's confession. The lights had returned to normal and the voice of Milu fell silent. They watched the proceedings, but never stepped out into the light.

"You killed our parents!" Nohealani shouted, moving from the throne. "Sent out the pulse, caused a civil war, killed Kai Malina and endangered all of us... to protect us? You're insane." She rushed to the old woman. "How many people died? My husband died. These people..." she pointed to Karen and the others. "lost hundreds of thousands and you claim to have done this for the gods. No. You did this for yourself. To keep us living in fear. Keep us from growing and learning."

"You are no Māhū!" Kaimi glared at the weeping woman on the highly polished floor. "And I'm sorry we didn't see this sooner."

"Guards, remove her to the cells." Koa demanded and returned to his throne. "Milu, we thank you, lord of the underworld, for your help here today."

The lights flickered again, then nothing as the figure of the god vanished.

Several people continued to look around the hall, but most had relaxed and focused on Koa. "We cannot let fear guide us. You have seen what fear caused." He pointed to Karen and the others. "The harm we caused them and for what? The vision of the future my parents had, gone because of one person. One person who had the power to destroy so much because of their beliefs. We are better than this."

Again, the room filled with hushed voices as everyone focused on Karen and the others.

"Dr. Linn, Mr. Donovan, Dr. Farmin and Captain Abbas. I have no words." Koa offered a nod of his head. "What happened here today and, in the past, cannot be forgiven, but I hope you will not judge us too harshly. I have decided we will not punish those who stole from us. I believe they, much like all of us here today, are victims of a much larger crime, one I don't think we will ever be able to amend for."

"What will become of Mana Lani?" Dr. Farmin asked.

"I cannot say." Koa rested his hands on his staff. "But again, please do not judge us on her actions."

"No, we won't." Karen offered. "We're all human. We all make mistakes." She forced every ounce of forgiveness into what she hoped to be a sincere smile. "I'm only glad we found out what happened. I'm saddened by the loss of life and how many lives have been ruined." She didn't know what else to say and when she glanced at Michael and the others, none of them spoke, only nodded their support.

"Go now." Koa gestured to the assemble. "Tell the others of what happened here today. You are the Council of Elders for Mu. We must speak as one and ensure nothing like this happens again." He addressed the Elders. "Know the Gods continue to look out for us, even the ones we fear the most, and speak the least of." He glanced at his brother and sisters and, with a nod, they left the throne room as the drums began again and the space slowly cleared out.

Karen, Michael, Rochelle, and Susan headed to their rooms, followed by two guards.

"That was..." Michael started, but couldn't continue with the thought.

"Unbelievable." Captain Abbas finished, licking her lips. A shudder had filled the space between her words. "Why would one person cause so much death and destruction?"

"One person is all fear and hate need." Each word pulling from Michael's mouth dropped with the weight of cotton balls falling from their bag. "Look at what's happening all around the world right now." He continued. "Sadly, people need to fight this kind of evil, and we rarely see that happen these days. Most people fall in line, finding going with what's popular and easy versus what's right."

"Fear is a great motivator." Dr. Farmin offered.

"But fear of what?" Karen asked with a shake of her head. "The fear of the unknown? The fear of change? Fear of the 'other'? The Gods? Everyone is scared of something; how do you fight off fear?"

"They were able to fight fear off today," Michael stated. "Even if for a short time."

"And an appearance by a god is all they needed." Karen pushed the loose strands of hair from her face.

"I don't think the same trick would work for us." Dr. Farmin pushed her hands deep into her pockets.

"I think you're right, and sadly, I think we might even be worse." Karen closed her eyes, needing a moment.

*****

Michael picked at the plate of food before him. He had witnessed some impressive acts of subterfuge in his life, and today was quite possibly the best. He couldn't figure out why only Karen, Dr. Farmin and Captain Abbas were allowed to attend today and not the others, but once they returned to the room, joined moments later by Tony, did Michael understand. Koa had enlisted Tony's help to bring a voice to Milu, which made sense, because Tony was native Hawaiian. He easily brought an ancient god to life, especially since he didn't sound native to Mu, or sound like anyone they might have heard before. Plus, Tony's imposing figure didn't hurt either, especially since he was hidden in darkness.

They terrified Mana Lani to confess.

He couldn't say he approved, but this was not his home, and the choice was the king's and the royal family's. Who was he to question? He did wonder what would happen to Mana Lani. Koa didn't and wouldn't say.

"How're you doing?" Karen asked from the door, the glow from the room casting her in a bright aura of light, almost a goddess in her own right.

"We can't stay here, but I'm not sure we can go home either." Michael played with the piece of fruit he hadn't managed to eat in the five minutes since he picked the papaya up. "What are we going to do?"

"Ulani came by with a message." Karen walked into the room. "We'll be meeting with the king tomorrow. I'm guessing to talk about this very thing."

"And what do you think about... well, about all this?" Michael pushed his plate away.

"His plan worked." Karen took a seat at the table. "The captain whispered to me she recognized the voice and when Kaimi delivered his question..." she smiled. "I don't think he'll win an Oscar."

"No, probably not, but his performance did what needed to be done..." Michael acknowledged, "but the fear from the council. They won't forget this, and if they find out the god was Tony speaking..."

"I think they'll be fine." Karen glanced at Michael's half eaten plate and picked up a chunk of pineapple, or what Michael assumed was pineapple. "I witnessed what you saw, but I also noticed many were much angrier with Mana Lani, and all the pain she caused. I think a majority of the Elders were in on the deception, so using the gods she so valued against her worked."

"I hope so," Michael huffed. "But to use a god..." He shuddered. *That screams bad idea to me.*

"If we don't leave, what do you think you'll do?" Karen poured herself a cup of water from the pitcher on the table.

"Well, I doubt they'll need or want anything I have to offer. I'm a businessman and a porn star, so..." He shrugged.

"I know." Karen beamed at him. "You can start an acting class."

They both laughed.

"Seriously, I don't have much to offer a place like this." He shrugged.

Karen beamed and rested a hand on his arm. "That's not true." She sipped her drink. "I can think of at least one prince who might find what you have to offer appealing."

Michael smiled at her. One potential good thing if they had to stay in Mu. Kaimi would be here and they would get to see where things went between them. Maybe staying wouldn't be too bad after all. "What about you?"

Karen sat heavily in the chair and glanced out the window. "Oh, I'd have plenty to do. There's a lot to study and research. Think of all there is to learn here, plus living with these people and learning from them, what an opportunity."

Michael watched her. "I think you'll fit in here. This is everything you've ever wanted, well maybe not Mu specifically, but all this. And you can teach them a lot about us." He waved a hand around. "I would be lying if there wasn't an appeal to this place. Staying here would be a fresh start, for sure."

"And are fresh starts a bad thing?" Karen's gaze narrowed on him. He chuckled. "No. I suppose not."

~ Chapter Twenty-One ~

"Now what?" Kaimi asked as he studied those at the table, his hands placed on either side of him. They were in the small council chamber today to discuss the future—*all our futures*—. The breeze off the bay brought notes of saltwater and lemongrass to the meeting space. Another day had passed since Mana Lani had been found out and sent to the cells. His brother's plan impressed him, and even more so getting to play a small part in the deception. But he worried given everything they had at stake, there might be long-term ramifications with their people, especially when using Milu. However, they would deal with that later, and the reward far outweighed the risk. Also, Koa showed great kindness in forgiving the thievery from Alister and the others. "Our people are not yet ready for the world laying outside of Mu."

"Agreed." Koa rested on his side in the council chair. "Yesterday's performance proved some of the council are still not pleased with me, but they understand... now."

He spoke with the council. Good.

"We can't alter your people's knowledge about us." Michael leaned forward, his hands clasped in front of him, "But perhaps we can keep ours from finding out."

"There are too many of us," Captain Abbas countered. "Not to mention all our data from the Pontus and Bob. There are twelve people with twelve points of view. We have to keep quiet, and given what already happened with…" she waved her hand, not finishing her statement.

"We would need to come up with something that caused the Pulse," Dr. Linn mentioned with a firm nod. "Something either manmade or from nature." She glanced at the monitors, images of everything they learned from Mu displayed there.

They were quite thorough. I would have loved to explore the ship and review all the technology inside.

"Agreed." Dr. Farmin reached for her full cup of water and took a sip. "But something to ensure no one comes looking again until you are ready for us." She glanced over at Koa.

"Like UAPs or UOPs," Captain Abbas stated.

Michael shook his head.

"Except people are always looking for those." Dr. Linn countered. "We need something dangerous. Something no one would be willing to risk their life for."

"Sorry." Koa held up a hand. "What are UAPs or UOPs?"

"Unidentified Aerial Phenomenon, or their counterpart Unexplained Ocean Phenomenon." Dr. Linn offered a smile, brightening her face.

"Thank you."

"Well, what about a freaking giant squid?" Michael waved his hands about in an attempt to mimic the tentacles and the creature itself. "I don't think I'll be back in the water for a long time after seeing that thing down here. Who knows what else is lurking in the deep?"

"You mean other than us." Kaimi faced him, his lips pulling up in what he hoped to be a proper smile.

Michael's face warmed with hints of pink on his cheeks. "Other than Mu and you."

"What about something from World War II or something from the Cold War?" Dr. Farmin offered.

"Do you think all this will be wise?" Kaimi watched each of the people assembled. There were risks with any plan they came up with, and to think otherwise would be foolish. They would not be able to hide forever, no matter what they did or whatever lie they told. A truth his parents fully understood, and thank the gods, Koa had quickly come to realize, as did the others. "What if you go and claim there was an accident and say nothing more?"

Koa's gaze narrowed on him.

"That is not what I meant." Kaimi added. "I understand the shore will never be the same now that the waves have struck, but an elaborate lie is too complicated and often fails."

"There were a lot of secret, off the book projects in the 50s and 60s," Dr. Farmin mentioned. "And not just in the US, but from other countries as well. The best lies, and the easiest to keep straight, are the ones having the most amount of truth in them."

"Given the nature of the pulse weapon." Noe stood as they addressed the group. "Such an accident, or attack, would need to be something plausible." Noe offered and moved to the monitors to enter information.

"Such as..." Michael turned to face Noe and the monitors.

"An EMP weapon connected to one of your atomic weapons, something lost and finally went off—"

"Because of an earthquake." Koa suggested, "This region of the ocean has many."

Dr. Linn nodded her head. "But everything we experienced couldn't only be a weapon. Something being tested and abandoned or lost."

Several folks around the table indicated their agreement.

"But how do we keep others from coming and searching for the ship and, by extension, this place?" Dr. Farmin shifted her seat, so she faced the monitors and the others.

"How deep do your submarines go?" Koa leaned forward.

Captain Abbas contemplated a moment. "Currently, close to eleven thousand meters, but that was a single man in a single sub, and he was exploring the Mariana Trench." She inhaled. "A standard sub can go about nine hundred meters, but the Pontus was designed to reach eleven hundred meters, give or take, deeper if all systems were secured."

"So deep, but not too deep." Noe nodded. "A little less than our Manō hae suits."

"What about a research vessel?" Michael started. "Something from the Cold War. We weren't able to tell if the ship was US, Soviet, Chinese or who. Our radar found the ship and we moved in as an underwater quake hit, causing a pulse, hitting the Pontus and we evacuated." He shrugged.

"The idea is simple." Noe nodded.

"But what caused the first pulse?" Kaimi asked.

"An earthquake." Dr. Farmin responded quickly. "Perhaps the vessel still had power, atomic energy. Maybe the quake shifted the rocks, hitting the ship, launching the forgotten weapon."

"And after the last, smaller pulse, the blast caused the vessel to sink deeper and become destroyed, too deep for anyone to reach." Captain Abbas offered.

"Do you think anyone will believe our story?" Karen rested her chin on her hands. "I wish Dr. Thomas' works could be more help. It would be nice to vindicate some of his theories after all these years." Karen shook her head.

"Who?" Kaimi asked, "Another scientist on your team?"

"No." Michael sat back in his chair, stretching his head and neck. "He was a researcher from 50 plus years ago, and he was right about Mu, well, sort of right."

Karen's lips pinched together. "Regardless, the idea sounds like a bad plot to some Sci-Fi movie."

"I've heard and read worse." Michael shrugged.

"I have no doubt." Dr. Farmin faced Michael and smiled.

"We can easily create data to match the story," Noe offered from their place at the monitors.

"We can?" Koa asked with raised eyebrows.

"Making the changes and creating the files wouldn't be complicated, as long as we don't have to provide visuals."

"Actually, visuals would be extremely helpful." Dr. Farmin added.

"Can we provide visuals?" Kaimi glanced at Noe.

Noe scratched their forehead.

Over the next couple of hours, and a hardy lunch later, they had developed a cover story simple enough and matching the events of what happened to the Pontus, or match close enough. There were still details to work out and Noe, Dr. Farmin, Captain Abbas and Karen would have their hands full, ensuring all the data they offered couldn't be proven to be false. They hoped a combination of data and missing files, along with their first-hand accounts, would be enough to keep the plan intact for all their safety.

Kaimi wasn't so sure about the idea. When he glanced toward Michael, his expression mirrored his own worry. A lot needed to be sorted, and they would need twelve people to agree on one story.

How was this going to work?
*****

"There's our plan." Karen announced to the group of twelve, her voice taking on a tone of finality. She rubbed her lips together, ensuring they weren't dry. The presentation had been simple enough, and the details were clear and easy to remember.

This has to work.

"Dr. Linn, Karen, this is a lot." Jiang reviewed the images on the screen. "The data and readings all seem reasonable, but…" She shook her head.

"Dr. Chen, between the visuals, the data and our own history, we can make this work." Rochelle offered. "We kept everything as simple as possible."

"And what will you tell your bosses?" Michael asked.

"The same as all of you." Rochelle shrugged. "I don't like the idea of lying, but I like the idea of our military coming and attacking Mu, or stealing their weapon even less." She shuddered.

"Well, I don't see a problem with any of the geophysical fluid dynamics; plate tectonics or the geology of the sea floor," Mason offered, putting the report down. "The fluxes of various chemical substances and physical properties within the ocean and across its boundaries all seem in line…" He laughed. "clearly none of this was tampered with."

"Actually…" Karen beamed.

Mason glanced at the documents, adjusting his glasses. "But I… I didn't see anything out of order…" He faced the group.

"Don't feel bad." Dr. Chen smiled, "I didn't see anything either and I've been at this a lot longer than you."

"Okay, so we can fool two oceanographers, that doesn't mean we can fool the rest of the world." Commander Levy countered. "I mean, I look at these few images, and I see a ship, but I can't see enough of the wreck to prove anything."

"Which is the point." Captain Abbas acknowledged with a grin.

"We don't want the ship to look too familiar to one country or be overly recognizable." Rochelle added. "We need to be vague. We can't tell if the vessel is Russian, Chinese, American, British, French or older, from World War II era Japan or Germany."

"You want to blame them all." Bianchi nodded. "In order so none can be blamed."

"Everyone will want to blame the other, and each will come out with statements the ship couldn't be theirs," Rochelle stated to the group. "However, with nothing definitive, no one will push too hard, as a vessel similar to the one we created could realistically have been commissioned by any of them. They all had a reason, and they all had, or have, the capabilities."

"And with them all members of the Security Council in the UN, they would be at a stalemate." Karen added.

"And we're left being the only eyewitnesses." Jayden shook his head. "And what keeps us from talking? And telling the truth?"

Everyone faced him and he held up his hands.

"I'm not saying I will, but you have to think about this," Jayden added.

"For one." Michael stood up. "You all signed NDAs to be part of this venture, even Dr. Farmin. So, there is that." He leaned forward on the table. "And I have one hell of a legal team. Whatever any of you might make with your fifteen minutes of fame would be lost in one hell of a legal battle..."

"And we hope..." Karen glanced over at Michael, giving him a slight nod of her head. He returned to his seat. "Given what's at stake, and all the people who can be hurt, you would be willing to keep this quiet for the good of everyone."

"Relying on our better nature." Karianne sighed.

"And threats," Tony added.

"Given the nature of the world I live in," Michael said and rubbed his chin, "I have to be willing to use all the tools at my disposal. I'm sorry if these revelations offend people, but this is the truth of how we are going to make the plan work."

"And what's in this arrangement for us?" Alister tapped his hands on the table. "We're sitting on a gold mine here, and the plan is all fine and dandy for you, but this scheme doesn't help us. I'm sorry, but I'm being realistic here. We all have just as much to lose, if not more, given what wonders Mu holds for everyone, not just for us."

"Considering the king has offered to forgive your indiscretions, I would think and hope you would be willing to return the kindness." Karen inhaled as her gaze narrowed on him, but not leaving out Jayden or Karianne.

"You misunderstand me, Doc." Alister raised his hands. "I'm playing devil's advocate here. Michael's right, NDAs and threats of legal trouble are the stick, but what's the carrot?"

She frowned and glanced at Michael.

"Money." Michael's tone fell flat. "Plain and simple if any of you feel additional compensation is needed there would be money involved; I doubt any of you read your NDAs, but I would be pleased to learn if you did, there is a clause offering you all lifetime settlements for your silence."

"Hush money." Jayden nodded.

"And every year when you cash my check, you reaffirm your silence and if you break the contract, all moneys, future and already received, are forfeited and will need to be returned." Michael added.

"Jesus." Karianne shook her head.

"I told you." Michael glanced around the room, "I have one hell of a legal team...but as Karen mentioned already, we hope, as there are 75,000 lives and families here in Mu, you'll keep quiet until the world is ready to learn the truth."

"And when will that be?" Bianchi asked.

"I can't say." Karen offered. "Look." She raised from her chair, making eye contact with each of the people in the room. "We've given you all a lot to think about and to go over. I know this isn't going to be easy, and I get we are asking a lot. But given what we know and what we've seen, what choice do we have?" She held up her hand. "There is one option still on the table, and that is not leaving."

"What?" Several voices called out at once.

Michael nodded. "The king has offered to allow anyone to stay who wishes to stay, and you would be listed as MIA, your families or whomever you delegated would receive a onetime payment. And my organization wouldn't dispute any reasonable claim."

Karen smiled at him and he nodded. "For now, we're finished."

And the rest is in their hands.

*****

There were so many things Michael wanted to say, but time continued to march on, faster, it seemed. How do you say goodbye to someone who you barely know and never got a chance to spend time with? Michael imagined the tracks he had worn into the white stone floor.

This is stupid. I barely know him. I shouldn't be this nervous.

He inhaled deeply and broke from his pacing and headed to...

Where?

He would figure that out as he went. The palace had guards, and he was sure they would know where to find Kaimi. He doubted the prince would be here in the guest area, so Michael made his way down to the main hall, figuring he would ask the first guard he encountered. On the stairs he came to a hard stop face to face with Kaimi.

"Hi!" Michael exclaimed.

"Hello." Kaimi took a step forward. "I was..."

"I thought I would..." Michael paused as Kaimi started, and laughed. "Please go ahead."

"Well..." Kaimi glanced around the corridor and the space before him. "I came to see how things went this afternoon."

"Oh." Michael raked a hand through his hair. "Well, we laid out the options and now the choice falls to the individuals."

Kaimi nodded and browsed the hall. "Would you like to go for a walk?"

Michael's heart picked up and he nodded. "I would love to."

The two made their way down the corridor, past the great hall. Kaimi pointed out a library and several smaller rooms used for various functions. The palace was huge, but this place didn't feel cavernous. After being here less than a week, he managed to remember the locations to go, and what halls led to what areas. He was going to miss Mu and this palace, but he was also looking forward to getting home.

And out of the humidity.

Outside the palace they made their way to the edge of the bay, seeing a few small boats out as the waves crashed on the crushed stone and shells making up the white beach.

"This place." Michael browsed around, seeing the white and gold of the palace building. The gardens. The ponds, the city proper. All the people. "You are lucky to live here."

Kaimi smiled at him.

"I mean. I know you've had your problems and I'm sure there are a lot of things we would start missing if we were here longer, but still." Michael inhaled deeply, the salty air reminding him of Monterey and Carmel, all the places he loved at home. Walking along Cannery Row, visiting the aquarium. The food; especially the clam chowder. There was nothing like the Monterey Bay.

"Are you looking forward to heading home?" Kaimi broke the silence. The spell his memories had on him now ended.

"It's time to leave." Michael didn't fully answer the question. "If we miss our return date, there will be questions and people will come looking." He stuffed his hands into his pockets, unsure what to do with them.

"Noe and I have been monitoring your broadcasts, and they have not mentioned anything."

Michael nodded. "We won't be overdue for three more days. Even with our communications down. All to be expected and wouldn't have triggered any alarms."

"The small sub will get you to the surface, but not to shore." Kaimi stated with a glance over to the orangish-yellow vessel.

"And once on the surface, we'll send out the S.O.S." Michael picked up a small rock and tossed the stone to the bay. "I wish we got to know each other better." He shifted his stance to take in all of Kaimi; his broad shoulders, toned skin, bright eyes, and smile. He didn't have near the tattoos as many of the other men here in Mu. "I know this may sound silly, but..." he shrugged.

"You could stay?" Kaimi offered.

"If only." Michael stuffed his hands deeper into his pockets, somehow finding more space than possible. He may not be anyone overly important, but people counted on him and, yes, his company would go on without him, but no one would take care of his people, his family, like him. Plus, he would need to be topside to ensure Mu stayed hidden. There were eleven other stories with the potential of one getting out. He had to keep their misdirection and their collective deception in place. No, as much as he wanted to stay and explore this place, he couldn't. "If I stayed, who would ensure your world stayed safe?"

Kaimi glanced around. "Dr. Linn. Dr. Farmin...Captain Abbas."

"All capable, strong women who I trust with my life." He bit his lip to keep from frowning. "But they can't run my company, which we'll need to help stay in control of for any of this to work." He shook his head. "I have to go home. The four of us; Karen, Rochelle, Susan, and I all have to return for any of this to work. Plus, there is going to be a lot of clean-up, needing the assistance of my legal team and my money."

Silence filled the space between them.

Finally, Michael laughed, freeing his hands from his pockets, then rubbed his chin.

"What?" Kaimi asked.

"Sharon, my assistant at my office, if she got wind of any of this, she would kick my ass. She reminds me of your sister; Nohealani. Not someone to be trifled with."

"If this Sharon is like Nohealani then no definitely not." Kaimi leaned in. "Of all my siblings, she is the one I have always feared the most."

"Definitely like Sharon."

"Since you leave tomorrow," Kaimi offered, his voice softer and there were touches of pink around his neck and ears. "let me take you to the Crystal Caves. The spot is something you should see before you leave. Maybe seeing such a special place will help you remember Mu and me."

"I doubt I'll ever forget this place...or you." Michael countered as he beamed at Kaimi.

Kaimi reached out his hand. Michael took the offered hand as they made their way down the path by the bay and to the entrance of the large caves. As they moved deeper into the space, instead of the cave growing darker, the area continued to fill with light and warmth.

Michael wasn't sure how long the walk took, but spending these final hours with Kaimi alone and enjoying this time together was worth every moment. The caves had large crystals the size of a man, jutting out in various forms and locations. As they passed one particularly large crystal, the cave opened into a huge cavern with a million points of light veining through the rock. The sounds of the ocean and of Mu cut off.

"When we were children..." Kaimi continued to hold Michael's hand. He stopped and found a place to sit. "We would come here and play." He beamed. "Oh, the trouble we would get into."

"I can't imagine growing up with brothers and sisters. Having a big family must have been wonderful." Michael sat deep in an outcropping and examined their surroundings, enjoying Kaimi's hand in his.

"There were times." Kaimi relaxed his shoulders and neck. "But I wouldn't change any of those experiences..." His face and expression dropped, "Well, I would change the years of the war, especially knowing those horrible events may have been avoided if we didn't give into our own fears and let Mana Lani manipulate us."

"Don't." Michael's word came out as gentle as the cool breeze off the bay. "Don't go down that path. Everything happened for a reason. These events, large and small, are the way of things. Each challenge is how life works. We can't celebrate the good without the bad."

Kaimi sighed. "Can we sit here and be present?"

"We can sit here as long as you want." Michael responded as Kaimi rested his head on Michael's shoulder. He tried not to think of the future or of them leaving.

Yes, staying here like this forever is a grand idea.

~ Chapter Twenty-Two ~

Karen ran a carved bone comb through her hair as she faced the mirror, looking at her reflection. She still didn't look bad given all they had been through; the next twenty-four hours were going to be difficult and Bob would be cramped, but the little vessel would take them home. She peeked around her room. This space was bigger than she needed, but she had quickly grown accustomed to her surroundings and the bed. She peeked down at the lip balm Ulani had offered her to try; the concoction was all natural and worked well. She glanced around the space.

I wonder if I can take all this with me for my home.

"Home." Karen huffed with another look around. "Saying goodbye to all this." She picked up the comb and ran her fingers over the instrument.

Think of everything we can learn and I'm giving it up... for what?

*****

Michael checked the dock. Even with his late night with Kaimi, he and Captain Abbas were the first ones there. Both dressed as they were on the day of their rescue. Everyone would need to be in the same clothes they wore on the day of the pulse. Stains, rips and markings all added. The messed-up clothing would ensure continuity with their story.

Despite not having a watch, he realized the others were late. The captain prepped Bob for the journey, but they couldn't take anything with them, only the clothes they wore. Luckily, or unluckily, his cellphone never made it off the Pontus, so one less thing for them to worry about, and he wasn't the only one. None of them had their laptops or personal devices. They didn't need them when they were being evacuated off the sub the first time, and since they were planning on taking the sub home, there was no need for them here in Mu. Leaving everything on the Pontus worked in their favor, he supposed.

"Good thing we don't have to worry about the tide." Captain Abbas pulled Michael from his thoughts as she stood next to him.

"Given these are our last few moments here, I guess people want to say goodbye." Michael sighed. "I am surprised there is no one from the royal family here or even Noe." He held his hand up to shade his eyes as he glanced toward the palace, the golden spires and white stone walls. Seeing the beauty of this place made finding reasons to leave much harder. As his gaze wandered to the gardens, he caught sight of Commander Levy and Jayden walking toward the pier, followed by Karianne. "Here some of them come now." Michael pointed.

"I hope we won't have to pat pockets and ensure everyone is sticking to the plan." Abbas's tone was harder than he believed necessary, but of everyone, the captain was a realist and understood people, probably better than he ever would.

"Given we can only take the clothes we're wearing, there aren't many places to hide stuff." Michael faced her, offering what he hoped to be a reassuring smile. "And I have faith in everyone."

Please don't let me be wrong.

*****

Kaimi met Timu's gaze. "Well?" Kaimi scrutinized his reflection.

"My Prince... Kaimi, you are as ready as I can make you." Timu stepped away and leaned against the dressing table.

"I can't believe we have to say goodbye." Kaimi played with his hair. "so much has changed and now..." He shook his head, pushing away the thoughts of Michael and the others.

"Are you ready?" Koa's voice broke the silence, filling Kaimi's room. "If you wish to say goodbye, now is the time."

Timu nodded his head and stepped to the side, making himself vanish through the servant's door. Kaimi wanted to thank him again, but the man disappeared, as was his nature, probably off to see to the midday meal, or perhaps his own meal.

"Saying goodbye isn't going to be easy." Kaimi turned towards his brother. A smile tugged at his lips seeing Koa dressed in his formal attire. "You are every bit the king."

"Are you sure you don't want the job?" Koa walked all the way into the room and stood next to his brother as they both faced the mirror. "If you wish, I'll step down for you. Relinquish the throne."

"No." Kaimi raised his hands and stepped back. "I never wanted to be king. Ruling was never my path. One I didn't fully accept until now, especially seeing how well you lead our people." His cheeks pulled up in a large smile as pride filled his heart and the rest of him.

You are what our people need. Not me.

"You don't want to have to worry about producing an heir." Koa tapped him on the shoulder, his smile growing and a sparkle danced in his eyes.

"Well, there is that." Kaimi inhaled, continuing to take up the open spot next to his brother. "Although I believe Makani and I would have made good parents."

"Or maybe another. A handsome stranger." Koa poked him in the side.

"Don't." Kaimi shook his head, inhaling intensely. "This is hard enough."

"I know. I'm sorry," Koa sighed as he peered around the space. "Come, we are going to be late."

Kaimi nodded and allowed himself to be pulled from his room.

Like when we were children.

*****

For as many people as were on the pier and surrounding the bay, nothing seemed crowded. Michael gulped in the salty air as he peeked around, seeing everyone. All of Mu must be present to say goodbye. They were here to get one final look at the strangers, who had been victims of a crime. A crime that none were qualified to punish adequately.

"Where are Karen, Jiang, Tony, Alister and Bianchi?" Dr. Farmin asked.

"Tony had asked to speak with the king." Karianne pointed to the palace. "He should be here soon."

"Okay, but what about the others?" Abbas huffed with a peek towards the cave, the Mouth of the Gods, and their way out.

"Karen and Alister like to make an entrance." Michael tried to laugh, but failed. "Here they come, along with King Koa." He pointed towards the large group of people accompanied by several of the palace guards. Michael tried to search the faces but didn't see Kaimi.

He must be there, but I'm not seeing him. He wouldn't let me leave without saying goodbye, would he?

"My apologies." Koa offered the group as he reached the gathered party. "There were matters to discuss, keeping us delayed."

"Is everything okay?" Michael stepped forward with a look around the pier; no rushing guards, no chanting, no angry mob. Even the scents of the ocean seemed a bit more mellow today, even the humidity, always present, seemed less at this hour.

"Everything is fine." Karen spoke but wouldn't make eye contact with him or any of the people who would be leaving. "But..." She fumbled with her hands. "I'm staying." She blurted out.

"You're what?" Dr. Farmin yelped.

"I see," Captain Abbas responded, stone faced.

"Mu, this place," Karen raised a hand and motioned toward the city, viewing the white stone buildings and golden roofs accented in blues and sparkling crystals. "Is too much of an opportunity." Karen faced Rochelle and Michael. "This is everything I've been looking for my whole life. Michael, this is what I promised my father I would find. His stories about Atlantis and a lost world. Yes, I...he...we... had a lot wrong, but look, we're here and to leave now..." She shook her head. "What kind of scientist would I be?"

"And this is okay." Michael turned towards the king. "But you'll be alone." He turned to her, reaching for her hand and enjoying the warmth radiating from her. "Are you sure about this?" He focused his gaze on her. Her dark eyes and jaw were set, but there was a peace and aura of ease around her.

I know that look. Her mind is made up.

"She won't be alone." Jiang's voice spoke out. "We talked this morning and..." She smiled. "Dr. Linn can't do this all alone. And to miss out on this opportunity. Not a chance."

"But Dr. C." Jayden stepped forward. "What about all your research? There is so much you can teach us. Teach me."

"Jayden," Jiang offered, her voice soft. "You've worked with me. What a year. You'll work with other doctors, you have a whole life ahead of you." Jiang nodded at him. "Plus, I think with all the data from our adventure, Michael is going to need some help, you may still be an intern, but who knows where you'll end up."

Jayden nodded and glanced around. "I'd hoped there would be more time."

"Who knows what the gods have in store for any of us," Koa offered by way of comfort. He and the rest of the assembled royal family were in similar outfits to what they wore the night of the welcome celebration.

Hard to believe it's only been a week.

"The two of you." Michael's cheeks pulled up as he draped his arms around Karen and Dr. Chen. "Well, I suppose you both staying isn't a surprise. But I'm going to miss you. Who's going to spend all my money on some crazy adventure?"

"Captain." Tony stepped forward, as did Bianchi.

Michael glanced at the two young men.

"I figured you would want to stay, Tony. These are your people and your culture, untouched by us." Abbas nodded and glanced at her ensign. "And if you're staying, I believe Mario is staying as well."

"But how?" Mario glanced between Tony and Abbas. "We were so careful."

Abbas chuckled, adjusting her collar. "Oh, Ensign, ask Commander Levy. The Pontus was my sub and you are my crew, and I know everything happening on her. I figured you would say something when you were ready."

"Thank you, Captain." Tony grabbed Mario's hand. "Being here, there is a lot for me to learn about my people. And maybe with the doc here, we can teach them more about us."

"I guess that'll give us more space in Bob." Rochelle's eyes dropped, but she kept her tone upbeat. "But, damn, I'm gonna miss you all. I never thought I would say that." She added and faced Karen. "I mean, given all we've been through. Who would've imagined a few weeks ago we would be here, Dr. Linn, now to think of you not returning."

Karen and Rochelle continued to talk and laugh. Karen rambled off some information about Mu, and how they might be able to protect the city with the information they found, and the mythology around this place.

"Michael." Alister stepped away from the royal family and guards, taking Michael by the hand. "I don't think I'm going either."

Michael glanced at the young man. "Are you sure?"

Alister bit his lips and peeked towards the city. "Not in the least, but I fucked up and I'm not so sure I won't fuck up again." He glanced down at the pier. "Plus, being here, this is a fresh start. I talked to Noe and asked if I might be able to help them. Maybe learn about all this stuff. I was pretty good in science class, and I'm pretty adept with technology..."

"And your family?"

"They'll have to learn to live without free handouts from me. I..." he swiped at his eyes and wrapped his arms around Michael, hugging him tight. He whispered, "They're good people, I swear, they're just... if you can keep an eye on them, especially my siblings, make sure they have a chance. I did everything for them, not for me, but for them. They're why I started performing and modeling. Now I can do something for me."

"You have my word." Michael kissed the top of his head. "I'll have David come up with a way to ensure your siblings get their chance. He's gifted when he needs to help people who deserve the help. They'll be fine. You have my word."

"Thank you." Alister stepped from their hug. "I didn't know Tom, but I know you, and I think he did a great job, and you got the best from him. Plus, I think we're too different." He laughed. "No surprise. Right? Still, I wouldn't have minded sharing your bed, maybe in another life."

A lump took up the space in Michael's throat and he couldn't speak, but he nodded.

"With only seven of us," Captain Abbas started calling everyone together from all their chatter, "Bob will be in better shape for our return."

"And speaking of returns." Rochelle pointed to Bob. "We should finish our goodbyes and get going. We still have a ticking clock on us."

"Agreed." Michael glanced at the sub, then at the group, not seeing Kaimi anywhere, but the guards and the royals were so close together who knew for sure he may have been hiding in plain sight. Or he might not be here at all. Still, he wanted to... no, he needed to say goodbye.

But maybe Kaimi couldn't or didn't want to. These things happen. Still sucks.

"Captain." Koa's words filled the space with effortlessness. The man easily projected his voice, something any good statesman needed to be able to do. "Since we will have several of your people here with us, it seems only right you have a way to communicate with them."

"Communication is too dangerous." Michael stepped forward, raising his hands to cut off the king. "We can't take any of your technology—"

"Mr. Donovan, I was not addressing you." Koa glowered at him, the full weight of his presence felt on every inch of Michael's being. "I was speaking with Captain Abbas."

Michael bit his lip but said nothing more.

"What do you have in mind?" The captain asked with a glance at Michael.

"Well, the plan isn't mine alone." Koa stepped to the side and revealed a man dressed in a baseball hat and a tattered crew uniform.

Who the hell...

Michael studied the members of the Pontus. They were all accounted for. At least, he assumed they all were.

Whispers and conversation broke out as the unidentified crew member stepped forward.

"I have the codes and know the frequencies to contact Noe," Kaimi's voice called out as he removed the hat on his head. "And since so many of your people are staying here, perhaps you can make room for one more. One of us from Mu."

"What?" Michael's heart tried to jump from his chest as he took several steps toward Kaimi. "You're here! I figured, maybe, you weren't going to say goodbye. And you want to come with us?" The words all ran together as Michael spoke. Even in his own mind, he sounded like a preteen talking to his school crush for the first time.

Kaimi's full lips broke as his bright white smile filled his face. "No. I want to join you." He took a step closer to Michael. "Learn about your world, if this proposal is okay with you, Captain Abbas. I worked with Noe on all our technology, so I can be helpful."

Abbas tapped her lips and her gaze narrowed. "Oh, I think we can arrange something, assuming this change is okay with you, Michael. I mean, his returning with us is a risk and might jeopardize keeping Mu secret, if only the Pontus had a crewmember of Polynesian descent who wasn't returning with us... Oh wait!"

"You..." Michael shook his head and pointed. His heart grew lite as his cheeks pulled up. "You approved this." He wanted to laugh.

"Mu may not be my ship," Abbas remarked with hints of a smile. "But any good captain knows her people and those in their orbit." Her grin grew, filling her with a beauty only a sincere and honest smile can. "Plus, I like to stay busy."

"Now Michael." Koa raised his hands, calling everyone's attention. "Kaimi is my brother and a Prince of Mu. I expect him treated well while he's in your care. If anything happens to him that I do not approve of..."

Rochelle smiled. "Mr. Donovan, I doubt we can afford any... what's the word? Diplomatic issues." She chuckled.

"There are worse things than our pulse weapon." Nohealani stated as her royal outfit of white billowed around her.

"Oh, brother." Ulani rushed over and hugged Kaimi. "I'm excited for you. Michael is very handsome and I get a good feeling from him." She kissed his cheeks. "Mother and Father would be thrilled with this. I know they would. And you being there, this is everything you wanted, plus..." she reached out and took Michael's hand.

"I'm fulfilling the dream my mother and father had, well maybe not completely, but..." Kaimi nodded, a deep smile pulled over his lips, showing all the joy he had on his face. "They wanted us to learn about the outside world, so this is our chance." He spared a glance at Michael. "Assuming you will have me."

Michael pulled Kaimi into him. "I'm glad you're coming. With everyone else staying, I was going to jump ship too."

"No, you weren't." Karen laughed with a brush of her hair, beaming at the two of them.

"We'll never know now," Michael countered. "Yes, I would be thrilled to have you join us and see what adventures lie ahead."

"Kaimi, Your Highness." Alister's gentle voice reached Michael's ears as he approached them.

Michael and Kaimi turned to the young man.

"Things might not have gone in the direction I had hoped with Michael, but he's a good guy." Alister beamed. "Don't screw your chance with him up. He's not what people see on the outside. Don't let his job define who he is to you or others."

Kaimi reached out a hand. "Thank you."

"Okay. Folks," Captain Abbas called out, clapping her hands together. "Your Majesty, with your permission, we should go."

"May the gods of Mu protect your travels." Koa raised his hands and his staff raised above them all. "Go with grace and may Kanaloa grant you calm waters and may Hikule'o ensure you reach your home safely." Drums started to play as did ukuleles, and what Michael had learned were ka'eke'eke. Off in the distance, by the entrance to the Crystal Caves, there were both regular dancers and fire dancers as music filled the giant cave, reverberating all around.

With the blessing, Michael and the group of seven made their way to Bob for the journey home. He reached out and took Kaimi's hand. "Are you sure about this? You may not be able to come home." His eyes darted around the space, the lapping of the water on the bay, the sparkle of the whites of the buildings. The glow from the crystals, everything was like something from a dream, his dream. "You'll be giving this all up."

"I've never been more certain about anything in my life." Kaimi peeked over his shoulder to his family. "If the gods see fit, this won't be the last time I see Mu."

"Aloha." Nohealani called out with a wave.

"Aloha." Kaimi turned and waved to his sisters.

Ulani waved to him, and Koa offered a nod.

Past the royal family, Michael spotted Noe and a young man. The younger man held up a hand and Kaimi returned the gesture. The man's smile shined like a beacon on a hill, even from where Michael stood, he noted how dynamic the smile was.

"Who's next to Noe?"

Kaimi inhaled a shaky breath, "A dear friend who I'll miss as much as my family." He mouthed *aloha* in the direction of his friend.

Michael nodded. "Well, maybe we'll have to look into ensuring you can return home. After all, anything is possible. Especially when it comes to our family and our friends."

I paid for one sub, why not a second one?

~ Chapter Twenty-Three ~

5 Days After Leaving Mu

Michael's eyes fluttered open. The soft scent of lemongrass and ocean mist tickled his nose, and he sniffed, enjoying the aromas before he exhaled. "You there?" He mumbled as the first rays of the morning started to break through the curtains covering his windows. He rolled over onto his back, a sigh breaking from his lips as the softness of the bed and pillow engulfed him, and the warmth next to him filled not only his bed, but his heart. The smile, the bare chest, his shoulders, and those beautiful thighs. "Is this all another pleasant dream?" He glanced at the ceiling fan as the machine spun, a soft moan joining each rotation. The cool air on his naked shoulders and chest both chilled and tantalized him, as did the hand tenderly holding him.

He glanced down, seeing the duvet tented up right below his mid-section. "If you keep your hand there, I won't be held responsible for my actions." He peered toward the ceiling fan as the blades spun around. He turned to be greeted by two beautiful brown eyes and a smile as white as the buildings of Mu.

He remembered each detail, the taste of his lips as they kissed. The playful bites at his ears and neck. Even how their tongues danced around each other for what seemed like hours. A gentle moment of passion shared between two people who desperately wanted each other, as their souls merged into one. Their embrace is how they fell asleep and now appeared to be how they were going to start the day.

"I love the way you feel in my hand, as you sleep," Kaimi whispered softly. "Soft and warm in those moments. Rising and falling like the tides of Mu."

A quiet chuckle fell from Michael's lips. "Not at the moment."

"Warm yes, soft..." Kaimi shook his head, giving Michael a playful squeeze, causing his manhood to buck in response.

"As much as I would love for this to continue." He leaned in and placed a kiss on Kaimi's full lips. "I have to get up." Kaimi's hand released him. He tossed his feet over the side of the bed, the cool of the floor on his bare feet sending a shudder through his body.

Kaimi exhaled and rolled over, tossing the covers off his tanned body, his own partial erection reaching to the sky. "Are you sure I can't tempt you?"

"You always tempt me." Michael teased as several chirps burst from his phone.

"I can't say I care for your cell phones or all your little technological gadgets constantly interrupting life. What's the point? Nothing is so urgent that one needs to be in constant contact with others." Kaimi sighed, straightening his feet under the covers, still keeping himself mostly exposed.

"They're annoying, agreed, but they serve a purpose and today their purpose is to ensure I'm ready for the press conference." Michael sighed and made his way to the bathroom to get ready. They had been in San Jose for five days. Once they left Mu, the journey in Bob was easy enough, and once they reached the ocean's surface, the sub's beacon went off and in a matter of a few hours, they were rescued. From there, Rochelle and he had bought the group some time, to recover from their experience and to allow their data to be scrutinized (and hopefully pass muster), but the media and the world wouldn't wait forever. After Rochelle briefed the President on their agreed-upon story, he was given the green light to hold a press conference and explain what happened to the Pontus. Luckily for him, the White House didn't insist on many changes to his speech. Thankfully they had little to say in the matter, but he still wanted them to all play nice. So, he did the same.

Michael would have loved to have had Kaimi there with him, but given they were trying to keep Mu and, technically, the prince secret. Keeping Kaimi at home was better for everyone, at least for the time being.

Home.

The image sent warmth through Michael's body, stopping at points in his cheeks and neck.

With a peek at his black suit, cream-colored shirt, and dark blue tie, he recognized he would, at the very least, look the part of someone in mourning.

And I am. We lost so many good people, and for what?

Michael pushed the thoughts of Mana Lani and her actions away, making a mental check of everything else he needed to focus on. Sharon, after she stopped fussing over him, had helped him pull all this together; she was so much more than his admin and he wondered if she realized how important she was...really appreciated how much he valued her. *A thought for another time.* Michael stood at the podium, only a few short weeks ago having been set up to celebrate the launch of the Pontus and their mission. The offices where Karen and her team had been housed would need to be boxed up, and everything would be taken to his office for now. All the lights made the space warmer than last time. They were moving on to April, which didn't help.

Mu's still warmer.

With all the cameras focused on him, he kept his expression as plain and as flat as possible, keeping the tone of the mood he wanted to present. Behind him stood Captain Abbas and Dr. Farmin, both dressed in clothes reflecting the somber note they needed to project. The rest of the survivors weren't needed, and they all were grateful for not having to be paraded in front of the cameras again, at least from what they told Michael.

Michael pushed a button on the tablet in front of him. Behind him the images of all the people who were on the Pontus with their names and their positions started to play. The video would circulate through all those lost in the accident in a continual loop, to ensure none would be left out or forgotten.

"Five years ago, we were hit by a pulse, throwing up all our garbage we had recklessly thrown into the Pacific Ocean. The event sent out an EMP wave, wiping out most of our computers, cars, cellphones, and even our power and water grids. This pulse sent the world into a tailspin, especially our Central American neighbors, who are still trying to recover from the event. Yet." He paused. "We never figured out why or how this happened." He stopped, allowing himself to fill his lungs. "There were theories, but no real answers." He pointed towards the bay. "Since then, Dr. Karen Linn tried to explain what happened. Her and her team worked for years trying to find the cause. This truth taking her from us, as well as fifty-two other brave souls who wanted to learn how this disaster occurred, and to ensure such a thing wouldn't happen again."

"Now some of you, based solely on Dr. Linn's passion for the mythology of Atlantis, and of other places, some call Mu or Lemuria, thought nothing of her or her theories. You thought nothing of the work of Dr. Chan Thomas either. Maybe nothing came of these theories. But as many on the Pontus said, there is a great big ocean out there that we know nothing about, and today, we may not have found these places Dr. Linn theorized existed but we did find what we believe caused the devastation known to us as The Pulse."

Several cameras snapped, as several members of the media moved closer, as did their cameras and lights.

Thank goodness for undershirts and my jacket. Maybe Kaimi is right, we wear too many clothes.

"In your press kits, and now on the screen behind me, are the photos of the vessel we found, this vessel from what we gathered from the Pontus' drones, before they were knocked offline, appeared to be some kind of research vessel." He paused and pointed to the images. "We didn't think much of this vessel until this happened." Michael nodded to Dr. Farmin and Captain Abbas. "Please note, what you are about to see are the last few minutes of lives for many of those on the Pontus."

Michael tapped a button on his tablet and several images and audios started to play. These were the minutes prior to the first hit of Mu's pulse weapon. The audio and video were a mix of everything they had recovered from when Koa and Kaimi, with their warriors, came to the sub. They were removed from the images and the fake vessel substituted. The images of an undersea earthquake followed by more images from inside of drone command and the bridge of the Pontus, these were the hardest for Michael to watch as this footage didn't need any movie magic. The engine room cameras caught the pulse hitting the sub and the explosive decompression and fire, as watertight doors crashed closed, and people screamed and rushed around to begin damage control. Michael couldn't watch the video; the memories of the event were too much.

Once the video stopped, Michael spoke. "We didn't know what hit us at first, but from the data we got, which I can now say has been independently verified by members of the White House Office of Science and Technology, from the Office of the United States Secretary of Energy, and several others including the Marine Science departments at Cal State Monterey Bay. We now know we were hit by the same pulse killing hundreds of thousands, and changing the ground we now walk on, five years ago."

Michael pulled up a blurred image of the vessel. "This ship," He pointed, the scowl on his face every bit real. "caused the Pacific Pulse. Based on our readings, the vessel must have been powered by some kind of nuclear engine, the only thing able to cause so much destruction." He let the words hang in the air for a moment. "We believe the weapon got triggered five years ago by one of the many earthquakes hitting this location of the Pacific Ocean. And we, unfortunately, were its victims again."

Michael paused and glanced at Captain Abbas before facing Dr. Farmin.

"We were lucky to get out." Michael added before facing the media again. This time wasn't the same feeding frenzy as before. In fact, the reporters seemed a bit more human. A bit more subdued. "Now I know you have questions, so please."

Several hands and voices called out.

"Go ahead." Michael pointed to a female reporter.

"Jody Marquez, CNN. The images of the ship don't appear to tell us who the ship belonged to. What else do you know about the ship and will there be another pulse?"

Michael nodded to Dr. Farmin.

You're up, Doc.

Dr. Farmin stepped forward. "From what limited imaging we have of the ship, we are unable to ascertain where the vessel came from;

however, based on the type of vessel and the nature of the Pulse, there are a few countries who have the ability to create such a weapon."

"And they are?" Jody called out.

"We believe the ship may have been World War II era Japan or Germany." There were gasps from the crowd. "Or even more recent; France, Britain, China, Russia or even the United States."

Arms and voices erupted at them, waving, trying to get their attention.

"Please." Rochelle raised a hand, calling the room to silence. "As for, will we be hit by another pulse?" She shook her head. "No. We don't believe so. One of the drones caught this image of the vessel dropping from the ledge where the wreckage had been perched. We believe the pressure would have destroyed any remaining threat the vessel posed."

"But you don't know, right?" A male reporter called.

"Mr..." Rochelle's eyes narrowed on him.

"Javier Garcia. NBC."

"No Mr. Garcia, we can't be 100% sure..."

There were rumbles from the media.

"But given..." Rochelle continued. "We have only ever been hit by a pulse like this once and the ship has been destroyed. We are hopeful and comfortable in saying the danger is behind us." She added a firm nod of her head.

Assuming Koa and Noe keep to their promises

Michael tried to keep his expression neutral. Given the risk they were all taking, this plan had to work. For all their sakes. With Kaimi here and the people of Mu's desire to stay hidden, everyone keeping to the plan should be a guarantee, but nothing was 100%. Giving themselves some wiggle room, another ship or something else may still be out there would be their only ace in the hole.

"Ali Nemazee, Al Jazeera, how can you be sure this threat *you* caused is destroyed? How is the rest of the world supposed to feel safe knowing the weapon is still out there?"

"Let me be very clear." Rochelle started, her voice raising with each word. "We do not know whose vessel we discovered. This information is based on our best guess. However, the possibility remains, the vessel and weapon were created by some rogue state who got their hands on technology they didn't understand. And, as I've already stated, we cannot be certain of anything. We are hopeful this won't happen again."

"What about these safeguards we've heard the US and Canada are working on?" Ali followed up.

"Both the US, Canada and Mexico, as well as the other countries affected by the Pulse, have all been working together since the Pulse struck to create safeguards." She focused on the crowd for a moment. "We've implemented EMP resistance systems in all our coastal infra-structures as well as having mandated all vehicles and other electronic devices have similar protection." Rochelle's gaze narrowed on Ali. "And, as I'm sure you're aware, all these initiatives have been shared with the UN. The World Bank has offered financial assistance to any country who may not be able to afford some of these additional safeguards."

The US government insisted on adding these additional protec-tions, and Michael understood why. Cast as large of a net as possible, when placing blame so fewer fingers point your way, and follow the blame up with all the good work everyone has been doing since to keep us all safe.

Thank you, Ali Nemazee, for making sharing this information a lot easier.

"Has there been conversation, at least, about trying to salvage the ship? Tomas Jackson, Fox News."

Rochelle moved out of the way and Michael stepped up. "Yes." He nodded his head. "But given the depth and what we went through…" he pushed a frown to his lips.

"And what do you have to say to the families who lost their loved ones on your sub, Captain Abbas? Under your command? Connor Walsh, BBC."

Captain Abbas stepped forward and removed her hat. "Loss is never easy. We left port with forty crew, fifteen Scientists, and four guests, each one of them someone I got to engage with and would have given my life for. They are all heroes, and I will never forget any of them."

"But you stand here and don't…" Connor countered. "The captain's duty is to go down with the ship?"

Captain Abbas's gaze narrowed on the reporter. "If not for Commander Jean Levy, Crewman Karianne Franco, and Crewman Kaimi 'Tony' Tupu, I wouldn't be here today. They pulled me from the bridge while unconscious. I owe them everything."

"And the lawsuit for their families. What do you say to them? Tiffany Cross, MSNBC."

"I'm sorry I can't comment on any potential litigation." Captain Abbas stepped clear of the microphone.

Michael stepped forward. "Regarding any potential litigation, you may reach out to my legal team."

Grumbles echoed about the space as expected. The potential for a lawsuit wasn't a surprise, but Michael hoped they would be able to settle things with the families out of court and under seal.

"Mr. Donovan," a male reporter called out, "What about the claims this is all a cover-up, and you and your team did find something down there and the government is helping to cover the discovery up? That Dr. Linn and, by extension, Dr. Chan Tomas's theories were correct."

Michael glanced at the sea of journalist, not sure who spoke. "To them I say. I wish. I wish this was all some big hoax, and maybe everyone survived after all." He turned from the mic. He didn't want this to get nasty, and he didn't want to entertain rumors, even if they were correct. The reporters got all the important information they needed, at least for now. "However," He faced the crowd, he was going to wait on this announcement but he wanted to give them something to chew on. "I would like to add. When we were hit, none of us were sure we were going to live or die. The Pontus was lost and those able to help did." He paused for a breath. "Because of our hubris, because of man's need to destroy or conquer nature, we did this to ourselves and no amount of finger pointing will ever change these facts. If we can take away anything from this event, it's simply perhaps we need to start treating each other better. Be more tolerant before we actually manage destroying ourselves and our world."

Michael tapped his tablet again, showing all the faces of every member of the Pontus who were lost.

"In that vein, in conjunction with Cal State Monterey Bay, we will be opening up the Dr. Karen Linn Marine Science Research Center. My hope is we can work to not only ensure something like this doesn't happen again, but we grow to understand our oceans and the world existing in its depths. Thank you all for coming." Michael tapped off the mic and the projections as Dr. Farmin, Captain Abbas and he left the stage.

And now we wait.

*****

5 Weeks after Staying on Mu

Karen reviewed the broadcast and all the additional information they provided and sent with Bob. Five weeks passed since Michael and the others returned home and luckily no one had come knocking. "I think our plan may have worked." She offered. "From everything we've seen, and sadly the lack of attention span of people..." She didn't want to say anymore. No point in jinxing things or tempting the gods of Mu.

"I wish we could've provided more data." Noe offered as they shook their head. "But any additional material at this point would be too risky. Even now there are bits and pieces we want to send but can't. Additional readings. Things that weren't so rushed."

Karen nodded her agreement. "I know a couple of the drones survived, and are still active, so maybe they can be updated and sent this new data?"

Noe paused a moment. "I like the idea, but..."

"But will additional data raise more questions?" Koa asked, watching the monitor and glancing at both Karen and Noe. "We've been lucky for now, but if we do anything more, there is a greater risk."

"Time will tell." Karen ran a hand over the work table she occupied. "But we'll be ready to help if and when they need us."

"Michael's announcement of the Marine Science Research Center was smart. A bit of information taking the focus from that reporter's question; did he say if they found out who asked the question about a conspiracy?"

"I think he said someone from Buzzfeed." Karen shook her head. "Luckily, most people don't take them too seriously, but they have been known to be correct."

"And in this case, they were." Koa shook his head. "Was he hoping to catch them in a lie or have someone break down?"

"I don't know." Karen rubbed her hands together. The lotion Ulani gave her kept her skin soft and her lips had never been so supple. "I'm not a fan of the media. And yes, I'm glad to see him announce the collaboration."

Noe nodded as he shut down the monitors. "Working with your university is a good way for him, and for us to know what might be coming our way."

"And to think." Karen started as her gaze narrowed on Noe. "He would have never thought of that if I didn't make the suggestion. Him attaching my name to the project is very sweet, so I won't be forgotten or some footnote in a textbook."

Noe picked up several files from the work space next to Karen. "Dr. Linn." They held up the files. "How many times must I ask you to keep the work station clear?"

"Those. There are only a few files." Karen grabbed them out of Noe's hands.

I didn't have this problem with Michael or the others, or when I was working on my own.

"Is this how you two are going to be?" Koa asked the group, a hint of a frown danced on his lips. "Perhaps I should have gone with them."

Karen laughed, waving off the king's comment. "Nah. We'll be fine, especially once I finish getting Dr. Chen and my lab set up. Thanks again for the space."

Koa nodded. "Well, seeing how you and Noe worked together over these last several weeks, this is a smart move."

"You're probably right." Karen dropped the files down on the workstation. "And I'm excited to start teaching again, so is Dr. Chen. I think teaching will definitely help to keep us all out of each other's hair.

And getting to shape the minds of Mu will be a huge step in bringing us all closer together.

*****

5 Months since Leaving Mu

Kaimi sat at the desk in the office Michael had set up for him at his business. The space was nice, and seeing the sky both at night and during the day had been wonderful. The sunsets were amazing, all the colors. He had never seen anything so beautiful. He would pull Michael out any chance he got to watch the sunset and if they woke early enough to rise. He spent hours viewing the sky, even from here. This place was so different from Mu. The technology alone was great to explore and working with Michael's IT staff had been fun. He had learned a lot and actually taught them a few things as well.

I'm looking forward to seeing what more we can do, not only for Michael's business, but in general.

In the five months he had been here in San Jose, he had found a passion he didn't know he had, working with computers, which he enjoyed. Also, he and Michael had been to see the giant redwoods in Muir Woods, traveled into the mountains by Lake Tahoe and Truckee to see snow. He had no idea how cold, cold really was. Michael shared with him there are places colder still. He wasn't so sure he wanted to experience all the cold; he liked the warmth and being comfortable. He found August reminded him most of the weather in Mu, still a bit dry and he and his skin were taking time to get used to this weather. Even with the summer heat, he found the morning and late evenings chilly.

I miss the consistent temperatures of Mu.

Kaimi reviewed his list, now that he had finished his work for the day. He was putting a list of places together for him and Michael to go. Places he had heard of or he found interesting. Yes, he had Hawai'i on the list and Samoa as well as Fiji, but those places would have to wait, and they took more planning, especially with how far these locations were. He had no idea the outside world was so big.

Even here in San Jose and the Bay Area, this place is huge, so much larger than Mu.

"Disneyland?" Michael asked with a hint of a chuckle from over Kaimi's shoulder.

"Oh, sorry." Kaimi peeked over at him. "I didn't hear you come in." He pulled out the ear buds he wore for his music so the noise wouldn't bother anyone. He had found hours of traditional Hawaiian and other Polynesian music reminding him of home. When he listened to the music, memories of Mu filled his mind. "I've seen many broadcasts about Disneyland and I want to see for myself."

"Hawai'i." Michael placed several folders next to Kaimi's workstation, then rested a hand on Kaimi's shoulder, giving him a squeeze.

Kaimi leaned his head so it touched Michael's hand.

"Fiji. Samoa."

"They remind me of Mu, and I believe we share a lot of the same culture and history." Kaimi offered.

"Well, I think I'm going to have to put restrictions on my offer to take you 'anywhere' you want to go," Michael laughed. "But, I will admit seeing you in your sarong again might make the hot and humid weather worth going through again."

"You don't like what I'm wearing?" Kaimi pulled at the button on his shirt.

"You look great, and I love the outfit. The light green shirt is perfect for you." Michael beamed at him.

"Well, good." Kaimi adjusted how he sat on the chair. "My crystals and pike are smashed with all these layers. These pants are annoying my legs and this shirt itches." He pulled at the neck to emphasize his point and reached down to adjust himself for the hundredth time.

I have not touched myself this much since I was a boy.

"I'm sorry," Michael offered with a shrug of his shoulders. "I know our clothing can get uncomfortable, especially in the heat."

Kaimi adjusted how he sat again.

Although my butt looks great in these pants, but I won't tell him.

"The pains of fashion." Michael rubbed Kaimi's shoulder. "Welcome to life in Silicon Valley. Hey at least we're not on the East Coast, like in New York or D.C., where they wear suits every day... the humidity. I would die."

Kaimi huffed. "I don't see why I can't wear what I normally wear. People would get used to how I look." Kaimi unbuttoned another button on his shirt, revealing more of his chest and feeling less stifled.

"Not too many men walk around in public without a shirt on, and wrapped only in a sarong. Not even in Hawai'i or the other places on your list, although your native attire might be more normal there, but still."

"I suppose." Kaimi ran a free hand over his shirt. "I do like how these garments help to keep me warm. This air conditioning keeps everything so cold. I had no idea how chilly this place gets." He pulled the sleeves of his shirt down before tapping the computer to open up a fresh window.

"I don't think of San Jose as cold or the office for that matter, but I guess compared to Mu, the South Bay is." Michael glanced at his watch. "Are we ready to meet?"

Kaimi maneuvered the pointer on his screen and tapped a few more commands.

Michael went and closed the office door.

"Is anyone still here? I assumed Sharon left a little while ago." Kaimi moved the mouse and typed in a few more commands. He pulled up an additional window and ensured all his encryption codes were in place and working as they should.

"She did, still I like to be safe rather than sorry." Michael returned to the desk, pulling over a second seat.

After a moment, an image popped up and staring at him were: Noe, Karen, Koa, and Nohealani. "Where's Ulani?"

"She's out with Timu," Nohealani quipped. "I guess since you left, he needed company." She covered her mouth with her hand to hide the smirk Kaimi was sure hid there.

"Really." Kaimi moved the cursor and enlarged the screens so they could see better. "I'm happy for him. I know he would often speak of her with fondness in his voice." He shrugged.

"And I'm not sure how I feel about this new friendship." Koa added. "He's a body attendant after all."

"And I'm a body attendant, remember?" Michael waved and sat closer to Kaimi so they were easily seen on the screen.

"But you're different." Koa countered without missing a beat. "Kaimi is my older brother, and Ulani is our youngest sister."

"Anyway." Karen shook her head, trying to call everyone together. "All this family drama. I think I should have come back with you after all."

Michael laughed. "Liar. You're loving being in Mu, and being part of this new family is a bonus."

She nodded her head. "I am. I really am. I've been teaching... and my lab, well, the lab Dr. Chen and I share, is terrific. Jiang said to say hello. She's off with her class studying the Mouth of the Gods." Karen's smile grew. "I wish you could have seen the location, Michael. Beautiful."

"And dangerous." Kaimi added, a tug of a frown on his lips. "You allowed this, brother?"

"They are being careful and respectful." Koa nodded. "Since you left Mu, more people have been curious about the place, seeing as the Mouth of the Gods is the only way in and out of Mu."

"Well, I'm glad." Kaimi leaned forward, resting his hands on the desk in front of him. "We need to change things in Mu, and here, for that matter, maybe this will all help."

"Or send us over the abyss," Noe amended. "There are still people grumbling about all this, and asking what the gods think."

"The council of Elders and I are listening to everyone's concerns," Koa offered. "None of us, even those raising questions, want to make the same mistakes we already made."

"How goes the legal battles?" Karen asked. "I wish we could offer more support from here."

Michael sighed. "I won't lie, the court cases are a pain in the ass and I wish I..." he waved a hand at the computer and the camera. "But... Anyway, we're trying to push for a settlement, and sadly, money is all these people want. They didn't think the death benefits we provided were adequate for the pain and suffering the loss of their loved ones caused. Keep in mind." Michael frowned. "As Captain Abbas reminded my legal counsel, most of these people never talked to or visited these supposed loved ones. A point we're going to be sure to bring forward, as well as any dirt we can find on these people. Luckily, we can get access to phone, cell, and email data. As well as social media. These people have no idea what they're in for."

"Ouch." Karen inhaled through her teeth, making an almost sucking-hissing sound.

"Please don't get him started." Kaimi requested and reached up and took Michael's hand. "There is no joy in this topic."

"Clearly." Nohealani commented. "Brother, what are all those coverings you're wearing this time?" She pointed and moved her head to view him better.

"New clothes." Kaimi offered with a glance over to Michael. "These outfits help me to fit in and keep me warm, plus the colors and textures aren't too bad."

"Good." Nohealani waved her hand in approval, or perhaps agreement. Might have been both. "I never believed one person would need so many clothes."

"I think you look very nice," Karen offered, winking at him, or at least the camera on their end. "And you should have seen all the luggage Alister and Michael brought." She laughed.

"Speaking of Alister," Michael peered closer towards the monitor. "Please pass on that David has been in contact with his family and they are doing well, and like all the other families, they miss him."

"I'll let him know." Karen tapped something on the device she held.

"And yes," Noe offered. "This outfit of yours today is quite nice."

"A compliment from Noe. Thank you." Kaimi lowered his hand to adjust his crystals and pike once more.

"All these changes are a bit of a learning curve for all of us." Koa leaned closer to the screens. "Tony and Mario are trying to teach us baseball. And Alister has been working with our dancers and storytellers to create a play about when the Pontus arrived. The concept's an interesting idea, and everyone, including myself, are excited to see performed." He shook his head and smiled. "With all these changes, I'm questioning our choices. Things were so much simpler before you arrived, and before you left, brother."

"Well, like Mother would say, we can't fight the tides." Kaimi motioned his hands in front of the screen and the camera.

"True." Koa's tone changed, meaning he had something important to say or ask, which he usually did. "Michael, has there been any word from Rochelle about the reports and the videos? Anything we need to be worried about? We're going on five months."

"Nothing." Michael smiled, glancing at the folder he brought in with him. "Everyone seems to have accepted our first-hand reports and the data we provided. Any irregularities are being chalked up to data corruption or damaged files, as we hoped. Susan, Captain Abbas, said her friends over in France aren't willing to question the reports, as they like the idea of people thinking France might have a piece of technology the rest of the world doesn't. The mystique is helped with the Pontus being French built, which has been a boon for them. Despite losing the Pontus, people want something similar for research." Michael held up his hand. "Not to find Mu, but for general ocean exploration. The new subs won't be near as nice as the Pontus, but nothing will."

"Are there concerns someone else will try and develop a pulse weapon?" Karen sat deeper in her seat, falling out of focus.

"No." Michael shook off the comment. "I don't think so. Rochelle hasn't heard of anything and neither has Susan, but who knows?"

"You already have nuclear weapons and EMP pulse weapons," Kaimi frowned and his gaze dropped to the keyboard resting at his hands. "You basically already have a power greater, if not similar enough." He sat a bit taller.

But without us and our crystal tech, you can't make a pulse work like we did.

"That doesn't make me feel any better." Karen countered. "Bunch of eager beavers up there trying to outdo each other. It's a giant pissing contest, or as you say here in Mu, pike competition."

Kaimi bit back his grin, seeing Koa do the same, while Noe smirked, and Nohealani rolled her eyes.

"I can't say for certain, but I believe there is a call in the UN to ban any further development of such a weapon." Michael continued as if the comment was never made, "But as we know too well, a UN treaty or resolution doesn't mean much."

"Is there anything else?" Kaimi pointed to the counter on the screen. "We should keep to our time until we find a better way."

"Agreed." Noe glanced towards the screen and counter on their end.

"I don't have anything." Michael offered as he ruffled through the folders he brought with him. "But I enjoy seeing you all."

"We miss you, brother." Nohealani waved, her white bright smile all but blinding in the light of the computer.

"Tell the others we say hello." Koa offered a bow of his head.

"Goodbye for now." Kaimi ended the communication with several clicks of his mouse and taps on his keyboard. He stood up, cracking his back and shifting his neck, causing several pops. "All this is temporary. We'll figure out better ways to communicate and to share information. This will all get easier."

"Oh, I know." Michael pointed to Kaimi's computer. "One of your special projects." He gestured to the various monitors and hard drives sitting about along with the tablets Kaimi was fond of using. "And I don't mind us going through my network. No one would ever think to track our signal through a bunch of porn sites." He tapped the top of the computer screen. "Do you regret being here? I know with the clothes. Me working, especially doing what I do, and you not getting to be with your family..." Michael waved his hand around the office. "I never even asked you what you want to do. I picked you up and plopped you here in this office, and put you on payroll. Hell, Sharon figured out you would be perfect for IT when she noticed how you handled yourself around the computer and with all the gadgets we have here."

Kaimi took Michael's hands. "I'm here with you. Thanks to you, I get to see and explore a world I had only ever seen in videos or heard stories about." He sneaked a quick look around the office. "In my home I was a prince. I had people to care for all my needs, so I only needed to focus on working with Noe, or for many years fighting my brother, this..." He beamed. The joy he had inside him filled him with warmth. "This is foreign to me." He plucked at his slacks. "And from here, I get to help my people. I get to develop better ways for us to communicate with them. I get to help your people find and explore your services with less fear of someone trying to sabotage their computer. I get to offer them greater ways to ensure what they enjoy doesn't harm them in their professional or family lives." He shook his head, not fully understanding why this bothered so many people. "Although I don't understand why people care or make such a big deal out of it, as long as no one is getting hurt and everyone agrees..." his shoulders raised and dropped. "Anyway, as for the rest, I have options, which is something I wouldn't have had in Mu."

"So, you're happy?"

"Definitely." The words, along with a smile, passed Kaimi's lips.

Michael's shoulders seemed to relax as he closed his eyes for a moment. "Well, I'm glad, because you make me so happy."

"Good." Kaimi leaned in resting a hand on Michael's warm chest, he barely made out the hairs underneath the fabric, he loved the fuzz on Michael's chest, a hairy chest a rare feature on the men in Mu. "We will be happy together and leave the rest in the hands of the Gods." The two shared a kiss and peace grew from deep within his heart, radiating out to the rest of his body. This magical new place, with this incredible man, gave him a joy he hadn't experienced in what seemed like a lifetime.

Well, not a lifetime.

Not since his time with Makani, before all the upheaval Mu went through.

Acknowledgements

This book would not have been possible without the support and encouragement from my wonderful writers group and my readers who keep pushing me forward and wanting more.

You are all fantastic. Thank you.

About the Author

M.D. Neu is an international award-winning inclusive queer Fiction Writer with a love for writing and travel. Living in the heart of Silicon Valley (San Jose, California) and growing up around technology, he's always been fascinated with what could be. Specifically drawn to Science Fiction and Paranormal television and novels, M.D. Neu was inspired by the great Gene Roddenberry, George Lucas, Stephen King, Alice Walker, Alfred Hitchcock, Harvey Fierstein, Anne Rice, and Kim Stanley Robinson. An odd combination, but one that has influenced his writing.

Growing up in an accepting family as a gay man he always wondered why there were never stories reflecting who he was. Constantly surrounded by characters that only reflected heterosexual society, M.D. Neu decided he wanted to change that. So, he took to writing, wanting to tell good stories that reflected our diverse world.

When M.D. Neu isn't writing, he works for a non-profit and travels with his biggest supporter and his harshest critic, Eric his husband of twenty plus years.

Excellent LGBTQ+ fiction by unique, wonderful authors.

Thrillers

Mystery

Romance

Young Adult

& More

Join our mailing list here for news, offers and free books!

Visit our website for more Spectrum Books

www.spectrum-books.com

Or find us on Instagram

@spectrumbookpublisher

www.ingramcontent.com/pod-product-compliance
Lightning Source LLC
Chambersburg PA
CBHW021334250626
47155CB00002B/697

* 9 7 8 1 9 1 5 9 0 5 2 3 9 *